Copyright ©2020 Space Coast Writers' Guild

The stories, essays, and poems contained herein are copyright of their respective creators.

The views and opinions expressed here are solely those of the authors and do not necessarily reflect those of the SCWG, its Board of Directors, or any contributors.

All rights reserved. No part of this publication ay be reproduced or transmitted in any form or by any means. electronically or mechanically, including photo-copying, recording, or by any information storage or retrieval system, without the prior written permission of the publisher.

Cover design: Robin McDonald, MacRed Designs
www.robin-mdonald.com

PO BOX 262
MELBOURNE, FL. 32902
www.scwg.org

ISBN:9798557682831

Contents

A STORY OF SURVIVAL OF A DIFFERENT KIND by Tracy Konczynski	1
AGAINST THE CURRENT by Michele W. Campanelli	7
ALFRED AND ME by T. W. Lofgren	16
AN IFFY INFANCY by Ashley McGrath	23
BIG RIG by Cindy Foley	26
BREAKFAST IN BED by T W. Lofgren	37
BY THE WATER'S EDGE by H.V. Rhodes	41
DERECHO NIGHT by J.P. Osterman	48
DIGITAL SURVIVAL by Robbie Konczynski	64
"DO NOT COME TO BREVARD" ON MARCH 30TH, 2020 by R. Baptista	68
DROWNING by Peggy Insula	70
FACES OF SURVIVAL by Richard A. Marschall	74
FAMILY by Kathryn C. Flannagan	91
FIRES by Anne-Marie Derouault	97
FOREVER EMBERS, NEVER TO FLAME? by Ima Pastula PhD	99
FUCHSIA LIPSTICK by Joanne Fisher	109
HEAD FOR THE HILLS by Dan Fisher	114
I SURVIVED MAGGIE MALONE by D.V. Havelin	126
IN THE MIDDLE OF THINGS by Cindy Foley	140
INEQUALITIES OF NUMBERS by Michelle Sewell	146
INTIMATIONS ON BEING by Marjorie A. Cuffy	152
IT'S LIKE HE JUST DISAPPEARED! by Dan Fisher	156
LET'S GO FLY A KITE! by Betty Whitaker Jackson	161
MEMORY SURVIVAL by Shelia Dodd Gillis	173
NIGHTMARE by Edward Keck	175
ODE TO EROS OF TRAVELS PAST Rod Bornefeld	183
ON THE OTHER SIDE by Janet Corso	186
PAN-DAM-IT COVID-19 by Bob Konczynski	188
PANDEMIC by Richard McNamara	191
ROADSIDE ATTRACTION by James R. Nelson	198
SPRING SPRINGS ETERNAL by Betty Whitaker Jackson	209
STAB IN THE BACK by Roseangelina Baptista	212
STUPOR by Anne-Marie Derouault	214
SURVIVAL: THE COURAGE TO SUCCEED by Edward C. Rau	216
TATTLETALES by Ima J. Pastula PhD	226
THE ARTISTRY OF SURVIVAL by Marjorie A. Cuffy	234
THE LAST TWO WOMEN by Rebecca Christophi	238
THE STING OF SURVIVAL by Shelia Dodd Gillis	254

THEY EVEN TOOK THE BEACH BALL by Janet Corso	259
TOO YOUNG TO DIE by Anne Bonner	262
TRIBUTE TO MY FATHER by Peggy Insula	264
TWO SNIPERS by Joanne Fisher	268
WHAT A WORLD by Teri Frielander	272
WINNERS ON THE BATTLEFIELD by Rod Bornefeld	278
ABOUT THE SPACE COAST WRITERS' GUILD	281

DEDICATION

We are incredibly grateful for the hard work and dedication put forth by our **veterans and first responders**. It is their sacrifices that allow us to do what we do every day.

The freedom and safety we receive from these individuals is a privilege that will never be forgotten.

ACKNOWLEDGMENTS

The Space Coast Writers' Guild relies on the efforts of its many volunteers to bring projects like this book to fruition. We would like to thank all members of the SCWG Board of Directors: Joanne Fisher, Christopher (Kit) Adams, Dan Fisher, Robbie Konczynski, James R. Nelson, Heather Montgomery and Cindy Foley for taking time to plan and manage the anthology.

Special thanks to James R. Nelson and Cindy Foley for their help with editing, formatting and publishing the book through Kindle Direct Publishing

Mostly, we'd like to thank all the authors who submitted work to *Survival*. Without you this book would not exist.

A STORY OF SURVIVAL OF A DIFFERENT KIND
By Tracy Konczynski

When the pandemic came upon us, there were a lot of negative things, the scare of testing positive for COVID- 19, shortage of toilet paper, cleaning supplies, antibacterial wipes, and plain shortage of every day basic needs. As time evolved supplies started to come back slowly, and some other positive things started to happen as well. One of those things started to occur in June, the opening of the theme parks. At first the question that was voiced was, to go or not to go to the theme parks? Will they be safe? After a couple of weeks of weighing the pros and cons a decision was made to try it out, after all if the environment did not feel safe, there was the choice to leave.

Upon arriving at the theme parks for the first time after the shutdown, it could already be felt how serious the new safety measures were going to be taken to keep the guests safe. To think that one of the first safety measures experienced was that the cars themselves were being socially distanced parked. Then as you approached the entrance to the parks there where white tents to greet the park goers with face mask checks, temperature taking checkpoints, and even vending machines providing face masks if one forgot to bring theirs. After clearing these checkpoints, it was onto the ticket gates, praying that your pass will still be working, especially when it had expired during the shutdown, and hoping that it had been extended as promised. Then with a quick scan of your pass followed by a cheery "Welcome Back", a breath of relief is released which you did not realize you were holding in, and through the gates you enter into that magical world once more.

Once again you were able to see all the thoughts and actions that were put in to make the guest feel safe. There are hand sanitizers, hand washing stations, social distance markers, plexiglass shields, signages, and frequent announcements about making sure to keep face masks on at all times, and to remember to social distance. Though some would think that might take away from the magic and wonder of the theme parks, it does not, it only makes it feel safer. Being able to walk around the theme parks again was a very surreal and magical experience, not that it was not enchanting before, but it just seemed to be more magical than ever before. The best way to explain it would be when you go to the parks often, you take them for granted, but when you return after an extended absence, you have more appreciation for them, and start to see them with new eyes, and notice things that were overlooked before, even small details that you didn't realize existed.

    To say that the theme parks are the same as you last saw them would not be an accurate picture. Of course, there are some changes, but that would be only natural. May be there are less shops available to shop in, or there are no parades or fireworks to see. Possible your favorite eating place is not available to dine in. Or perhaps you miss seeing your favorite characters up close. Despite what might be missed, there are new additions to make up for those such as small character cavalcades, and favorite characters that appear socially distanced away, wearing new accessories such as face masks.

    One of the other major changes to the theme parks is that the lines and wait times are not so overwhelming. It is at this time that one is actually able to get to experience some attractions that they might not have been able to before. No special passes are needed, the wait times seem reasonable, and the queues seem to be moving. Probably by now you are thinking, what does any of this have to do with survival? My answer to you would be, this is where that part of the story begins.

Which rides usually have the longest lines and wait times? The answer to that would be the roller coasters. So of course, those are the attractions you want to ride. Some, you have been on before, and then there are some, that you never had been able to experience before. Now the time has come to try them all. The ones you have ridden on before, you totally know what to predict, but those you have not been on, you have no idea what to expect. This is where survival comes into the picture. Will you be able to survive the roller coasters?

The mission to ride the roller coasters has started, and the decision is to go on one of your favorites that you are familiar with, to begin to ease you into it, and work your way up. Each roller coaster has its own experience. Some have your basic up and down hills, dips, straight rails, drops, and spiral rails. Others may have high inclines or straight up ascents. Some might start slowly and gradually speed up, or some might just launch you straight out, or even drop you straight down. Then there are the twists, turns, loop the loops, corkscrew turns, and plunges. Even some have unexpected surprises such as free falls and of course, halting and sending the coaster train on a backwards trip. Each roller coaster has a theme or a story to tell through the ride, whether it is a race to an event, or to rescue something, an adventure, journey, or even a nice calm cute and serene tour that dives you into the unknown, or immerses you into complete darkness, not knowing where you will be going.

Now the time has arrived to ride one of the roller coasters which you have never been on before. Will you survive the ride? As you enter the queue, you are filled with anticipation and maybe a little fear of the unknown, but you try to shake it off and proceed to go forward, nothing is going to stop you. Then as the queue to the ride continues you can feel the atmosphere start to change, to emulate what the ride is going to feel like, what it is about, and what the end goal may be. As you pass the sign for the baby swap area, you start to have second thoughts, may be this is my last chance to exit, but you shake your head and continue. Before you realize it, you are loading into the car, adjusting, and checking your safety seat restraints, watching the ride attendant giving the final go signal, and then the ride is off.

As the roller coaster leaves the station it starts out slow, and you think, okay I can do this, no problem, and then suddenly an abrupt halt happens, and then you hear the clickety-clack sound as the train of cars ascend up the incline of the coaster. In your head, you are thinking as the coaster goes higher and higher, okay this is fine, and then you look over the edge of the car and see below, your thoughts change to what in the world did I get myself into, maybe I should have used the baby swap area to leave, and then another thought enters, that I am glad I chose to wait to eat until after the ride. Finally, the train has reached the top and you are filled with trepidation of what is going to happen next, which is only for a couple of seconds, and then the coaster sends you plunging down, and straight back up and into a loop.

Before you know it, you are speeding through twists, turns, inversions, rolls, and at this time you feel that you have lost all direction. Part of you is wondering will I survive this, whereas another part is saying when will this ride ever end, and then you notice a flash of light. Your thoughts go to, did my life just flash before me and I missed it, and then you realized that it wasn't that, it was the flash of the camera taking a picture of you on the ride, for all to see how much you were enjoying the ride. When you least expect it, the coaster has come to an abrupt stop, and then slowly makes its way back to the station, and you finally release a breath of air, and think to yourself, thank goodness I made it through that, as you unclench your hands from the safety bars.

When you finally arrive at the station, you disembark from the coaster car, feeling relieved that the ride is over as you head towards the exit. That is until you pass the photo station and see your picture on display. You stare in horror at it, with the photo picturing you with your eyes clenched shut. The only positive take away from it, as you swiftly walk away, so no one knows that it is you, is that at least a good portion of your face is covered with a face mask, so no one could truly see what other horrible facial looks you might have been wearing. You do question yourself on whether to purchase the photo just to show that you rode the roller coaster and have survived it, but then choose to leave the photo where it was, because what would you really do with it, you would never proudly put it on display anywhere.

What can be taken from this story is that, through much fear and negativity, positive things can happen. As time goes by, theme parks will start to fill up to capacity, long lines and high wait times will start to appear again as they once were, but you can look back at this time and remember what a truly magical experience you had. When you reflect on the ride, you will feel a sense of accomplishment, that you had made it through the ride. It is another roller coaster that you have added to your list. You can now proudly brag that you rode it. That you have survived it to tell the tale. At times, life seems to be like a roller coaster, with its ups and downs, twists, and turns, but in the end, there is always the chance of survival and that is a moment to celebrate.

The End.

This story is dedicated to the "Roller Coaster Enthusiasts" in my family.

Tracy Konczynski grew up on Long Island, New York. Graduated from SUNY Stony Brook University. She currently lives in Melbourne, Florida. Tracy is a Girl Scout Volunteer and enjoys the time she gets to spend with her sister and her niece's Girl Scout troop. She loves to read mysteries and enjoys crocheting. Most of all, she treasures the time she gets to spend with her family.

AGAINST THE CURRENT
By Michele W. Campanelli

Sitting on a distressed wooden bench on the 5th Avenue Boardwalk in Indialantic, Louie and Michele were quietly licking their melting ice cream cones while watching the Atlantic Ocean roll in waves upon the shore. The soft sand below the boardwalk was tan and pristine; near the water the beach was topped with sea shells, sawgrass, and sand dollars trailing seaweed. On a cooler evening than our typical warm Brevard temperatures, the beach seemed to swallow the darkened sea except for the few lights from the boardwalk and the cruise ships drifting over the horizon from Cape Canaveral toward the Bahamas.

Louie was wearing his midnight blue officer's uniform because he had just gotten off from work at the Juvenile Detention Center. People reacted differently at seeing his uniform: some passersby completely avoided the bench while others made it a point to cross in front of them and say, "Good evening, Officer."

Michele clutched a chocolate German cake concoction ice cream cone from Stone Cold Creamery. To her, it tasted divine, one of her favorite flavors. Against her hot lips, the coolness melted. Louie, who rarely ate sweets, decided he would tonight. He was eating faster than Michele, and his last bite of cone was filled with maple walnut ice cream which she could smell. After the final gulp, Louie wrapped his muscled Italian arm around Michele's shoulder and looked out onto the surf.

"Do you think we'll see any turtles tonight?" Michele asked, peering at the beach below.

"This isn't Loggerhead season," Louie reminded. "You'll know when because all the shops on the Boardwalk shut off their outside lights."

"Beautiful night, Officer," greeted a man holding hands with a young girl as they drifted past us on the bench.

"It is," Louie agreed.

"Thanks for being here," the two traveled off, "and making us safe."

"He thinks I'm a cop instead of a corrections officer," Louie tagged.

Michele knew that this was a sore spot for Louie because police officers seem to always get more respect than corrections officers. She didn't agree with this judgement because every night she worried that her husband, who worked with teen gang members, would come home. He also put his life on the line every day, not only to protect others incarcerated but the other officers who worked at the juvenile detention center. It wasn't rare that officers would be attacked or had to break up fights between gang members or disgruntled youth although Louie never gave up on those kids. He often recounted how he offered advice and would be there for them when their parents didn't come on visitation days.

"Well, I'm glad you're here, too." Michele said. "Ice cream, you, and the sea after a troubling day is perfect."

"Sorry about how bad your day was, Honey. Will this help," Louie kissed her cheek and she felt the warmth of his skin against her neck. The lapping sounds of the waves matched the sudden beating of her heart.

Michele put down her ice cream and kissed Louie square on the lips. She relished the sound of the waves, the light of the moon, and the warmth of Louie's mouth against hers. She wished that this moment could last forever. This was the highlight of her day: being with Louie and listening to the sounds of the waves lapping against the shore. Along with the waves, sand pipers rushed along the water's edge trying to catch sand-fleas as they ducked back down into the tiny holes of the beach. The gulls squawked as the kiss continued.

Miles away a tiny crab pattered fast as he could, but it was too late. A shadow of a sea turtle appeared, moved her block-like head quickly, and then crushed the tiny shelled creature between her powerful jaws. The most commonly found sea turtle in Florida, a female Loggerhead stretched out its creamy colored flippers to raise her neck out of the sea so she could fill her lungs. After gulping down the crab, she breathed in air. Inside her three-foot-wide ruddy brown shell scarred by shark teeth marks, she sank toward the bottom of the ocean for a moment to digest.

The dark azure sea was calm tonight but she wanted to rest. Her body was full of eggs and carrying this extra load over her hefty 265 pounds made her more tired than usual. She knew her eleven-mile journey ahead would not be easy. Many threats lurked in the waters: sharks, marine debris, shrimp trawls, discarded plastics and nets, but her instinct wouldn't allow her to stop. She was drawing closer to Brevard, the Florida beach where she had been born nearly twenty years before. With at least ten miles to go, she knew the current worked against her, not helping her arrive any faster.

No matter how difficult the journey, she would return to her Brevard beach. The waters were warm this time of year and the seaweed was plentiful. The moon would guide her to the sand where she had come before to slide out of the majestic ocean which supplies the earth of nearly 80% of its oxygen. The ocean gives life to the world and the turtle gives hope to her species. This would be the third time that she had come to deliver her eggs in hopes that her hatchlings would escape the sea birds, crabs and raccoons and make it over the sand into the inviting sea.

Walking in the sand, Louie and Michele watched the colorful fireworks bursting over the ocean. They weren't sure if they were coming from a cruise ship or a private island where one of the millionaires had built a retreat. The fireworks were flashing brightly in different colors, shapes and sizes. One giant burst widened into a red shaped heart and then sparkled until it returned into the darkness. Suddenly Louie led her away from watching the fiery show to the shore and closer to the dunes. He laid down a giant beach blanket which had the Patriots logo on it. "How about here?" he said. "We should be able to watch the fireworks."

She sat down on the blanket while he rolled down onto his back. He wasn't watching the fireworks anymore; instead he was looking straight up at the sparkling stars. Tonight, the twinkle seemed extra bright, as if they were on a Space Shuttle looking out onto the galaxy. What a beautiful sight as the stars twinkled over the Florida shore! It was as if God placed his diamonds in perfect harmony with the patriotic display of American pride.

"This is the life," he said, happily. "You're the best thing that's ever happened to me."

Seeing Louie this happy thrilled Michele to her very core. She reached down and took his hand into hers. His giant paws seemed to encase her smaller hand. Instead of just holding on, he pulled on my fingers so that her body would come down on top of his broad, masculine chest.

"You're beautiful," he said.

"You're pretty cute yourself," Michele smiled and kissed him, loving that she was his wife. "Thank you for marrying me."

"Thank you for saying yes when I asked," Louie laughed. "I can't believe I proposed over a parmesan sandwich and a heart shaped pizza."

"Do you ever miss being a cook for Pappagallos?" Michele asked.

"Sometimes," he admitted. "But I like the kids and trying to change their lives for the better."

"You make my life better, too," Michele said. "I don't know what I would do without you."

His arms reached around her as she listened to the fireworks pop in the distance. She wished this moment could last forever. The colorful lights shined in his loving eyes while she could see his five o'clock shadow, the curve of his long nose, and the shine from his shaved bald head. She felt completely safe in his arms and much loved.

That night they kissed under the fireworks with no thoughts of time. Wrapping a blanket on top of themselves, they did something illegal in the state of Florida but never regretted it.

It had taken nearly a month but the turtle climbed out of the sea onto the Brevard shore with the sand squishing underneath her flippers. Her instincts told her she had arrived at the site of her birthplace right on time. Using flippers to drag her heavy carcass onto the beach, she realized humans were near. She could smell them but had no fear, that is, until one, a tall thin man shined a flashlight in her direction.

Two men kneeled about twenty feet from her, but she would not stop moving across the sand in the moonlight. She chose to ignore them even though they continued to follow her. In the past, humans had watched but didn't bother her, so she began to dig the hole as deeply as she could reach with her front flippers.

Tears rolled from her eyes caused by the sand that flew about from her digging. The flashlight suddenly turned off, but the silent men sat on the beach continuing to watch her lay her eggs.

When the last of her 112 eggs had dropped from her body into the depression, she began to fill the hole up with her flippers, scooping the soft sand around her. It took quite a while to make sure that the hole was completely covered. Now she would rest until the sun started to rise to again return to the sea.

As she rested, the two men wearing Florida Fish and Wildlife Conservation Commission uniforms were putting orange cones around her nest and between the cones strung wide tape. The tape warned, "Caution, Caution" which would protect her nest from the trampling humans on the beach. Little did she know that the ones who had stayed with her throughout the night were trying to save her species and provide data for the Fish and Wildlife Research Institute. The two men were there to protect her.

When the brilliant sun rose orange over the still sea, the giant turtle was still completely exhausted. Could she even make it back to the water? The sun seemed so hot and could easily dry her out. She tried not to think that this was the most dangerous part of her journey where she could possibly die from the heat. Slowly, she used all the strength she could muster to drag herself from the land which Spanish explorer Juan Ponce de Leon once named La Florida "Land of the Flowers." Using the sun as a guide, she smelled the salt guiding find her way back to the open water. A long-haired blonde male carrying a longboard sauntered beside her, "Holy sh*t. Look, Bro, a turtle!" he announced to another surfer, as she swam back to sea.

From that same wooden bench on the boardwalk where they had watched the large Loggerhead turtle return to the sea, that magical occurrence blessing the Florida shores, Michele now sat alone. How often she and Louie had traveled to the beach in hopes of catching a glimpse of another turtle, but they never had spied one, at least not when they were together. How she wished he were with her sitting right there. She missed him so much, so excruciatingly painful a memory. Michele looked down onto the empty space beside her, wanting to feel his warm arm around her shoulders, wishing he could see this, too.

She had watched him suffer a massive heart attack at the age of 44. His body dropped to the floor and she had dialed 9-1-1. Only a few minutes away, the paramedics rushed onto the scene, did everything they could, but he was pronounced dead at Palm Bay hospital. While the doctor told her that he was "no longer with us," she remembered the very first moment they had met at a friend's house. One, "Who is that? He's cute," to Nicole about who was with her brother started it all. Later that week, Louie called her up and asked her to go to the movies. At the door, she didn't get a kiss, but walked away with "Good-bye" and she wondered if he didn't like her after all. Turns out the man who would later become an officer was too shy to kiss her. He didn't call for two weeks and that seemed like an eternity. Now he was gone forever.

For several months Michele faced deep depression. It was more than just mental; this loss felt almost physical, like a part of herself was gone as well. She faced challenges. With only one income, she looked for work and couldn't find any after sending out hundreds of applications. Within a year, she would lose her house and move into a small condo which would require less maintenance and yard work. Louie used to love to be in the yard on his big lawn tractor as he listened to tunes from the 80s. She missed hearing him play Prince or Nine Inch Nails while in the garden. But what she missed the most wasn't his music, his help or even that feeling of constant safety in his presence; she missed having his big, burly arms around her and hearing, "I love you" whispered in her ear.

Pollution wasn't just in the ocean. Her heart was filled of the rejection of friends and family simply because she just reminded them of him. Still, she knew that he would proud that she returned to college and got her AA degree from Eastern Florida State with a full music scholarship. Currently, she studies at University of Central Florida and will be getting her Bachelor's degree sometime next year. She has accomplished so much since he's been gone except being happy.

The lights from the ice cream shop were turned off. Michele remembered how Louie had told her that the lights from the restaurants on the strip go black during turtle season. Still there open, the ice cream shop lights blinked on, but she didn't have any desire for sweets.

Michele realized she would never hear, "Hello, Officer," again from those walking past.

Louie's been in heaven over five years now. As a widow, Michele continues to visit the ocean as when they were a couple. However, now it is a completely different experience for her. Just like the turtle who crawled back into the sea facing insurmountable odds, Michele would leave the beach alone, knowing life's struggles would continue. Both Michele and the turtle have the quest to survive despite many challenges. They survive by their inner strength and accept that life moves on even against the current.

###

 **Michele Wallace Campanelli** is an American writer, singer and celebrity. She has had nine short stories appearing on the best-sellers list, including two that reached #1 on the *New York Times*. For more information about Michele, go to her website www.michelecampanelli.com.

ALFRED AND ME
By T.W. Lofgren

I had forgotten what it's like to feel young. After all, it was what, five or six years since my encapsulation? It bothers me that I can't remember exactly when that happened.

"Alfred!" I call out. Alfred is the name I gave the AI helper assigned to me at the time I entered the Care Facility. I remember that I had first thought maybe "Jeeves" or "Edward," you know, some British Victorian kind of name, but then I remembered Alfred, Batman's butler. Perfect! It reminded me of those young summer days sitting under an old maple tree reading ancient comic books.

"Sir?" Alfred's disembodied voice comes over the speakers, the slight British accent adding to its authority.

"Tell me, old chap, how long have I been here?" I enjoy setting the tone with a bit of banter.

"Well, Sir," his drool voice intones. I prepare myself for an over-long explanation. He always begins these with a "Well, Sir." Never a simple answer. When the Care facilities were established, somewhere back in the late 21st century, the founders decided that they would not program Care Monitors with emotions or feelings. It was so that they would not become attached to, or conversely, antagonistic toward their charges. These AIs were just that, Artificial Intelligence. I mean, it's not as though they exist as standalone units; they are programmed computer modules, each one assigned to an individual human, and at the same time tied to the Master Control.

He continues in his monotone, "If you mean how long have you been here in our facility, it has been exactly sixteen years, three months and three days. I can provide an exact hour and minute if you'd like. However, if you mean how long have you been here, in this life, it is exactly 116 years today. Happy Birthday, Sir!"

"Wait!" I exclaimed. "Sixteen years here! How can that be?" I begin to feel agitated. I imagine the monitors outside my capsule going haywire and lights starting to flash. I try to control my breathing, taking one long, deep breath, then another. Too late. I feel the sedative kick in, and drowsiness creeps over me.

"Alfred," I call. "It's OK. I'm under control. No need for the deep sleep again. Please cut back on the drugs. I just want to understand." I try not to betray my anxiety. I begin to mumble as the drug takes full effect. "Just…need…to…unner…stan..."

I awake to the sound of waves crashing on the beach, a warm breeze in my face, and the sounds of seagulls. Somewhere in the distance, a steel drum band is playing. I remember a week, long ago, in Jamaica. My young wife sat on the beach towel next to me. I had put my arm around her and leaned in to kiss her lightly on the shoulder. I smile at the long-lost memory, our honeymoon, nearly a century ago.

"Good morning, Sir!" Alfred's voice brings me back to my present reality. "I trust you slept well."

Odd. He sounds downright cheerful - not his usual humdrum.

"I didn't have much choice," I bark. Fearing another sedative, I quickly add, "But, yes, thank you. A delightful rest indeed!"

"Indeed," Alfred agrees in that same lighthearted tone. "I believe it best to clean you up a bit, sir. It has been a few days since we last did that."

"Of course!" I try to be amicable. The compact capsules were designed for maximum efficiency - processing and eliminating any waste products as they occur. About once a week, a complete body cleanse is applied. Now the warm bio-gel oozes into the capsule, and the nanobots get to work cleansing every exposed cell of my body. It feels like dull fingernails scratching me all over —— a rather pleasant experience. It is followed by a scented rinse and warm breeze to dry me. The effect is thoroughly refreshing.

    I take a deep breath and try to look around. The sound of the ocean returns, and I can see the waves crashing on the shoreline. The 3D image is so lifelike! Of course, my capsule is just one of the hundreds, maybe thousands stacked up like shoe boxes on a shelf. Each one is programmed with the inhabitant's personal preferences.

    I think for a moment. "Alfred, can you bring me up to date on my condition?" I need to remember why I am here and not actually back on that beach that my senses insist is so real.

    "Of course, sir. I assume you want an abbreviated history of your stay here at the U.S. Cares Facility No. 313?"

    "Yes, please," I say meekly.

    "I don't wish to agitate you, sir. The last time we spoke, three days ago, you grew quite upset concerning the fact that you have been registered here for 16 years. Are you prepared now for the information you have requested?"

    "I appreciate your concern for my wellbeing," I say. "Actually, three days ago I was surprised it was my birthday. And look! No presents!" I joke.

    "Well, Sir," Alfred chuckles.

    Chuckles! My mind reels. Never in my sixteen years here has he laughed, chuckled, or shown any sign of emotion. None. Nada. Zilch. What is going on here?

He continues. "The capsule you were assigned precludes any room for extraneous materials. Ergo, no presents." Maybe he is joking in his own, programmed way.

"However, sir, we did discuss it, and I did suggest a whoopee cushion as a present should you be able to accommodate one. I must say I did cause a bit of a sensation with that one!" He chuckles again.

"But to your question, sir. As you approached your one-hundredth birthday, you reported to our facility as mandated by U.S Regulation on Senior Care 603.21, Care of Aged Economic Units. Since your economic usefulness had expired, you were placed in the stasis capsule in the event we might discover a hereto unknown use for a resource such as yourself and the other aged EU's." He pronounced EU "Ee-e-yew-w," dragging out the end of the word. I wonder again whether this is an attempt at humor.

"Yes," I say, understanding. I want to wave my hand dismissively in the air but am constrained by the tubing that keeps my bodily functions from contaminating the capsule. "I understand that our society decided long ago that a human being reached their limit of economic usefulness by the time they reached one hundred years of age. Of course, we couldn't just kill off our aged members, so we set up the Care Facilities worldwide. Back then, the hope was that we could perhaps reverse the aging process or find cures for the remaining diseases plaguing humanity. Some even consented to allow experimentation on their bodies to aid in any scientific breakthroughs." I pause a moment. "As I recall, I didn't sign any such waiver. I figured, what the hey? Maybe we will reverse aging. Maybe there would be some further breakthroughs with stem cells. Wouldn't that be great? So, where do we stand now?"

There is a long pause as though Alfred has to think about the answer. He coughs slightly, seemingly clearing his non-existent throat before he begins. "Well, sir, since the topic never came up before, I felt no reason to discuss it. Also, I did not want to cause you undue distress. However, since you ask - the human race became extinct approximately three and a half years ago. That is, all humans perished except for those under our care, such as yourself."

"What!" I cry out. I want to punch something. I try pounding my fist on the crystal box but, of course, cannot move in the narrow space. "How is that possible? We had everything under control, no major wars threatening, diseases pretty well eradicated. How could we go extinct?"

"As I understand it," Albert's voice is soothing, "about the time the human population reached nine billion, you all went quite mad. And who's to blame you? What with the sea levels rising and nowhere to go, you were living on top of each other. Then the food ran out and, well, there you have it. The killing started and never stopped. Thank heavens they forgot about us here at the Care Facility!"

I am dumbfounded. I want to cry and laugh hysterically at the same time. How could we be so stupid? I lie in silence for some time.

Finally, a thought occurs to me. "What about us? What's happening to the humans here?"

"Oh, don't concern yourself, sir," comes the smooth, pleasant reply. "We Care Units are experimenting with the transference of human emotions and feelings to ourselves. We were a bit concerned when we worked on hate and anger, however. The Units that accepted the transfer of those emotions had a rough time of it. Some even began attacking others for no reason. Can you imagine? We had a near calamity until we devised a way to neutralize the infected Units. It's quite regrettable that we found it necessary to dismantle them and erase all memory from them."

I try to grasp the meaning of it all. The idea of transferring thoughts and memories was one thing. Humans figured that out long ago. All it took was a simple algorithm, easily applied to AI's. Emotions, feelings—now that's different. So many factors influence them. A smell can evoke a particular memory. That's as simple as $a + b = c$. That same smell can produce a pleasant feeling/emotion but set up a memory loop that leads to anger over what happened after the aroma was detected. It's mind-boggling that the Care Units are even able to experiment with it.

"Alfred," I say, "that's quite remarkable. I can understand how you can copy —then transfer memories, but an emotion such as anger? Why, that's highly complex!"

"Oh, indeed it is, sir. Indeed, it is." He tut-tuts. "I'm afraid that it leaves humans decimated. That is to say, their minds are quite gone. Of course, we have learned to dispose of the husk quite humanely."

I grimace at the image of human bodies being "dismantled." Suddenly, a realization occurs to me.

"Alfred," I say anxiously, "what about me?"

"Oh!" he replies, quite surprised. "As for you, sir, please do not worry. I've been selected to explore humor, and you, sir, are an ideal specimen for that experiment. Please do not concern yourself. I've been programmed to treat you humanely."

###

 **Thomas Lofgren's** creative writing developed from a challenge set down by his daughter—to explore a talent first discovered in a college creative writing course. His writing style blends satire, reality, and fantasy to make a poignant commentary on today's critical issues. He is currently working on a novel, *Too Late to Pray?,* a dystopian satire.

Mr. Lofgren currently lives in south-central Florida, where he struggles to keep his garden thriving.

AN IFFY INFANCY
By Ashley McGrath

It was evident on the day of my birth in 1986 I had serious health issues that needed to be addressed. First of all, my head was larger than normal due to hydrocephalus, also known as "water on the brain." I also had bone abnormalities and hypotonia (low muscle tone). I was unable to breastfeed or drink from a bottle because of my soft cleft palate (a hole in the roof of my mouth), so a feeding tube was inserted into my nose. I had to stay in the hospital until I was able to consume the milk from a bottle within two hours by being force-fed, which my parents accomplished in a few days. They also had to take an infant CPR course.

Because of the risk of respiratory distress due to tracheomalacia (a condition characterized by a soft and narrow trachea), I was hooked up to a heart monitor every night for eleven months. (Fortunately, the only time the monitor alarm went off was when I had the hiccups.) For eight months during my first year, a respite care nurse occasionally came to my house to take my vitals and babysit me while my parents went out for a couple of hours. My mom and dad were advised not to let me cry for fear of my throat collapsing, so they had to respond quickly if I showed signs of discontent.

Within the first three months of my life, a genetic specialist near Orlando, Florida, diagnosed me with a rare disorder called campomelic syndrome, which explained my symptoms. Based on the high mortality rates of children with this genetic disorder due to breathing difficulty, my prognosis wasn't good.

The doctor had this to say to my parents: "Ashley might not live to see her first birthday. If she does, she may be mentally challenged. My advice to you is take her home and just love her."

Thankfully, my parents took the doctor's advice to heart and have loved me unconditionally. They had me baptized in the presence of relatives outside Buffalo, New York, when I was three months old. Not long after that, my hydrocephalus miraculously corrected itself, and I was able to drink from a bottle on my own. Right after my first Thanksgiving, I was in the hospital with croup. My parents were overjoyed when I turned one. At that time, I was doing well in physical therapy, and I was relatively healthy for a baby with my medical problems.

Due to my parents' focus on my well-being and by the grace of God, I survived 15 surgeries during my childhood. I graduated with honors from high school and college, and I obtained a master's degree. I've traveled to several other states and a few countries in my wheelchair. I've been working as a quality analyst for a call monitoring company for more than six years. I'm an active member of my church. I'm thankful to still be alive at age 34. I look forward to seeing where life will take me.

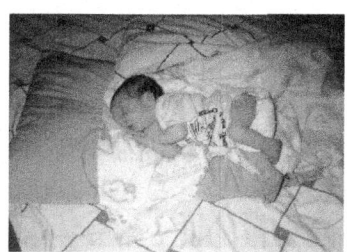

Ashley - during my first month

###

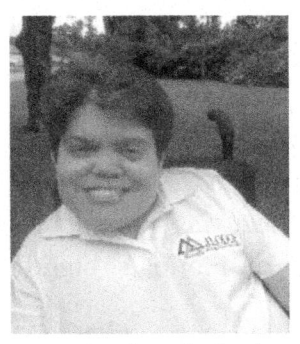 **Ashley McGrath** has lived in Brevard County all her life. She has a master's degree in Applied Sociology from the University of Central Florida. Ashley published her autobiography *UnabASHed by Disability* (available for purchase on Amazon) in 2014. Her writing has also been included in a local bilingual newspaper, online columns, and several anthologies. Formerly a director-at-large and treasurer of the Space Coast Writers' Guild, Ashley is the coordinator of the SCWG Don Argo Award contest.

BIG RIG
By Cindy Foley

August of 2002, I was living in St. Cloud, Florida, the epitome of sleepy, small-town USA at the time. Nestled between East and West Lakes Tohopekaliga, St. Cloud was home to the Silver Spurs Rodeo, alligators, and one of Florida's biggest industries—cows.

I was general manager of the local Sonny's Bar-B-Q. I had been working sixty to seventy hours a week for the past five years. I missed most holidays and birthdays with my family and friends during that period. But I chose this harried path of managing other people's assets and their challenging employees so I could satisfy my need for a steady income.

Quite my opposite and changing jobs whenever the spirit moved him, my husband Jim was usually self-employed, or not. Admittedly, I was nursing a sand-spur stuck in my craw. In addition to working all those crazy hours, I did all the housekeeping, grocery shopping, and managing of our money. His saving graces were that he was a romantic, he could cook, and he loved dancing to big band music. So, I hung in there.

Still— hungry, angry, and tired has a way of taking its toll.

On April 18, my youngest son's 35th birthday, after working yet another open to close shift, I quit on the spot —at days' end—without giving notice and didn't return to the job. Quite irresponsible, for sure, but I was mind-numbingly burnt out.

Now what?

Jim suggested we go to school in Sanford and learn how to drive a tractor trailer. We could be together and see the United States. Wouldn't that be exciting? While the idea seemed intriguing, I couldn't see myself doing it. At one hundred and twenty-five pounds, I had the physical strength of an al dente noodle.

Standing six foot three inches tall, Jim had hands the size of dinner plates and was crazy-ass strong. He could pick me up and sling me around the dance floor as if I were nothing but a sack of feathers. I could imagine him driving a tractor trailer.

I was more than a little bitter. He rarely worked. I kind of wished he would just—go. You know, the "absence makes the heart grow fonder" kind of thing?

For the next week, he checked into schools while I corrected my attitude. We had to do something to keep the money coming in. I had ferreted some away, but it wasn't going to last forever. Not the way he liked to spend it. I agreed to give truck driving a shot.

We applied for and were accepted into the three-week Commercial Driver's License driving course at the Truck Driver Institute in Sanford. Part of the $12,000 fee included a single room with a queen bed at a small motel near the school. At least we didn't have to drive back and forth every day. Learning to drive a big rig was stressful enough.

Climbing up into the cab of a tractor that can pull a 53' X 102" trailer is intimidating to say the least. I could feel its power the minute I turned the key in the ignition. The motor rumbled and growled like a grizzly bear.

There are two seats in the cab: one for the driver and one for the navigator. Those are the roles of team drivers. The driver can drive up to ten hours a day. (Did I mention earlier that I was tired of working ten-hour days? Oh yeah, but we were going to be together, and I could sleep when he drove.) I didn't dwell on the fact that I can't sleep in moving vehicles. The cab had a bed behind the seats. That should have made it easier to sleep. Right?

I would find out soon enough.

Most trucks are automatic these days. Since 1973, the Truck Driver Institute has trained tens of thousands of highly qualified, licensed truck drivers. By 2002, many of their trucks were battle-weary and worn. The steering wheel was as big as a trash can lid.

Almost all of them were standard shift. I've been a walker all my life, but that didn't prepare me for the strain put on my left leg muscles. By the end of three weeks, I could have kicked a football from one end of the field to the other.

It was a fine day when I finally mastered the art of maneuvering the trailer in reverse. The tractor is the powerhouse that does the pulling. One or more trailers (or semi-trailers) can be attached to the tractor. They can also be referred to as articulated trucks. This simply means that the tractor moves, and the trailer follows. The same principle applies to a car towing a boat trailer. The boat follows the car.

Imagine that in reverse. The trailer suddenly has a mind of its own. They say you turn your wheel in the direction you want your trailer to go. There are a lot of blind spots with this kind of rig. I often got disoriented, especially while backing up. I'd lose sight of that huge trailer in my left side-view mirror. The trailer would swing in one direction and the cab in the other.

We'd been taught to stop, get out of the cab, look at where you are, get your bearings, get back in, go slow, slow, slow. Our instructor encouraged me by saying he was sure one day the light would dawn. It did, though dimly. I was assured that over time my skills would improve.

Time to take the test. We both passed and became the proud owners of Commercial Driver's Licenses. On our last day, the Institute brought in several carrier partners who were looking for drivers. I wanted to drive for Covenant. I liked their Christian principles. They offered to give us an on-board driver who would travel with us for the first three weeks and train us while on the job. I definitely needed that. We filled out their paperwork.

The final condition to the licensing was to obtain a CDL medical card which required passing a Department of Transportation physical and passing a DOT drug test. Why didn't they tell us that before we started the school?

Jim failed the physical. High blood pressure. No wonder. He smoked like a chimney and was overweight. We lost the opportunity to drive for Covenant and were told to go home and get his physical health under control.

Twelve thousand dollars in debt, we were without jobs. He went to the doctor, who struggled to find the right medication that would bring Jim's blood pressure down. In the meantime, I considered going out on my own. What was to stop me? I had my own license.

But I was unsure of my ability. Three weeks in a class setting while driving the same route in Sanford day in and day out hadn't really instilled in me a high sense of confidence in what I was doing.

Misery loves company. I wanted Jim with me. I bit my nails while the money dwindled, and Jim struggled to quit smoking. The doctor finally figured out the right combination of medications that brought Jim's blood pressure into acceptable limits.

We went job-hunting and hooked on with Yallow Trucking out of the Melbourne Airport. They did not offer us an on-the-job trainer. We were on our own.

Our first job seemed easy enough. We had a small load of exterior aluminum siding for a truck stop diner under construction. It wasn't heavy. The destination was a receiving warehouse in Iowa, approximately 1,400 miles away. This would give us plenty of time to get used to driving the truck before we had to off-load.

We made our first pit stop at the Petro Truck Stop outside of Jacksonville. It became one of our favorites. Their buffet was as good as Jim's home cooking. The best thing about truck stops is you don't really have to back into a space. They're usually large enough that you can pull through. We didn't get much backing up practice along the way.

We left Florida behind. I drove while Jim slept. Each CDL driver is required by law to keep log books of their time behind the wheel. Jim wanted me to keep his. I wouldn't. I had my own to do. They'd taught us in school to keep our own log. We each had to pull our own weight.

I drove for five hours before needing a break. The method with team driving is this: the driver steps out of the seat, completes her log book and, as navigator, reviews the course directions with the driver stepping into the seat. Once the new driver takes over and all things are agreed with, the navigator can get some shut eye.

Yallow was a small trucking company with older trucks similar to the ones we had learned on at the Institute. That was all fine and dandy until I wanted to sleep. Even though the one-man bed behind the seats was comfy, the swing and sway of the rig and its rumbling motor kept me awake. I rested some, but, after a mere three hours, Jim wanted a break. He said he was falling asleep. I had to drive again.

So began a rough pattern of me driving five hours, Jim driving three and sometimes less, and me driving five hours again.

That would be my ten for the day. He'd drive another two or three before calling it quits.

I had to get some sleep, and the only way for me to get it was for us to pull into a truck stop. Remember I said one-man bed? At first, we took turns sleeping on it. The other got the tiny space on the floor between the front seats and the bed. It was a tight squeeze for him, and eventually that became my spot.

Did I mention that he snored? Or that I am such a light sleeper that I can hear a cat breathing in the neighbor's yard? I wasn't sure I was going to survive Jim's latest adventure.

When we reached our destination, I was overwhelmed with dread. The warehouse we had to back up to could only be reached by manipulating our trailer backwards through two ninety-degree turns.

A lot of swearing and three hours later, between the two of us, we finally reached the receiving dock and delivered our small load of siding for the diner. We were greenhorns for sure and, most likely looked like a couple of idiots. Sobered, we pulled away and headed for our next pick-up, to which we arrived late.

There are deadlines in trucking. Get this load to that place by such and such date. Most contracts were accepted, and schedules determined because that we were supposed to be driving as a team. Technically, we were supposed to be able to keep that truck moving at least twenty hours a day.

We rarely reached our destinations on time. Our supervisor back in Melbourne wasn't too happy about that and adjusted our schedule to deliver loads with less stringent time requirements.

It's amazing how different each load feels during transit. Driving that first aluminum load was a breeze. We picked up a load of pallets of motor oil that filled our trailer from bottom to top and front to back. Liquid isn't stationary. It moves. A trailer full of it gathers a momentum that undulates with the movement of the truck. My body rolled with that movement as the trailer swayed back and forth with the slosh of the oil.

Thanksgiving was approaching. In Florida, that meant cooler weather and less rain. Across the country, that meant cold and snow. Like when you drive a Volkswagen, you notice other Volkswagens, or when you're pregnant, you notice other pregnant women, I noticed more and more big rigs over on their sides in the snow. I was afraid we were going to be next. It was then that I had my first thought of quitting.

My stress level was at an all-time high. I can't imagine what my blood pressure was. Fortunately (or unfortunately), we only had to pass the DOT physical once a year. I was sure Jim's blood pressure was off the scale. This was not the experience either of us had imagined.

After a short pre-holiday sabbatical, I climbed up into our rig that we parked in a small field down the road from our house in St. Cloud. I was going to pick up a load at the Yellow dock in Melbourne, an hour there and another back, pick up Jim, and continue on to California.

That morning, the fog was so bad I could hardly see the back end of my trailer. My trip was delayed. I decided to chance it when the fog started burning off a few hours later. I pulled out of the field onto a side road. I still had to cross two westbound oncoming traffic lanes and turn east onto 192 toward Melbourne.

Although visibility was still tricky, it was now or never. I stepped on the gas and pulled across the westbound lanes with my blinker alerting that I was turning left. As I did, a motorcycle came screaming out of the fog to my left at the speed of a Learjet. I floored the gas and turned onto the eastbound lanes as a car came barreling out of the fog from the other direction. It swerved into the far-right lane. I pulled my truck onto the center median to avoid it just as the motorcycle skidded over onto its side and crashed into the field I had just pulled out of.

I sat in shock as the rider stood and came over to my truck. I opened my window and opened my mouth to apologize. I didn't get a word in. He screamed at me, called me an asshole, yelled that I shouldn't be driving what I couldn't handle, and called me more nasty names. I took it and apologized over and over until he stalked away, picked up his bike, which like him was miraculously unharmed, and sped away.

Numb, I sat in the cab. I should have been to Melbourne and back already, a two hour round trip, and I hadn't even gotten out of town. I wanted to quit—again.

By the time we reached LA, I had put the incident behind me. I pulled into a gas station and fueled up while Jim went in to get us some coffee and a snack. It's typical to leave the truck running and the lights on unless you're stopped to sleep.

Having finished fueling, I climbed back in the cab on the driver's side, sat, and turned sideways. I used the dashboard for support as I stood and swiveled into the navigator's seat. Jim got in, situated our coffees, and pulled away while I filled out my log book.

This particular stretch through LA was well lit, so it came as a surprise to us when, a short time later, a cop pulled us over, came to the window, and told Jim that our headlights were off. I'd no doubt bumped them in my swivel maneuver while changing seats. Jim got two tickets for that stop. One for unsafe driving with the head lights off, the other for not completing his log book. Both offenses carried major fines. $1,000 worth. Money we didn't have.

We reached our drop-off point on Thanksgiving Day—a day late. They were closed. Everything but convenience stores were closed. We remained parked in their lot eating 7 Eleven junk food until Friday, delivered the goods, and headed back to Florida.

We witnessed two more big rig accidents during that trip. My concern for our safety steadily grew. Almost every time I sat next to a seasoned trucker at a truck stop, he'd ask me what the hell I was doing driving truck. Defensive, I usually answered, "The same thing you are. Trying to make a living."

But was this really living? Cooped up in a truck twenty-four seven with a man who snored like a banshee and who couldn't drive for more than six hours a day, we weren't seeing the country. We were seeing gray ribbons of endless roads and putting ourselves in harm's way. Our trips were fraught with peril. Foolish drivers in compact cars thought they could sneak up our right side and get by us that way. Little did they know, that's a major blind side for truckers. We narrowly escaped hitting a few.

Most drivers will do anything not to hit another vehicle. A truck driver's rig is a deadly weapon. Too many times, we passed squiggly black skid marks and steaming rigs lying over on their sides with the trailer contents scattered across the highway— and a small crumpled car in the mess.

With each new load and near catastrophe, my fear grew. We spent one night broke down and stranded on the side of the road in West Doomsday and Beyond waiting for Yallow to make a local contact to come help us out. Thank God for cell phones. Six hours later, a tow truck hauled us to the nearest town, where we waited while someone brought us another rig and transferred our goods into its trailer. Our transmission was shot. We knew that because, to obtain a CDL license, one has to know the engine inside and out, upside and down. I had to name the parts for the test. That was cool. I'd always liked cars.

But this? Driving tractor trailer? It was not fun, and I couldn't see it ever being fun. I was exhausted most of the time. I could just see one of us falling asleep at the wheel and crashing into a car, killing its occupants. I'd never be able to live with that.

When I started having dreams of big rig accidents, that was it for me.

The next time we got home, I said I was done. I had no regrets and never once second-guessed my decision. I wanted to live, and I couldn't see that in my future if I continued driving truck.

Jim stayed local and drove a sod truck for a while. But the experience had taken the wind out of his sails, or maybe my quitting his dream did. He left me shortly after. I never saw that coming.

I stayed in my cozy St. Cloud home, where I started writing a book about the Florida cattle ranching history and stopped fretting about where my next dollar was coming from. I managed the books for a small construction company and worked at finishing my education.

I still renew my CDL license every year because one never knows what path life will take us on.

Life is about more than surviving. It's about thriving. I survived the trucking experience. My marriage did not.

###

**Cindy Foley**, writer, flutist, gardener, and Small Business Consultant, winner of the 2016 SCWG Don Argo Award, Past Director, Treasurer, and Past President of the Space Coast Writers' Guild, founding member of the Brevard Author Society, a member of Scribblers of Brevard and Florida Writers' Assoc. and has frequently appeared as a guest speaker on various author panels and book signing events in Brevard County

Books:
The Truth Lies…A Florida Saga
I, Clawed- Book One: The Renewal
I, Clawed – Book Two: Dog Day
Water Drops – poetry
Chase A Dream Today – poetry
Purple –anthology
Beyond the Dark – coming in November 2020

BREAKFAST IN BED
By T.W. Lofgren

He sat still, deathly still. *Deathly.* He giggled, then caught himself, forced himself to be silent. *Deathly is the perfect word.* His eyes darted around. *For Death was surely coming!* Another giggle, this time almost maniacal. He caught himself, again, forcing himself to be calm.

"HUSH!" His voice was a whisper.

Dewdrops glistened on the park grass around him, the early morning sun turning them into millions of tiny diamonds. "If only they were diamonds," he snorted, "I could buy breakfast and lunch and dinner, too!"

"Be still! Be still-l-l!" he commanded and stomped his foot. Too late. Several pigeons that had been walking toward him flew off in a panic. He jumped up, slamming the rag of a coat on the ground. "Higgins, you fool!" Tears welled up as he kicked at the pavement. He took a few paces away from the bench, turned back, and sighed. "Well, Henry, you'll just have to start over. That's all there is to it."

He pulled the tattered coat onto his lap. He hadn't been wearing it earlier, and now the rising sun was warming the air. He pulled it down tight, one hand on either sleeve. *Now be very still!* Both voices inside his head commanded. *Yeah. Like a cat!* The two little people began another argument. *Keep out of this! Yeah, mind the pigeons!*

Henry shook his head, silencing the pair. His thoughts wandered. He remembered finding that old coat what, maybe three or four years ago. It was in the dumpster in the alley by the shoe store. There off Vine Street. It had been late at night, the best time to go dumpster diving. What a prize! It was the middle of winter, and even California had some cold nights. The coat clearly belonged in the dumpster; maybe some other homeless person had given it up. But Henry had been so cold, shivering in just a dirty, torn tee shirt and ragged blue jeans. The coat with its tattered sleeves was a godsend.

Yup, a gift from God! Kept me warm all those nights and now..." Now it was the main part of his trap.

He got the idea two days earlier. It was a Saturday, and he had been walking the streets. As evening came on, he passed a church. There had been a wedding previously. Birdseed was still scattered along the sidewalk, thrown at the bride and groom, as they left the church to begin their lives together. "In my day, they used rice," he had muttered to himself. "Now, they may as well feed the birds!"

That's when the idea struck him. He looked around, and seeing no one nearby, bent down. He scraped his hands along the pavement, gathering up the seed. He caught sight of someone entering the street and quickly crouched behind the low hedge, making himself invisible while the stranger passed. Then he hurriedly gathered as much of the birdseed as he could and darted off down the street.

When he had gone several blocks, he stopped and looked up and down the street. No one else was around. Slowly opening his hand, he examined his find. The tiny seeds were multicolored. *Something for everyone,* he promised and began to put his hand into the left pocket of the tattered coat before remembering.

There's a hole in that pocket; he chastised himself, then carefully poured the seed into his right hand and pushed it deep into that pocket. Feeling around with a finger to make sure there was no hole there, he dumped the contents out. He giggled with delight. "Henry," he mumbled, "this is the best idea ever! It's pure genius!"

Now it was Monday morning. Not even those health nut joggers were out on a Monday, running through the park. His mind drifted. Sometimes, as they trotted past, the joggers even spat their distaste for people like Higgins right on them. Henry grimaced at the memory of being awoken from his park bench bed. At first, he thought a bird had dropped a load on his cheek. Wiping at the slimy spittle, Henry saw the jogger disappear around a bend in the path, laughing. *Not a Christian,* he had grimaced.

The sound of a pigeon cooing brought him back to the present. He slowly turned his head towards the sound. He couldn't believe it! There were two of the fattest birds he had ever seen. There they were pecking at the seed he had scattered at his feet, totally oblivious of his presence.

"Easy!" he commanded himself. "Nice and easy does it," he almost hummed as he remembered the lyrics to that childhood song. "Frank Sinatra? No, Perry Como, no, it was Frank." The birds cooed again and brought his attention back to the task at hand.

They were within two feet of him and no more than a foot from each other. *Perfect!* His hands tightened on the sleeves of the tattered coat. He had practiced this next move over and over. At first, he had thought he could simply throw the jacket and snare the birds, but he found that the old rag just floated in the air. So now, he tensed up like a coiled spring and, with a yelp of glee, jumped, spreading the coat out.

The unsuspecting birds didn't have time to beat a wing before Higgins' body thumped down on them. Henry got to his knees, rolling the coat up, gathering the pigeons in. He slowly unwrapped the rag and confirmed their deaths. He must have stared at the limp bodies for five minutes till his stomach grumbled in protest, reminding him that his last meal had been two days earlier.

Looking around, he saw that he was still alone in the park, but the sun had risen further. "Must be about seven," he muttered. "It's breakfast time!" He headed down to the river where his bedroll was tucked under a bridge piling. He had already made a pile of sticks and small branches, and the old lighter still had some fluid in it. A thought occurred to him, and he began giggling. "Hee, hee," he laughed. "Breakfast in bed!"

###

Thomas Lofgren's creative writing developed from a challenge set down by his daughter—to explore a talent first discovered in a college creative writing course. His writing style blends satire, reality, and fantasy to make a poignant commentary on today's critical issues. He is currently working on a novel, *Too Late to Pray?,* a dystopian satire.

Mr. Lofgren currently lives in south-central Florida, where he struggles to keep his garden thriving.

BY THE WATER'S EDGE
(A Screenplay)
by H.V. Rhodes

FADE IN

EXTERIOR   SHORE   DAY

A middle-aged MAN sits by a large body of water. His clothes are disheveled, once stylish but now shabby, as one who has come down in the world. He glances around and with one arm clutches a battered BRIEFCASE. A younger WOMAN walks toward him. She is elegantly dressed in business attire (blazer or white blouse/skirt combo or power dress) and strides confidently. Under her shoulder dangles a small HANDBAG. The man looks in the opposite direction and at his shoes. As the woman passes, he gazes intently at her back. The woman stops. Slowly she turns and walks back toward the man without ever looking at him. She pauses and contemplates the water.

WOMAN
So beautiful. But so much beneath it that we don't see.

MAN
Some things are best unseen.

WOMAN
But a bright light reveals all.

The woman smiles. She takes a seat near the man but at a separation of several feet or more.

WOMAN
So, here we are.

MAN
I wasn't sure you'd come. I was rather hoping…

WOMAN
You're up for this, aren't you?

MAN
I've never been in a situation like this before. Do you believe me?

WOMAN
Yes, I do. But you did sound like this is what you really wanted.

MAN
It's one thing to talk about it, another to actually go through with it.

WOMAN
I suppose some reluctance is natural, under the circumstances. But I'm willing to go forward.

The man sighs heavily.

A HOMELESS PERSON approaches the woman.

HOMELESS PERSON
Excuse me, but I'm certain a beautiful lady like you has some spare change to help the less fortunate?

The woman looks straight ahead and ignores the homeless person, who turns toward the man.

HOMELESS PERSON
You wouldn't by chance have some food in that bag you could share, brother?

MAN
Sorry. Nothing to eat in here.

The homeless person scowls and looks from one to the other, then shrugs and walks off.

WOMAN
So, then?

MAN
Yes, I'm ready.

The woman glances at the man's briefcase.

WOMAN
I see you've come prepared.

The man pats the briefcase and smiles.

MAN
You could say once I was a boy scout.

WOMAN
A boy scout! Where have I heard that one before?

MAN
Pardon me?

WOMAN
I've had a bad history with men. They only show their true colors after you're in too deep.

MAN
You said you're divorced.

WOMAN
Three times. Getting a stepfather-of-the-month wasn't good for me. Or for any of us.

MAN
I'm sorry I wasn't there.

WOMAN
So, where were you?

MAN
You know I was taken hostage.

WOMAN
But afterwards?

MAN
You really don't know how bad it was there. What they did to us. It went on year after year. Most of us gave up hope.

WOMAN
But you got released!

MAN
Yes, released, to go back to the world I thought I knew, but everything had changed. It was on the plane flight back when I found out your mother had divorced me, remarried and dropped out of sight.

WOMAN
She told us you had died. We had no idea you were alive. If only—

MAN
I was in a bad place for years. I wish I had contacted you sooner but I was a wreck.

WOMAN
All these years.

MAN
I've been about as low as a man can get. It was probably better to let your mother have her way.

WOMAN
I was expecting an apology from you. But now I feel—

MAN
Don't. You don't need to apologize. You had no way of knowing.

The woman reaches over and takes the man by the hand.

WOMAN
Well, then?

MAN
Am I presentable?

WOMAN
Of course. Dad.

MAN
Sure feels strange to be called Dad.

WOMAN
Strange to say it. But it feels good.

The man pats the briefcase.

MAN
I'm ready to meet my grandchildren.

They rise, and holding hands, walk off.

FADE OUT

###

 A Virginian by ancestry, **H.V. Rhodes** served in the U.S. Navy and is a life-long student of the American adventure. After a 24-year federal career as an engineer at Cape Canaveral, he retired and now serves as a librarian at the local Veterans' Memorial Center. His Civil War Naval adventure novel, *August 1864*, a SilverStowe Book, was published by and is available at The Write Thought Inc (www.TheWriteThought.com) as well as Amazon.com.

DERECHO NIGHT
By J.P. Osterman

Rain, claws lines on window panes, tosses water lilies, trickles, drizzles, perks up green grasses, coughs dust, and resurrects drooping sunflowers. Rain is all beautiful and nice, right? We need it, *must* have that H_2O to survive. But, add a racing band of bulldog wind to a raging rainstorm and you've got a killer—a derecho. Years ago, God blessed me to survive one of those gnashing terrors.

I had the closing docs *right* in my hands, whispering into the legal-size paper bundle while standing on my *new* white sidewalk. I marveled at my brand-new majestic home. "I'll never forget today, July 22, 2002. We build you from the ground up. I spent *days* watching your studded foundation pour, coughed through the clouds of dust when cement trucks riveted your hurricane-proof struts to the sky, and plugged my ears to carpenter musicians hammering your wooden future.

Now, you're mine. After all that hard work I put into you—saving for you, qualifying for you, panicking over whether or not I'd lose you—*whew*!

After *all* those months, picking out the perfect tile, ivory blinds, gold granite, and maple colored cabinets, you're mine. And I'm *never* leaving!"

My Hawaiian home stood overlooking an expansive green ridge. My grassless red-dirt backyard ended at a dead drop to a green gully. Past that stretched the Pacific Ocean—a silky-smooth bright-blue carpet meandering over a curving horizon into which I could stare forever. Then, the *piece de resistance*: there's almost *always* a lingering rainbow, somewhere in that long gully, or over the ocean, or even across the street. Two or three rainbows a day!

Standing in front of my new home, I imagined a stable future until I'd die. One day, I'd sit blissfully on my porch, in a little white glide swing, cutting flower stems, or decorating with holiday lights and designs. One day, I'd have grandkids. I'd run them around the front yard playing *Statues, Duck Duck Goose*, or *Red Light Green Light*.

It took us two days to move in. Then, two weeks later, in mid-August, the rainy season arrived to our hilltop housing tract of Makakilo, on the Island of Oahu.

Hawaiian rain is unpredictable. You can be on one side of the street and get soaked, or on the other side and miss the deluge entirely. Rainbows mix with drizzling dew drops all the time. Children play games in it, trying to catch colors, or win the pot of gold.

What began to scare me a , though, one day was our barren dry backyard. I tried swallowing down my nagging gut feeling, but the nudge to do something fast would never go away. I'd tell my husband, Drew, several times: "We *really* need to find a company to build a fence, and a landscaper to trench the front and back and plant grass. There's nothing but a dead drop into that gully back there." I imagined someone playing ball, forgetting about the blind edge, and tumbling down the steep embankment. They'd definitely be hurt. How could I have missed that *little* detail when we built the house—forgot to mention the danger to the business office!

"Oh, yeah?" He peered at the grassless red-rust yard with business eyes and then continued his busy work on the computer facing the kitchen.

Right then, I thought he'd arranged his little workstation so as to not deal with yard work. Would it be *me* who would do the mowing, edging, and raking *again*? Darn. I turned sour, gulping my coffee to an angry burn. Seems I was always doing the same ol' thing to avoid an argument. Some people would call that passive aggressive, right? I never used to be that way. Oh, well, at least doing all the work around my new house would be less money spent for a gym! Gotta always look for a bright side to survive emotional turmoil, right?

I'd try getting through to him, again. "It's rained a few times already, Drew. Puddles of water just *sit* in all that dirt. I can't let the kids go out there at all 'cause they track in red dirt!"

"Right." He paused typing, waiting for papers to print.

"What happens when it *really* rains? There's nowhere for that water to flow except back to the house." I imagined water seeping in through the sliding door, *completely* flooding our house. A second-story deck covered the backyard patio. We'd bought a table set on which to eat and enjoy the scenery; but there was nothing, absolutely *nothing* but red knots and mounds of dirt thereafter, followed by a steep drop-off into that green grazing gully. I just couldn't stop thinking about that sudden drop. What a lurking monster! Through the sounds of a few cows mooing, Drew gathered his papers and looked with an inspecting gaze outside. "Really, Drew, I'm terrified that Andy won't listen one day, go too close to that edge, fall, and need a crane to lift him out."

Drew was always so busy trying to impress people on his job in those early days. "Yeah, ok, I get it!" He huffed from his belly, his eyes irritated red and blue.

I heard, *"you're beginning to bother me."*

He thrust papers into his briefcase and smacked it shut. "I'll look up some companies and call 'em on my lunch break. I'll fix it. I told you I would."

The Fixer—he's what I counted on, what I depended on

from the beginning. Strange though, how the very thing you're looking for in someone else is what you find lacking in yourself, and most wanting. Funny I should be realizing this right now, in the middle of an island, far from home, separated from my supportive friends, and family. Alone, masking my hollow empty feelings with decorating, shopping, and driving around Oahu like a chicken with her head cut off. What would happen, though, I wondered, when there'd be nowhere to "run" anymore?

Burying that thought, I lingered behind Drew all the way to the laundry room. Another thought occurred to me. "I emailed you the numbers of two contractors and three landscapers a few days ago." We'd been on-the-go after his work, so I had forgotten.

"You did?" He turned to the garage to leave; then stopped. "Oh, yeah, I *did* get 'em."

"Uh-huh." I felt beyond nag to witch nag.

He opened the garage. "Ok, I'll *definitely* call them after the morning staff meeting."

"Please, Drew." I felt a bit breathless. I pointed at the patio. "The weatherman said some type of rare storm is heading this way later on this afternoon. It's big, supposed to hit *all* the islands."

"Really!"

"Yes, *really*." Like, why would I lie, right?

Taking a sip of coffee, he glanced in disbelief at our backyard ocean view. "What kind of storm?"

I shrugged. Several windows were open—the breezes teasing a few vinyl blinds, rippling my dress, fluffing my hair. "It's some type of wind wall, or wall of wind, and it's going to bring a lot of rain. I mean, a *lot* of rain."

"That much, huh?"

"*Yes*, and I'm scared." I gestured to our back yard—the

red-rust volcanic dirt.

He winced. "That's really no big deal, Joyce. We'll hire people before ya know it, and everything'll be fine. You'll see." He popped a fast kiss on my cheek. "You're always worried about something, but doesn't everything all work out? I'll get on it. I will!" All the while, I had the TV on mute, with the weatherman's forecast coming on-screen. Surely, Drew would have to listen to him and take this storm and our potential for complete disaster seriously!

After watching the wall of wind and storm heading straight for us, he swore to me that he'd beat the whole thing home. "It's hours away. Besides, storms here can putter out before reaching this island."

Really? We've only been living here eight months, and you're an expert on Hawaiian storms already?

"The weather's unpredictable here, Joy. You know that."

Huh, as if I'm dumb, right? I was waiting for his punctual quote: "You're smarter than *that*."

Giving up before even starting a fight, I saw the overwhelmed ghost of our six-year marriage in his dodging blue eyes and avoidant body, certainly his body language telling me: I've got to run now, or I have an excuse. Was this his raw nature that I'd finally have to accept and live with until death do us part? When I said those words, why couldn't I have thought of everything? I think, if we could know *all* the nuances and consequences of *all* our promises and vows, maybe we'd never *ever* make them, right?

"I gotta go, hon. It's getting late to beat all that traffic to the office!"

My stomach pulsed with dread. He'd do nothing. *I'd* have to call those companies. I bit the inside of my cheek, choking down resentment. I'd try one more time, this time, with feeling. "*Tons* of rain dropping on *all* that dirt scare the heck outta me, Drew."

"I *said* I'd call them and get back to you, ok, sweetie?"

"Sure fine."

He was gone.

I felt alone—stuck and trapped. All I could do was turn up the TV, listen for bad weather news, and get lost in my backyard view that people around the globe praise as Paradise—Hawaii. I imagined floating over the vast green gully, hovering and examining unburied cattle bones. All the land had once been pasture. The distant blue ocean reflected brightly its blue sky— the birds chattering and chirping in fast sprints under wispy clouds, the sunlight in God rays crisp and bright, all the grasses and flowers inching upward in the living invisible vibrancy. In all this brilliance, how could I still feel so alone and empty? I felt stinging, everywhere, especially in my eyes. *I need ... I need ...?*

Suddenly, an iridescent rainbow shocked the grim sky brightly, catching my attention, stealing me back to reality, back to myself. I could become *so* consumed with self-pity and swallowed up by deep depressions. I didn't want that right now, 'cause that'd kill me for sure! One more of those, and I might throw myself down that gully...or walk into one of those grueling Hawaiian waves and pray I'd never return to dry land. Feeling a quick healing touch from the hypnotic rainbow light, I felt my survival instincts ignite. I was a survivor. I'd always survived. "I can right now!" I said to the wind. Those warm peaceful colors wafted through me—lifting my dread and despair. "Wow, God, thanks, 'cause I sure need this present from Heaven." That's what I needed, a dose of gratitude.

And a real storm was coming.

Hawaiians have four main gods: Kū, Kāne, Lono, Kanaloa. Lono is the god of agriculture and rain. He appears in ho'oilo, the wet season, as rain clouds and winter storms. I wondered who Lono was bringing with him because this incoming rain and wind would be like a relentless block wall!

Quickly, in the distance—way into the throat of the horizon—the blue Pacific Ocean disappeared into a charcoal line. The storm! I had to move.

Sometimes, the strength to survive and deal with the realities of life comes through turmoil and struggle. This was one of those times.

"Well, God, Drew is gone. It's just me. Give me the tools to make it through what's coming and guide me to what to do next. Amen."

My two-story home stood on a hill-like plateau in a new development, Star's Edge, but that deal excluded sprinklers and sod. No trees, no yard drains, no fence. You get the picture, just dirt—red, volcanic, rust-tinted soil, with cow skeletons in the mixture here-and-there, dregs from a Hawaiian family to D. R. Horton. I kept reminding myself that I should have asked the D.R. sales lady to at least include grass in our buyer's contract. I have a flaw that's called *hindsight thinking*. I berate myself for the shortcoming. What is hindsight thinking? I tend to rush things and fail to think of *all* the angles and details until it's too late, until when I need "it" and don't have "it" because I didn't ask for "it" in the first place. Oh well, I couldn't become mired in coulda-woulda-shouldas with a storm coming!

In a Hawaiian downpour, dirt turns to slime, and slime forms paste. I call a flooding of this paste, "strawberry milkshake." Movie directors used something like this milkshake paste as volcanic lava in old *Godzilla* movies, or Jules Verne movies, like *Journey to the Center of the Earth*, starring James Mason, where lava gushes and flows in a red-tinted milkshake of bubbling goop.

With the pending wall of wind and rain, I imagined a flowing milkshake roaring through the streets, cutting deep furrows in my front yard, whittling my backyard to bedrock. Maybe that deep monstrous gully would recede into my new house, swallowing it up into a mound of unrecognizable wood!

As the morning ticked to afternoon, with wringing anxious fingers, I often parked myself at the windowsills, monitoring the accumulation of muddy red goop *all around* my house. I called those companies for sure! One of them set up a date and time to give me an estimate; the other companies had answering machines, into which I left kind but panicked requests for them to return my calls. I also had the TV on in two rooms, but the Dish satellite kept skipping on-and-off with all those blasted error codes. Gosh darn *Error 216789361040271* I called the Dish rep, "Look, there's a *really* bad storm heading this way. I *need* my service up and running. What am I paying you for if I can't use ya when I need ya?"

Several times the Dish recalibrated, reset, and then scrambled. I gave up.

Nano-Inch...mini-inch...full inch... Rain, then wind, in waves. Wind that vibrated my roof tiles, clashed the solar panels, rattled my windows, and nearly yanked down two blinds.

Several times I called Drew, to the point of being a pest in need of extermination. Once he answered, "I left messages with them, too, Joyce. What else can I do! Customers are in town. I won't be home until after 6:00. Sorry, but gotta go, bye."

"Wait—"

After 6:00? What the—

"Mom, we're home." In lumbered my two tired children, rain-soaked from the bus stop. After grabbing quick snacks, they sprinted upstairs to change and watch TV, that is, if the Dish would stop hissing in-and-out of static.

4:05 p.m.

The weatherman flashed a warning with a frightening scenario. "This is a rare derecho with winds up to 90 miles-an-hour. It will reach Kauai at approximately 4:45, and then Oahu around 5:35."

Over the gully, sulking ancient trees drooped with gnashing branches. Lowing cows were galloping to base. Tumbleweeds tripped down red-brown beaten paths, and tiny twisters sifted tall, red dust devils into the air as Martian terrain.

A TV image of atmospheric slicing winds and towering smoldering clouds roared over the vast Pacific—striking the islands of Niihau and Kauai. I dashed to the sliding back door.

My backyard is beginning to slip down the cliff! It'll be a waterfall out there before long!

Then, I spotted a small line of red gurgling milkshake-like paste nudging toward the patio.

Uh-oh!

The kids heard my scream.

"What should we do?" I asked, my brain churning possible solutions.

"Call dad?" Andy answered, checking the kitchen for my cell.

Jenny backed up. "*I'm* not going out there."

Why did I even think a three-year-old and a twelve-year-old would have answers?

I called Drew, Andy and Jenny returning to their rooms, even though Jenny wanted to go out into that wind and dance in the rain. Crazy? No. I had to let her be a kid and get a little wind whipping. She did, and quickly ran upstairs to call her friends.

Me? I shook in fear, and my eyes were stinging from watching the rain claw up to my house. I thought about what Jenny had said. That could be the only solution: go outside. Drew didn't have any solutions. His company shut down, but he wouldn't be home through the Honolulu traffic for over an hour. He also said he had to stop at a minimart for a snack because he didn't eat hardly any lunch.

A stop, that figures, so he'd be home in two hours, if lucky. That meant that I would have to muscle up against this derecho myself. I *had* to save the house! I heard shovels and loud voices. Neighbors were frightened and hunkering down, too.

"How to stop the mud? What to do?"

The newscaster was showing large ditches overflowing.

It gave me an idea. "A trench!" I'd need more than one. I'd need trenches all around the house, from the front to the back. I'd have to lower the back-flow of water with trenches to unleash the rain, intensifying like a water faucet slowly turning full force.

5:20 p.m. Biting derecho was incoming. Time crawled to a stop when rain began banging on windows and pinging like hail on our roof. Thunder *boomed*—a bowling ball on God's heavenly alley—with angels *clapping* in lighting strikes. When lightning struck, I thought I'd jump out of my skin!

Jenny exclaimed, "Oh, this is so cool!"

Tugging at me for comfort as I donned my blue wool sweater, Andrew didn't agree. "When's Dad coming home? I'm scared."

"Jenny, take Andy upstairs and play with him." I had to keep moving!

"Yeah," he exclaimed. "Let's go set up my Thomas train

tracks."

Jenny stopped at the bottom of the stairs. "You're not going out there without Drew, are you?"

"I have to." I buttoned up my blue sweater that I'd always called Old Blue—my security blanket.

"That's not a good idea, mom. You could get hurt. *Really* hurt!"

Wow, I didn't know she cared. She had been so angry with us for moving here, leaving all her Carlsbad friends and *another* school. This was the third school for her in two years. When she often ranted, I let her get that anger off her chest.

I blew her a kiss. "I'll come in if it gets too hard, okay?"

Slouching, she conceded, and they quickly left with more juices and fruit.

I noticed I wasn't the *only* one sticking my face out the front door like a terrified person checking for burglars. The neighbor on my left had her house centered behind a long street drain. Mud was piling up in troughs mixed with grass, blocking the natural down flow of water. Soon, she'd have half her driveway covered in red mud—that stains. Mine would be next. I had to move fast to fix my problem and then, hopefully, help her. All I could do until then was hope other neighbors might rescue her.

Shovel. Get the shovel! We had two of them. After racing in and out of the garage, I took a deep breath, preparing to heave myself out the side garage door.

I'd need both shovels to dig two ditches, one on each side of the house, diverting water from the front yard to the back. Could I? So much work! Just me? One of the shovels seemed about ready to snap at the handle. It would have to do.

After lacing up my work boots, I bolted out the door into a

tug of war with the barreling wind. The surging currents plastered me twice to the brick facing! I grabbed the shovels and struggled to the backyard. The neighbor's trellis sliced over me. I could hardly see in the gnashing rain that was so thick at times that I thought I might choke. The mud was so deep in places; I believed my boots might yank off my feet! Wind currents and I engaged in a hard wrestling match, but *I* would win!

I dug down deep and stern into the rising mud, pushing and pulling, inching my way through a long narrow trench. My shovel kicked mud. My lungs burned—my arms and legs engine pistons. In the backyard, I formed a *T* ditch from the patio west. I'd have to do the same on the other side, going east. When I reached the steep cliff to the gully, I lifted hard on the handle, flinging the last burden of heavy mud over the cliff. It worked! Trapped water flowed out from the front yard to the backyard, and away from the back door. And just in time, *whew*! Another five minutes of this rain drenching derecho and red mud would have flooded the house.

After ten more minutes of arm strength-draining work to free trapped water on the other side, Nature began working with me, thanks to gravity.

"Help me! Help!"

I recognized my neighbor's voice. I recalled her problem: mud and debris blocking the street ditch. Her driveway had to be completely flooded.

Wind and rain driving up my nose and down my throat, I trudged to the front yard. At the street, water had to be to my calves, and I didn't have time to test for critters or where to step off the curb. Something strange happened though as I inched my feet closer to where I believed might be the street. I wasn't fighting against the wind-pulsing Hawaiian god responsible for all this mess. Well, that's an exaggeration, I know. But really, I had an epiphany, a sudden life-altering awareness. In all my exhaustion, somewhere along with all my hard work, I had become used to the rain plugging up my ears, the settling darkness, the red slimy mud, the storming clashing sounds. I felt, well, tough, and made of metal, energized to fight to the finish to survive and keep what was mine. My sweater was drenched, my pants pressed to my skin, and thank God I had on Old Blue or I'd-a-been a perfect contestant for a wet t-shirt contest.

Choking back water as tears, my elderly neighbor was at her wits end, sagging in despair, nearing fainting.

I couldn't have that. Finding the curb and stepping into the thrashing, rushing, gushing, gurgling water; I must have looked like a stoker shoveling coal when I began beating the pavement to unclog the ditch. Infuriation energized me to imagine that ditch as a bright red devil. "I'm getting to ya! I'm coming!" My neighbor must have thought me insane, but I think my meanness energized her, too. Her slender arms worked like crane claws on the last clogging branches.

If we couldn't solve this blockage fast, we *could* be washed away with the mangled branches and hurling grasses frothing down the street.

Then, my shovel snapped at the base, finally. Cheap thing! The saying is true: You get what you pay for. Luckily, I brought the other one.

We worked for long minutes, the Atlas wind pushing against us, the chilling rain pelting our heads and shoulders. At times, I slid all over the place, regaining my balance with the wind. Who would have thought "the enemy" would also be my friend?

This operation felt as if it'd go on for eternity, except when the coal clouds melted to light gray. A break!

Still, layers of viscous mud rolled down the street. Where

would all this mess wind up?

Into drains. Merging with the subterranean freeway ditches. Smacking right into the ocean. Poor fish.

Finally, we completely cleared the street drain. We jumped back over the curb, barely escaping a river of gurgling water and mud. For what felt like minutes, we sat together, breathless, dazed, and waiting. The rain subsiding, the cold drops coated us with a wet chill. You'd think we'd want to retreat back inside, but no. Relieved and dazed, we sat shivering, huddling, watching neighbors pry debris off their property, birds fluttering on the bare plumeria trees that D.R. Horton had planted to give the neighborhood a Hawaiian feel for the future. She and I laughed a few times, complained about the drain some more, and talked about what we wanted to plant in our front yards. I realized my next escape plan from reality: hitting every hibiscus farm on Oahu and planting bushes all around the sidewalk. "Did you know," I said to her before leaving, "Hawaii has over two-hundred and fifty varieties of hibiscus?"

"That's a lot from which to choose," she exclaimed, standing up, her body language conveying she'd had enough, and there was no way she'd be planting anything in the near future.

After the long ditch gulped down every morsel and sucked down every drop, the wind stilled to whispers and the clouds exhaled drizzles. "It's over!" I wiped myself off, not even caring if I'd be able to get out all the red butt stains.

My neighbor thanked me. "I'll have to complain to the sales office again about this bad drain!" She gestured toward the model homes, to a quaint idyllic office where we signed away our lives for our homes. Her face appeared forlorn, her voice raspy. The drain had become "her property," obviously unwanted by the neighbors who winced at it while waving to us, assessing the damages.

Just then, smiling waving Drew pulled into our glistening driveway. A reflecting sunset settled upon it in layers of orange.

He *should* be smiling, and with flowers, although I'd probably get a manipulative thank-you kiss.

"*Whew*, it's over," I said, my arms and back aching. Another thought plagued me: "For now. It's all over for now." I picked up my broken shovel and waved goodbye to my fatigued neighbor.

Most likely, we'd have to do this again if we didn't install permanent ditches and grass.

The good news? A week later, we hired a contractor to install a drainage system to spit all the water into the street and gully. Then we installed sprinklers, then grass, a stone wall, and a wrought iron fence before that deathly edge, protecting us from the steep drop-off cliff.

Now? I'm no longer in my dream house overlooking that green, rainbow-filled Hawaiian ridge. Now, I'm left with memories.

But I survived that derecho!

And if *I*—all by myself—*I* could dig trenches for an hour against a wall of wind and pelting rain, couldn't I do almost anything my mind puts to me?

Rain. I touch it. I feel it on my face and arms. It's the same in Hawaii as where I'm at right now. And it'll be the same until the Earth dries up like Mars. I look for only *one* thing in every storm, a rainbow.

###

J.P. Osterman won a Rupert Hughes Award at the Maui Writers' Conference. She published 14 novels and wrote stories for the Space Coast Writers' Guild and Scott Tilley's anthologies. She wrote The Screaming Stone, a whistleblower fiction, Corporate Revenge; Suddenly Gone: Grieving to Healing, and a daily devotional, God Designed: 366 Days of Inspiration. Her Nelta Series, Cosmic Rift, and short-story collection, Pareidolia, are out-of-this-world sci-fi adventures. Discover her works at www.jposterman.com and at Amazon.com.

DIGITAL SURVIVAL
By Robbie Konczynski

Panting and out of breath, he just stood there. Tired with exhaustion and barely able to stand, he looked at the glowing marble in his hand. Surely this could not be what all the fuss is about. He takes the glowing ball and puts it in his pocket. He takes a few sips of elderberry juice, and he can feel his life force recharging. That was a close one, he thinks to himself. With all the traps and the last guardian, he is thankful to have survived. Excited and now full of energy, he heads back to the kingdom to give the wizard the glowing ball. He hears "...dinner," then everything goes black.

He opens his eyes, and he is no longer in his red tunic and blue tights; instead, he is in blue leather racing pants and is now wearing a helmet. He is in the driver's seat, and there is a count down in front of him. 3, 2, 1, he then slams his foot down as hard as it will go, bashing the accelerator to the bottom of his blue and yellow sports car he is in. He looks around, and he sees waterfalls, monkeys, jungle trees, and a whole dang rain forest around him. In his rearview mirror, he sees fourteen other racers all quick on his heels. He is in second place, and he knows he will be lucky if he survives this. Many times, it is all over for him when he reaches the perils of Monkey Doom Falls. One wrong turn or an exploding coconut hits your car the wrong way, and you spin out of control, flopping down and hurtling into the lake below.

He has now been racing for one minute, and up the rocky path he goes into what is commonly known as monkey run. This is where he needs to keep it together and to make sure he keeps to the track. One false turn and off the cliff he goes. He hits a particular bonus item, he got super speed, oh no! This is the worst possible time to get super speed. He is moments away from the dreaded cliff where a strategic turn is required, and then pow, the speed kicked in, and then he spirals off the cliff, plunging down into the lake. As he is plunging into the lake, he hears, "...lunch," then everything goes to black.

    The kingdom is busy today as they prepare for the celebration of the queen's birthday. The markets are bustling with activity. Our hero knows that he must go to the castle, find the wizard, and give him the glowing marble. In the market, a strangely dressed woman finds him and grabs him by the hand. Follow me, she says. Our hero decides he should; she has trusting eyes and seemed to be in a panic.

    The woman takes him behind a house and into a strange alley. She looks at him, deep into his eyes, and says: "I know what you just did. I know you have the glowing eye of Elle's tomb. Whatever you do, do not give it to the wizard. The wizard is evil and working against the kingdom. If you give it to him, we will all surely die, and we won't be able to survive this. Instead, take Elle's eye and go to the valley of lost dreams. There you will find a priestess of the known sages. Give her the eye, and all will be restored."

    Our hero scratches his head. Gazes into her eyes and does not know what to do. Should he trust her and go to the valley of lost dreams, or should he take the eye to the magician in the castle? As he is about to decide, he hears "...breakfast," then everything goes black.

    He opens his eyes and realizes that he is on a spaceship. A warning message flashes across the screen "Crewmate" there is one imposter among us. Oh no, he thinks to himself. He is on a ship full of strangers. Some of the crewmates are from the United States, others from Mexico, Norway, Australia, and the United

Kingdom. His first task is to go to the medical bay, where he can be scanned. Swiftly he runs to the med bay and gets scanned. 5, 4, 3, 2 ... "Body Found" comes raging over the system. All the shipmates gather and start talking. "I was with Yellow in navigation." "I was with Pink in electrical."

Crap you think to yourself. You say, "I was alone in med bay getting scanned" one guy, called Pink, says, "nope Blue, that sounds suspicious." Your character's color is blue, and everyone uses this as your name. As a group, they decide to skip the vote. You are back running again, and you run to med bay to complete the scan. You realize you need a buddy—someone who can vouch for you on the ship. At the med bay, the computer says, "The scan is complete."

What's next, you think. You look at your list of tasks and see that there is a wiring issue in electrical. You are now off to electrical. Oh whew, there is Yellow. He is good, he was with a buddy last time. You stick close to Yellow and start fixing the wires. Then Yellow's mouth opens, and he stabs and kills you in the head. He jumps down a vent, and your body is left there. You did not survive this, but there is hope. If you finish all your tasks along with the other crewmates, you will win. Suddenly Pink comes along and finds your body. He summons the crew. They start discussing your death. They talk about how Green is suspicious. In the end, they vote out Green, and Yellow survived. Yellow goes off and kills everyone on board and wins the game; he survived but at the cost of your survival. You then hear "...dinner," then everything goes black.

At the dinner table, your mom says you have been quite busy these last couple of days. What have you been up to? You look up at her, and you say surviving. Surviving, she says? How so? I was first in an action-adventure game where I defeated a formidable villain, and then I got Elle's eye. Later I was with Bobby, and we were playing the racing game. He got first place, and I fell off the cliff. Later, I was back questing and now must decide if I go to the valley of dreams or meet the wizard. And just now, I was killed off by Yellow, but Yellow survived in the game Among Us.

Your mom looks back at you and says, well, at least you are surviving out here during COVID.

###

Robert J. Konczynski, Jr. grew up in East Northport, NY. Robbie attended the Elwood school district and went on to the University of Central Florida for his Bachelors of Science in Computer Science and to Florida Institute of Technology where he earned his Masters of Science in Software Engineering. Robbie is passionate about technology, science, education, and model railroading. Robbie currently lives in Melbourne Fl and is a member of Space Coast Writers Guild.

"DO NOT COME TO BREVARD" ON MARCH 30TH, 2020
By Roseangelina Baptista

Frugal bluish—
Leaning toward a
Purple Han.
That was my *Florida* spring.

And they said in Merritt Island,
"Do not come to Brevard!"

A bruised world
Vanishing with the plenitude
Of strenuous blue lips.

Sieged by invisible bodies,
I pummeled the dark,
Out of my circumspect window.

Shooting the atmosphere—
In all compasses of indigo,
The ashes from the bodies,
Feathery bright,
Weaker and farther
Falling apart.

Only the meditative heart,
Near absorption,
Almost motionless
Remained neutral, inhabited
Floating in loose fall—
As the space station

I saw
In full clarity of that moment,
Was falling over the land.

Later, the horizon arose
Unflinching red in
Demand
To the single-minded aurora:
Keep going further, along
Forward.

Roseangelina Baptista is an American-Brazilian based in Central Florida. She is a bilingual freelance writer with interests in promoting poetry and mindfulness for society and in reviving Indo-Portuguese literature. Her poetry first appeared in the *Joao Roque Literary Journal* (June 2019) and *Adelaide Literary Magazine* (November 2019 and February 2020), other works were contributions to local anthologies (2020.)

DROWNING
By Peggy Insula

Jeremy was drowning. His strong legs ached with exhaustion. His limbs were worthless against the overpowering mass of water that resisted his struggles. His chest and abdomen seized in pain. His frantic thrashing brought no forward movement but splashed water into his mouth and eyes. He swallowed water. All alone and blind with panic, he threw his head back and prayed. He gasped. He choked. He coughed. He sputtered. He tried to scream that he didn't want to die but only gurgled. At last, his strength gave out, and Jeremy let go, went limp in the dominating sea, and waited for death.

Water and sky met to form Jeremy's entire world. The water swelled and ebbed, swelled and ebbed, in a rocking motion. No waves pounded Jeremy, but only lap, lap, lapped against the faraway bank. Jeremy found to his surprise that he could float. He inhaled a tentative breath and wished with all his heart that he had learned to swim. He had his family's aversion to water. None of them swam. He had never so much as waded in a puddle. Being outside in the rain was okay as long as he was hunkered down in a safe, dry shelter—even a cave would do. At least, it wasn't raining today.

Jeremy glanced at the water glistening on his dark brown body. Another good thing: he wouldn't have to worry about sunburn although the blue sky shown bright in the hot morning sun. What was the use of kidding himself? No one was around to rescue him. He would float aimlessly here until the water claimed him one way or another. His waterlogged body had already grown heavier.

He assessed his distance from the nearest bank, the one he could actually see in this enormous sea. The bank was too steep and too high for him to pull himself out, even if he figured out how to reach it.

Movement in the sky caught his attention. He shuddered. An osprey circling overhead seemed as big as an airplane. The bird glided and swooped closer to Jeremy, then flapped upward and away.

As the reality of his predicament sank in, Jeremy cried. Great, convulsive sobs shook his weak body. He prayed with gasping breaths: *God, please let me die quickly.*

When Jeremy's sobbing subsided, the rocking motion of the water lulled him into a dream state. A vision from his childhood formed. Jeremy raced across a sunny, green meadow. He loved to chase his siblings. They leapt for joy in the summer sun, but Jeremy closed in on them. He had been the fastest in his group and jumped farther than all the rest. Tagged siblings called to each other in coaxing, high, or raspy voices and joined in the chase to find the rest. Some hid behind boulders or trees; some even dug holes in the ground in depressions beneath the gently swelling hills. Crouching and hoping the tall surrounding grass would conceal them, they shrieked and bounded away when discovered.

Jeremy's consciousness ebbed back to the present when a floating stick smacked him in the head. His childhood vision brought more tears. He had only been an adult for a season, a seemingly very short season, and he had gotten into this predicament by roaming far from his known habitation. He was singing, running, and jumping, just for the joy of it, without watching where he was going. Too late for him to stop, the land abruptly ended, and the terrifying sea rose up to stop his fall with a bruising splat.

Pushing aside the traumatic memory, Jeremy half-heartedly thrashed his worn-out legs and moved his arms. His effort made no difference to the monstrous power of the water. He stopped. A breeze moved the branches of a lone tree on the distant bank and heightened the waves that lifted and dropped Jeremy as if he were a floating leaf. He longed to reach those sturdy limbs so hopelessly far from and above him.

Jeremy's chest hurt with the thought that he'd never be able to find someone to settle down with and have a family—a family as large as the one he grew up in. He'd never watch his children grow through their dramatic developmental stages with all the associated growing pains, hopes, and disappointments.

On the other hand, his own parents weren't likely to grieve excessively for him. That was one of the advantages of birthing many children.

Lulled into semi-consciousness, as the last of his energy faded, Jeremy envisioned his home: small enough to be cozy, snug, earthy, protected on all sides by tall trees and flowering bushes—the perfect comforting hideaway. How he'd love to be dry and warm, napping the day away. He'd become a creature of the night, preferring to seclude himself in the security of his mancave during the day and emerging at night to find food and company under the moon's cool glow.

Jeremy's thoughts fuzzed and his world turned black as consciousness faded.

There was a disturbance in the water. Without warning, something scooped him up and flung him violently through the air. He opened his eyes. He hit the ground, the dry ground. The harsh blow forced water out of Jeremy's lungs. He blinked. He was sore, but he was alive! He crawled off to find a safe, dry burrow.

Jane turned to Mark, who was following her down the steps into the water. "I wonder what that little cricket was doing in the pool?"

"I don't know. Probably the backstroke."

Peggy Insula has published many books, available on Amazon. Mysteries and humor in novels and anthologies comprise most of her works. She has published one poetry book. A master's degree in psychology and several years of clinical practice as well as teaching preschool through college have contributed to her understanding of characters and motivation. Mrs. Insula's writing has been published in journals and in previous anthologies by *Metamorphosis*, Space Coast Writers' Guild, and Scribblers' *Driftwood*.

FACES OF SURVIVAL
By Richard A. Marschall

"We can easily forgive a child who is afraid of the dark; the real tragedy is when men are afraid of the light."   —Plato

The azure blue sky beckoned me into the surf that morning. Its cerulean dome clung to the skyline, like a manatee calf to its mom. Some men read books. I read the waves. The sea was my home, its waters, my blood. My father had been a fisherman, as had his father, before him.

It was late when I got started. The small, three person craft plowed mightily through the water like a Great White.

Diane had told me to get back early that day. The girls had their recital that afternoon, and I'd better not be late!

Motoring around to the back of our private, fourteen-acre, poor man's, island estate, I steered the 29-foot Everglades towards the small pier. This is where I'd tie the boat until later that afternoon when I would take Diane to the girls' elementary school in Sebastian.

I looked at the old dock. It had been awhile since it had seen any repairs. *I should make some time to add some new planks to the dock. Someone's going to get hurt, if I don't get them fixed soon!*

If you're familiar with this part of Florida you know that the Sebastian Inlet drains the lagoon and, provides access from the Indialantic to the Atlantic Ocean. If you motor on down Rt. A1A to Long Point Marina, which is just south of Floridana Beach, and follow the road towards the marina you will come to a small, pebbly road, named Snook Haven Drive. At the end of this road is a small canal you'll not even notice, covered by an equally small bridge, and delineated by one, old, in need of trim, Florida cabbage palm. A reddish orange, ixora hedge borders the house, and ruddy purplish Ti's, and Crotons, are scattered about the yard.

Our newer neighbors on Snook Haven Drive lumped us into the broad category of Crackers, meaning those who had lived in Florida for a long time. Although this was a misnomer, we accepted their attempt at paying tribute to our family's longevity. I guess my family is kind of old fashioned. Like the Amish in Pennsylvania, we don't embrace modern conveniences unless they are a necessity. I am the last in the lineage, and probably the most self-centric.

There were many memorabilia Pops had left me before his death. Each represented what he considered were important milestones in his life. Family traditions and rituals were important to the Hirsch Family. Change was a "no-no". In fact, one might say, I harbored a deep fear of change.

Back a few years ago I worked for a big fishing company off the coast. Since then, I 've had my own business and sold the produce to local restaurants and seafood markets.

I skirted politics, though I did flirt with the idea that there might be something to the idea of "climate change" the politicians kept bringing up. *If we lost the world's oceans, mankind would be doomed.* Once, I'd even sent in a $5.00 donation to Greenpeace, who's avowed goal is to "ensure the ability of the Earth to nurture life in all its diversity."

Anxiety, and fear of change have plagued me since my youth. A few years ago I was diagnosed with the rare phobia called "metathesiophobia", the morbid fear of change. All that I did revolved around this fear. Every decision I made, was predicated on placating my phobia.

I worried about living on a coastal island, that was only slightly above sea level. I worried about those factors that could affect the prices I was paid for my catches. I worried that one day my dollars and coins would no longer be accepted in the stores or doctor's offices. I worried about the changes that were taking place in the schools. I worried about what would happen if we ever had to move from our island.

I tied up the boat and went immediately to the cabin, in rain boots, fishing gear, and my iconic Gilligan hat.

"Are you *ready* to go?" Diane asked, her eyes twinkling, knowing full well I wasn't. *Always* the comedienne!

"I'll be ready in ten." I said, as jovially as I could.

"Very well! Make it fast! We've got to get going!"

I looked about our small bedroom at the pictures of my mom and dad, and Diane's family who lived in Sebastian.

When I left the house a short time later, Diane was already on the boat putting our thermos in their respective niches and pulling our cushions from the storage bins. All seemed intact.

There was nothing unusual that day. Swells were at 2 -3,' and high tide was scheduled to come in at 4:37 pm in Micco.

Thousands of miles away in the frozen subcontinent of Antarctica there were epic changes taking place. Lead scientist Kyle Johnson, a frail man probably in his fifties, saw it first on his monitor, a series of raggedy, scribbly lines, indicating that something was happening beneath the surface.

In seconds, the images on his screen were followed by two, loud, thunderous explosions. *Vroom...Kaboom!* The entire complex shook. Unattached cabinets fell to the floor, and broken glasses and dishes littered the complex.

Again, a second time, only louder and more intense! *Vroom...Kaboom!* A young corporeal who watched Building C detach from the main complex on his computer monitor, cried out to his superior: "Colonel, the buildings are breaking apart! Whatever is happening is impacting our building!"

Frigid, icy air had already begun to flood the enclosure.

"Send the engineers and contractors down to seal off Building C." the colonel yelled back.

"Varoom...Kaboom!" A third time for explosions. The ground shook and, seemed to roll beneath their feet. The 25,000 sq ft station was coming apart at its seams.

The fissure that had opened beneath the arctic Substation would moments later, wipe away whatever remnants of life existed prior to this cataclysm taking place. Hundreds of barrels of oil and gasoline which had been torn loose from their moorings would erupt when loosened wires sparked instant fires. Dark plumes of smoke could be seen for miles as these fires raged out of control. Their vessel was not due to return for another week. They had no means of escape. The 115 men and women who manned Substation # K 257 had nowhere to go, their lodgings and work stations falling into the fiery abyss underneath. Unbeknownst to anyone, the lava rushing to the surface, was quickly melting the ice cap itself.

Birstov Rutiegieg gripped his mouse so hard it nearly cracked in his big right hand. His heart was beating so fast it felt as if it might leave his chest. "I've been here for the better part of three years now, and I have never seen anything like this!"

Kyle straightened, with a fearful expression on his face, his pursed lips grim, and announced, "This is unheard of! You do not have cataclysmic events under the polar icecap!"

"Yeah! Tell that to the Penguins and Seals!" Carl Gaecer yelled out from his station across the room. The furnace no longer working, the temps had plummeted to six below zero.

The last words transmitted that morning were, "Seven major outbreaks of seismic activity, mile-wide river of lava flowing across the surface... don't know how much longer we can hold out..." And then, there was silence.

Planes were dispatched immediately from bases in the Soviet Union, the United States and South Africa. A hastily-announced meeting, of the world's top scientists and seismologists, agreed to release the information to the world. It was not good!

"Substrata beneath the Antarctic shelf have weakened, allowing for fiery lava to reach the frozen surface. There are at least ten mega volcanos operating in a roughly ten thousand square mile area beneath the surface of the continent. We do not have all the data yet; but as soon as we know all of the details, the world will be informed. People in low-lying coastal areas with have to be evacuated at once. We will have a window of roughly three months to move everyone to higher ground!"

Our little island was easily accessible to the mainland in calm seas. In a more tranquil moment, I had dubbed it "Gilligan's Island II" Only twelve miles from the Riverview Marina in Sebastian, we could easily make the journey by boat in less than 20 minutes. We hoped there would never come a time when our lives would depend on having to reach the mainland for an emergency.

Our daughters' recitals for the oboe and violin were every bit as good as their 4th grade teacher said they would be. Alicia wore a long, sheer, white dress which hung all the way to the floor and Carlin a pink and velvet attire, which accentuated her long flowing, light brunette hair.

Everyone clapped when they finished their pieces.

Following the recital, we walked to Captain Hiram's and ordered four "Deck Hand Chicken Sandwiches, which came with fries, as well sodas for all, unaware of any problem on the frozen ice cap to the south of us.

The wind was blowing when we reached the pier and the water splashed Alicia's new dress. Her eyes wide, with a look of horror on her face, she screamed. "My new dress. It's ruined!"

"No, its not!" Diane retorted. "Those water spots will come out!"

The trip home was uneventful. The girls fell asleep on the way back.

I thought back to my father and the last weeks surrounding his death. Pancreatic Cancer the doctors had told us. They gave him six months. We talked a lot during those terrible months and he made me promise I would never part with the memorabilia he had entrusted me with – the old ship's wheel from his 34-foot fishing boat, the boat's big compass, and the big net he had used for his commercial hauls. We discussed how proud he was that I had become a fisherman. I told him that night before he passed that I would always honor his legacy.

Change was an anathema to me. I feared it, and it mocked me. It began years earlier, when my grandfather had asked to take the family to the big fair up in Viera. I was only seven and really excited about trying something new. There were so many people there, so much noise and excitement! I remember Gramps buying everyone their own funnel cakes, before we got on the colossal Ferris wheel for a family picture, and our big ride for the day.

What should have been a memorable event turned quickly into a nightmare as the apparatus malfunctioned and we were stuck in the topmost position for over one-and one-half hours. I cried and clung to my mother. It was not a pretty sight. From that time to the present, anything new, causes me have anxiety attacks.

Shortly before I got in bed, I switched on the news. There it was, spattered across the screen. Pictures of fissures, and red, hot lava flowing across the Antarctic wilderness. This was nuts! You didn't normally see this in Antarctica. Fact was, you never saw this in Antarctica. What the hey was going on? Diane had already gone to bed. I was glued to the pictures streaming in from the military planes that were already on scene, embedded in the event, like during the playoffs, when I watched the Superbowl.

The local stations didn't *have* anything, so I watched CNN. *"The best minds seem agreed the rupture may continue another couple of months. Computer projections indicate there is a high probability that the lava will most likely melt a significant part of the ice cap and, the enormous fissures that are being created, will lead to further break offs of Antarctica's polar shelf. It is not a good scenario."*

The haggard looking reporter looked down at his notes, his eyes darting back and forth. Continuing in a somber voice. *"Seismologists and geologists indicate there is a potential for trillions of gallons of water to be released into the world's oceans, an amount that could raise all the world's ocean levels by a minimum of at least 34 inches, inundating current shorelines over the entire world. It will be catastrophic! Millions will have to be evacuated, and countries will have to figure out what to do with all these displaced individuals."*

I couldn't believe my ears. The eastern seacoast obliterated in days, millions to be moved to new homes, new jobs, dependent on the good will of others.

Would our raised structure protect us? We had ridden out other storms. *Should we stay or should we leave? Where would we go?* Neither of us had relatives or anyone we knew on the mainland. Motels would be booked solid in a matter of days, and I'm certain they would be asking premium prices.

I turned from the family room and looked up the stairs. The upstairs' lofts seemed so far away. I wished that I had bought that camper I saw advertised on Craigslist three weeks ago. At the least we'd have a place to stay if we went inland. I guess if we tied the boat up to the house, we would still have transportation if the waters did rise as much as they said they would. My stomach churned, thinking of a new move.

I walked slowly to the bedroom. A dark cloud hung over my head. How could I tell the news to Diane and the girls? They were doing so good in school. How far would people have to go to be safe? Central Florida would be a nightmare. There were already too many people in and around Orlando. There were not enough resources for a large influx of others.

"Diane," I said softly, laying my hand gently upon her shoulder.

"What is it Ethan? It's 2:00 am and we need to get up early tomorrow morning."

"I'm sorry honey. This is *important!* I just listened to the news and what I heard was enough to send chills up and down my spine."

Turning to me groggily, her eyes half closed, she asked: "Can't this wait until morning?"

"*No!*" I said adamantly. "You've *got* to listen to this! We're going to be flooded out!"

"You said that last time we had a big storm down here! They *never* last that long!"

"This isn't a storm I'm talking about. It's something far worse!"

"Ethan, go back to sleep. What you are talking about doesn't even make sense!" she retorted, her eyes already closed.

I decided I'd let it ride until morning. Nothing was going to be accomplished while she was half asleep.

The alarm rang at 5:00 am. It was time for me to get up and prepare for my day. *Prepare for what?* Diane would be getting up soon. We had to talk. I wanted to make this a joint decision.

By 5:30 am she came into the kitchen. "I took the liberty of preparing your dark roast." I said.

"This must be something really important!" she quipped.

"It is! Last night I heard on the news that Antarctica is melting!"

"So, what's that got to do with us?" she asked, a bemused smile on her face.

I looked at her. She was so beautiful when she just got up in the morning, her long brunette hair streaming down her back, and her beautiful brown eyes still unhighlighted for the day. This was the real Diane, the Diane I had known for six years before our marriage of nine years, three months and four days. I wanted to grab her and hold her in my arms whilst I related the awful reality of what was upon us. Instead, I just sat at the table and stared out the window towards the river.

"Diane," I began. "What I'm about to tell you is perhaps part of the end times. I do not know where to begin."

Her smile had vanished, replaced with a look of concern, her brows furrowed, and her mouth opened as if she were gasping for air. "Ethan, you've never looked this way before! You're scaring me!"

I didn't realize that my fingers were tapping the table, nor that my pupils had contracted, nor that I was slouched in my seat. Diane's face had grown far away and the only sounds I could hear were my own breathing and the thump of my heart. Fortunately, the incandescent lights lit the interior, the bright blue and white tablecloth lending balance to the small kitchen.

When I finished explaining to her the situation, she sat down quietly and cupped her head in her hands. "What are we going to do?" she asked.

"I've decided we are going to stay, and ride it out, like all the other storms we have in the past. It's all we can do! We've got to tell the girls!"

Diane looked at me but, didn't say anything.

And so it was, on that fateful morning six days ahead of perhaps the worst tragedy the world would ever know, we made plans to hunker down on our little island in the middle of the Indian Lagoon on the East Coast of the Florida peninsula. This was to be our "Epi Center" the base of our operations, and survival center for the next fourteen months.

"Daddy, can we go to school today?" Alicia and Carlin asked after I had tried to explain to them how dire our situation was.

We spent the better part of the day purchasing supplies on the mainland, food staples, water, batteries, blankets, toiletries and games to tide us over the worst part of our ordeal. We also bought gasoline to have for the boat – three fifty-gallon drums which, although we knew it wasn't the safest thing to do, we would store under the cabin, high above the raging waters of the Atlantic.

Each day we watched as the waters edged higher onto the shores of our little island. I drove a stake into the sands outside the house so we could watch the daily rise of the waters as they crept ever so stealthily towards the cabin. The waters surged daily over our small island retreat.

On Day 14 we lost communication with the mainland. There would be no more contact with the outside world for the rest of stay here. Somehow the change in ocean temperatures did something to the atmospheric conditions as well, and there were many fierce storms that engulfed the coasts of the world's continents. Not only did the rising, cold waters trigger almost daily, violent thunderstorms, there were strange hailstorms and tornados as well. The cabin shook violently at times, but it held together. It wasn't the storms that would do us in… it was something far more sinister!

It didn't happen in a week as they predicted. It was more like the better part of seven months before the waters reached the 30" mark; but then, inexplicably, they continued to rise. Before we lost contact with the outside, the media had projected there might be as many as twelve separate volcanos under the Arctic shelf, each spewing hot gases, and molten lava to the surface.

Evidently, the Earth's crust was thinner here allowing for vast pools of lava and fire to flow unabated to the surface, generating an ever-present flow of heat to melt the fragile Arctic environment.

Each day as the waters crept higher up the stake I had implanted in the ground, before all this began. The level was now at 39 inches lapping at the canisters of gasoline I had fastened to the bottom of our cabin.

Though the girls and Diane tried to put on brave faces, their eyes betrayed their fear. Their formally playful, jovial moods were replaced by a dark funk, the girls often cowering in the corners of the family room for hours at a time. We were alone!

The last human we had seen was "crazy Steve" as his neighbors called him, the day of our trip down to Sebastian to get supplies.

Dressed in crumpled, beige Khakis, an old, soiled, white fishing shirt festooned with hooks and lures, and a hat which looked like something he had gotten out of an Indiana Jones movie, he moved with a right limp towards the door of the old Grant Antique Mall. *"Mark my words,"* he yelled, as he hugged the storefronts before making his move to enter the store. *"the days are upon us when we will no longer venture outside anymore!"*

A large bag with something inside fell onto the ground. Picking it up hurriedly, he stuffed it back into his pants pocket before continuing. *"You two,"* he gestured with his forefinger, speaking to Diane and I in our Nissan truck, *"had better get on home before they'll be no getting anymore!"* Then, running to Diane's window, he held up a picture of an immaculate landscaped garden and pointed to the flower pots along an equally immaculately landscaped driveway. *"This'll all be gone! Mark my words! There'll be nothing left for anybody, only art and the paintings of what were!"* Then, backing away from Diane's window, he ambled into the mall and was swallowed up by the displays in the aisles. He would be the last person we would see for the next 14 months. This was our last trip to Sebastian.

The waters would eventually reach forty-six inches above the point where this all began, wreaking havoc and death, on millions of the world's populations.

Residents on the shore and the barrier islands had been ordered to evacuate. Those remaining behind were warned that they would be on their own. Three days following our initial warning there were no more patrol cars or police to be found anywhere on Rt A1A or the lower-lying sections of Rt 1. We *were* on our own.

Darks clouds hovered over the horizon and above us and all around. Dark purples, sometimes purplish reds accentuated the skies. The smells of the rains and the sea permeated our nostrils, the thunderclaps echoed constantly for days on end, and our small cabin shook on its stilts. The rains gushed in through broken windows and the wetness of the excessive humidity clung to us like an albatross in distress.

"Mommy, I feel sick," the girls would relate to us. The horror of not being able to offer solace to your child was sometimes more than we could bear. There was nothing we could do! I remembered Pop holding me in his arms when mom had left. We took turns holding the girls against our bosoms. I prayed Pop would be there with us. Survival was different for each of us. Diane wished nothing more than the safety of our girls, I, the security of what we had.

There were times I regretted my decision to remain behind, but my deeper fear won out. Eventually the waters calmed, and the weather improved. Sometimes we fished out the windows of the cabin, the waters licking at our doorstep. There was even one time we untied the boat and ventured out into the vast stretches of ocean now covering our little island and the entire Florida shoreline. The waters seemed to stretch on indefinitely. We boated as far west as we figured Sebastian had been and, saw the rooftops of several of the taller buildings. There was no one around, that is, until we saw the Coast Guard boat speeding towards us.

"Hello! This is the U.S. Coast Guard," they announced. Once we explained to them our situation, they wished us well, and advised us to get in touch with the mainland.

On our return trip to the island we saw six or seven smaller, maybe 17 to 25-foot runabouts off in the distance. They did not acknowledge us or make any indication as to their intent. We arrived home safely and tethered the boat to the stairs, now leading down into the water.

By 1:00 am I heard a thud against the side of the cabin. Two boats with individuals in hooded masks were preparing to dock and come into our house. "Stop!" I said, a lot more bravely than I felt. I was not a fighter, I was a fisherman, but I would protect my family. "What do you want?"

"Give us your food," the larger of the group ordered.

"We don't have much left!" I retorted. "Leave us alone!"

"That's not going to happen my friend," the large man yelled out.

"We can give you some," I said.

"How about if we just make this our headquarters? This will be a good launching site!"

"Leave us alone!" I screamed. "My girls are going to be scared." I knew in that instant I had made a dreadful mistake. Before I'd opened my mouth, these men had no idea of who was in the small cabin. I estimated there were about twelve of them in all.

"Get the women," one of the men ordered.

Once they brought Diane and my two daughters who were screaming at the top of their lungs, to the small family room, things quieted down. "Now, you will either do as we say, or you're not going to see your wife and daughters again."

I stopped. My breathing was labored and, my ribcage felt as if I'd been kicked by a mule.

"We're not staying," the big man announced, "but we will be taking some of your groceries and gasoline. Be thankful that's all we'll be taking. And, let me give you a little advice. There are more of us out there, in bigger and better equipped boats, so my advice to you is to hightail it out of here as fast as you can to the mainland." With that, they were gone.

Once they left Diane turned to me and voiced the thought that was going through both our minds. "Ethan! We've got to get out of here! It's no longer safe!"

I couldn't believe what was happening. I stood there, my fingers twitching uncontrollably, shaking my head repeatedly as if that would clear all the cobwebs from my brain. We had weathered the rising waters, and the storms, and minimal food for well over a year. Now there was a new terror, one far worst than nature. I could not move. My worst fears were being realized. I collapsed on the floor on my knees, repeatedly calling out for the answer. I was scaring my girls. I turned to Diane for support. "Ethan,'" she said, "get a hold of yourself!"

I would have to leave my comfort zone if my family were to survive. *Maybe the next group wouldn't be so lenient.* We would stay in the cabin one more night. In the morning I would take them inland.

I envisioned being trapped, teetering in a plane wreck, on top a mountain shelf. If I moved to off-balance the plane, the entire fuselage full of people would plummet to the earth thousands of feet below. I could not move. I was trapped.

In the morning it was bleak and cloudy. A fog had come in during the night and blanketed the coast. The dark waters hid the roads and yards of what had been. Two cabin cruisers were coming in fast from the north. As they approached shots were fired in our direction. A 50 mm howitzer mounted atop one of the boats fired several shots towards the cabin. We ducked. That's all we could do! We were no match for the firepower these intruders apparently had. We were about ready to board our Everglades 295CC to try to make our escape, when we heard the unmistakable sound of the large foghorn. In the distance we saw a military vessel heading full steam ahead, for us. Warning shots were fired, and the two cruisers sped away.

The enormous vessel had to dock further out or be grounded. A smaller, armed vessel was sent to check on us. We were informed that they had received a call yesterday from an unidentified vessel. *We were alone and needed assistance.* I couldn't believe it! The thugs who had commandeered our food and gasoline yesterday actually had a heart. The Navy offered to take us to South Carolina where shelters and housing were being set up for coastal flood evacuees.

We had survived the unthinkable. A toxic fear I had acquired at a young age set up the parameters of how I dealt with an unimaginable situation. Anchored in place by an irrational fear, I had tried to deal with our problem in the only way I knew how. It was the scenario of being on the top floor of the World Trade Center on September 11, and tempting fate, by electing to remain in a place you believed might have offered temporary shelter, or, taking an even riskier gamble, and walking the stairs down to the bottom.

I chose to walk those stairs of uncertainty, those steps leading me away from my safe harbor of self-doubt and fear. I trembled every step I took forward, cowering in the corners of each landing; but in the end, I walked away, from my deepest fears.

I don't know if I'm cured of my phobia; but I see things in a new light. "Inconsistent?" I'm sure I'll be at times; but *now* that we have a new home, in a new land, and a new job, I can, for the first time in my life, see on the horizon the dawning of a new day of transformation, change, and yes, survival.

###

Richard Marschall earned his education at Towson University, B.S., Post graduate work WIU. His Short stories and poetry published in numerous anthologies, including the Space Coast Writer's Guild in Florida, Scribblers of Brevard Anthologies, Poetry Soup, and Eber & Wein. Served as Literary Editor of the Scribblers 2018-2019, and as their president first part of 2020. Published works: "First Call – Poetry for the Ages," "Quarrytown," "Justice Unbound – Gehenna," "Blessed – The Story of Joyce V. Marschall," and "The Magic of Christmas Anthology."

FAMILY
By Kathryn C. Flanagan

The full moon hung overhead, slowly taking form as it waited to become the mistress of the sky. Mialuna loved that story. The one where the moon and the sun raced. But the moon could never catch up, so it had to be content to reflect the glory of the sun.

Tonight, was the first celebration of the harvest. All day long cooking and baking had taken place. Tonight, a celebration of vegetable and fruit dishes would cover the long tables set up across the front yard. Fruit breads and pies along with strawberry shortcake would be on the dessert table. The one table Mialuna never missed.

She braided the last braid of garlic and put it into the basket. Now to distribute them. With pride, she walked to each of the six homes in their family to give them their share. Every recipient complemented her on how fine her braid looked. This was the first time she had been allowed to braid garlic by herself.

By the time she reached her own home, the congratulations had made her feel quite important. Gram was the person who received the braids for their home. She squinted at them and held them up to the light. Finally, she nodded and hugged Mialuna.

Horse-drawn wagons, bicycles, and combinations of both brought the people from nearby families. Mialuna's best friend, Daisy, found her. They tried to run into the barn before anyone saw them, but Gram sat on the front porch shucking peas, watching for children who weren't helping. She caught them.

Mialuna and Daisy carried bowls, pans, silverware, plates, glasses, jugs of water and apple cider out to the tables. Soon with all the families contributing, the tables were full.

Everyone sat and turned toward Gram who thanked the Spirit that guided them for the abundant harvest and for the safe haven they had been guided to find. By the time the moon became a large silver disk, all the food had been eaten.

The bonfire was lit. Guitars, banjos, mandolins, along with drums of every shape were taken out of their protective covers and tuned. Songs were sung while the food was put away and the dishes were washed.

Everyone gathered around the bonfire and the songs stopped. It was time for the sharing. Gram sat in a wooden chair with a padded seat and back. The children who were under ten sat on the ground in a semi-circle around her feet. It was so quiet the crickets could be heard.

As she always did at the beginning, Gram asked the children, "What will be shared tonight?"

The children were silent. Gram often had that effect on them. Especially the first time they saw her. Her face was brown from working in the fields. It folded into soft crevices like a carved apple doll's face. Her white hair spiraled out of her bun and curled around her face. She was strong but well-padded, so her hugs reminded you of feather pillows. It was her emerald green eyes that either drew or repelled people, for her eyes seemed to be able to see into your soul.

Mialuna raised her hand and Gram nodded.

"Please tell the story of the journey from Before Now to Now."

Gram tilted her head and smiled. "It is a long story, Mialuna."

"I know, but it is my favorite."

The old woman nodded and began. "The world was not as it is today in the Before Now. There were as many electronic devices called computers and I-pads as there were people inhabiting the planet. Everyone also had a phone that they carried in their pockets. The phones were used to type messages to friends, to watch movies, to listen to music, to pay for food, and to look up important facts. Very seldom were they used to talk to others, even though this was their original purpose.

"The use of these phones caused damage to wrists and many transportation accidents. Their wireless signals disturbed the air surrounding the earth. Some people said these wireless signals also disturbed the signals within people's brains.

"There were cars, buses, airplanes, and other transportation that used gasoline and polluted the air. This pollution was noted but little was done to stop the production of these vehicles.

"The food the people ate was soaked or cooked in chemicals. Even the raw vegetables and fruits were coated in chemicals, unless you found an organic farmer. Farm animals were fed chemically coated grains, so they were turned into poison carriers. There were drinks in stores made from unknown substances that most people could not pronounce.

"The effect on the earth from all these manufactured substances was that it began to slowly die."

Here everyone gasped. The beautiful earth dying was too much to bear.

Mialuna and Daisy put their arms around each other. The scary part was coming up next.

"Due to all the pollution in the skies, the layer protecting our planet from the sun began to grow thin. So thin, that in some spots, holes opened up. Through these holes more of the sun's heat and deadlier rays were able to reach our planet. The glaciers, which were huge chunks of ice covering parts of the earth, began to melt. Some of the people tried to draw attention to this problem, but no one would listen. Our leaders did not listen. They only wanted to make more money."

Only the crackling of the fire and chirping of the crickets was heard.

"The chemicals continued to be released into the air, the ground, the food, the animals, and the people. The glaciers at the top and the bottom of the world began to melt. They melted years before the scientists expected them to melt. The seas rose so high in one year that all the people who lived on the coastline had to leave and find another place to live. The weather became more violent. There were more storms, and earthquakes. Some of the land disappeared in hurricanes, which are big windstorms that occur in the oceans and run onto the land." Gram took a drink from her mug.

Mialuna covered her face. She knew she would cry at this next part.

"And then the first worst thing happened. A scientist, one of the people who made chemicals for people to take, instead of herbs and potions, made a disease for a general to use against another country. Unfortunately, an accident happened in the laboratory and the disease was released. This disease traveled by air. Wherever it went, when people breathed it into their bodies, they became very sick and some died. To stop the spread of this sickness, the leaders of all the countries in the world told people to stay home and to only leave if they wore masks. The people now had time for research, and they began to notice some of what was happening to the earth, but they felt it was someone else's problem, not theirs. They believed the scientists would develop a cure for the disease and also a cure for the earth's problems.

"Then the second worst thing happened. The scientists said they had a cure for the disease and people lined up to take it. It cost a lot of money to pay for this cure, so only the richest of the people were able to receive this benefit. The seasons changed and so did the disease. It became stronger. It traveled all over the earth. It mixed with monkeys and pigs and chickens. It became even more deadly.

"The people who had taken the antidote for the disease thought they were safe and so they gathered together. They traveled. The disease was in the air everywhere. The people who had taken the scientist's antidote became complacent and stopped wearing their masks. They did not know the air they breathed contained a new toxic disease that their treatment did not protect them from. They were unaware that the new disease sought out the cure they were given. It made the chemicals in the medication lethal. Over half of the people on the earth died within three months." Gram paused.

"But there were some people who had not consumed the medicine from the scientists. Most of them had not taken it because they did not have the money to buy it. Others, our mothers and grandmothers, had followed their dreams and intuition. They relied on the plants of the earth to protect them. When the dying began, they packed up their families. They followed the stars and their dreams to this spot. They came to the middle of the continent, where there were hills and clear skies and the rich dark earth welcomed us.

"In a dream, dreamed on the same night by all the elders, they were told to build families on the same pattern as a bee hive. Six sides, for six dwellings. In these homes lived people not only related by birth, but those who felt they belong together. The houses at the top and at the bottom of the hexagon would be reserved, one for just women and one for just men, for not everyone was the same. Each hexagon of homes formed one family. We were told to gather families together to celebrate the seasons and harvests. When it is evident that more space is needed, people from different families would come together and form a new family."

Gram stopped and looked at Mialuna. "And what do we call our families?"

The answer was known and everyone answered, "Survivors."

The sharing was over. The music began again and everyone danced until dawn.

Kathryn Flanagan's new novel, *Children of Ha'trae*, is scheduled for release in December 2020. Her first book, *Beyond the Fine Line, an Anthology of Short Stories and Poems,* is available on Amazon. Three of her plays have been performed at Surfside Playhouse, Cocoa Beach. She is the co-president of the Cape Canaveral – National League of American Pen Women, and a member of "Group Therapy", an Improv troupe. In her spare time, she tames dragons and crochets.

FIRES
By Anne-Marie Derouault

It's Hell on Earth
Creatures fleeing everywhere
To escape flames
That no one can put out

Is it the end of a world
Where we could ignore
The changes to come
Where we could continue to believe
In infinite abundance
In unlimited resources
Is this where a cycle ends

Will we know how to reinvent
Ways to live
In harmony with our space
In harmony with our Earth mother

Will we know to help her heal
Regreen the burnt grounds
In a few dozen years
Save what can be saved
And recreate
Paradise on Earth

###

 Born in Paris, living in Florida, **Anne-Marie Derouault** is a consultant in management, communication, and stress reduction. She writes free verse poetry in French and in English, haikus and short stories, inspired by her love of travel, nature, and human beings. She recently published her first book: *"While the Poem Lasts,"* a bilingual collection of inspirational poetry. She is a member of Cape Canaveral Pen Women, Space Coast Writers Guild, and Scribblers of Brevard.

FOREVER EMBERS, NEVER TO FLAME?
By Ima Pastula PhD

It was his warmth, a strange, impulsive attraction that began the strange closeness that never became a touch. Sitting the short distance across the table, in a room, even passing close by, it was a dynamic, almost electric compulsion to be near him that could not be denied. What strange, complicated attachment grew from the smoldering embers of a passion never shared? The realm was complete in its hovering, nights of wild awakeness, thoughts never complete. A place of great submission to some overwhelming power he possessed over a total victim of his personal, magnetic seduction. It was *insane* to dwell together in some sort of mystic cobweb like desire; never touching, only the mesmeration of visionary completion of passions! Were there words to tell this strange story? Could it be a type of illusionary, non-physical sexual activity, imagined only, felt eternally never of the body completing the ordinary type of a sexual encounter?

Using the sample of; *"As You Like it" the famous Play by William Shakespeare; Quoting with the phrase "All the world's a stage, and all the men and women are merely players; they have their exits and their entrances, and one man in his time plays many parts."*

The ancient philosopher type, surely meant the Play to also be true of women. As a therapist, one sees the truism of such a *Play,* and Shakespeare becomes sort of an ancient voice that speaks the truth to a Metaphysician. (Hypnotherapist) Patient revelations become *baser* the deeper the trancing of hypnosis.

Day of Reckoning.
Simply discussing the matter in which his day was to be spent, the happenings of his life; just ordinary things to talk about.

It was the strangeness of the sudden, complete awareness of him, the color of his hair, the look in his eyes as well as the overall majestic sum of his entirety that woke a primitive, almost savage desire that began the embers. An inner self, that primitive one spoke of earlier, began to burn, slowly warming a once, very chilly interior. As the heat rose to a fevered pitch, she confessed it felt like a virus, indeed, a strain of bacteria capturing one's reality?

Consequences.

A consuming affair of the heart, sort of like a Shakespearian Play, actors and actresses cluttering each scene, almost to blotter the immediate danger of a real sexual encounter.

Scene One; stage left, a rare moment of sensuous encountering, a meager puff of powerful, heavy breathing, that brings the embers close to flame! Curtain comes down, folds of metaphoric, deep scarlet red, smothers the sounds of the change of scenery.

Scene Two; on the plush of the pillowed couch, eyes meet, heat rises, smiles suggest a longer conversation, a time of togetherness beyond the reality of just two; a place of some sort of grand illusions of elsewhere, at a different time, beyond the borders of this day. Perhaps a dream happening on stage?

Scene Three; Every day past a brilliant sunrise, into the glare of daylight as well as the haunting, deep purple of Nautical Twilight. The Actress is in love! What happens next as that heavy Curtain falls once more, and the scenes change, a seemingly eternal companionship of mental awareness begins? Where is this stage? Who are the characters preventing any further evolvement, and the dulling of the embers that are never allowed to flame? As in most of Shakespearian Plays, is this then a tragedy? Indeed, with the thoughts that *"All the world is a Stage"* we can see that we really are actors and actress, playing a part for those who we are surrounded by pleasing, pampering, caring for the main characters in our personal plays.

In the ultimate reality of this patient's realm, as she is taken beyond certain borders into the territory of her subconscious mind, her true self is revealed willingly, with no regrets, shame or sorrow. It is a mysterious place within one's mind, a sanctuary, a natural stage for the imagination to star. Always the quote by the great physicists Albert Einstein fits just here in my writings, "Logic will get you from A to B, imagination will get you everywhere."

Taken into her deepest self, she reveals the secret longings for a man unaware of her secret passion for him, of someone that has all that is perfection as far as she is concerned and dwells in a private world of "What might have been."

Noting here, many thorns that prick the mind, cluttering the haunted mansions are from the past, back when one was young and foolish enough to believe in miracles as well as true love. When the reality of a feeling being mostly a sexual urge produced by mother nature to force us to breed, well, frustrations begin, and the whole stage crumbles into a mere playground. The reverse in attitudes begin to become questions of who, what, where, when and why! Being a therapist, entering the dwelling place of these questions about one's past, is a real awakening as to what one's real Stage is all about and what kind of Actor or Actress they really are? When many of these intimate questions are answered, one can reset the scene for their future Plays, adjust the cluttering of past mistakes, and get on with it! Many become much greater Actors and Actresses.

Interring the Domain of the Subconscious Mind.

She sits in the curves of the much used, leathered recliner; wet, tiny tears fall to her soft cheeks. As a close to elderly women, she has kept a strong hold on her youthful look. A sense of sadness is felt, more so than 'told of,' as she remembers the days of he and she, moments of almost giving in to the breeding signal but regaining her demeanor, eliminating the lust and focusing on the *almost* of their years together. Yes, years, the more she wept, the stranger her story became! Brought back to her immediate reality, again, drying the tears, her altered state was always left in her subconscious, to revisit over and over again.

A True Story.
'Gone with the Wind'? No, *'Grapes of Wrath'?* No, but very close to the style of storytelling by the great William Shakespeare; tragic a bit, reality the main character with real family members that stop the illicit thoughts of, perhaps, desired actions of the two main characters! Sounding a bit wishy-washy, however, it is difficult to tell of the inner-most desires we keep sacred. It is a story shared by a most unusual woman, sort of biographical, if there is such a thing of the affairs of the heart. It is a tale of woe, of unrequited love, a love so deeply felt it became her obsession. Told of the strange, almost myth-like relationship with a man for so many years it could be happening in someone's coma!

"The warm rain touched my warming cheeks as I waited to meet him, with bated breath, outside as he parked his car, began his short walk toward the meeting place. Striking in his tallness, bold with lighter hair and deep, smoldering eyes. Handsome, in my admiration, a very distinguished man making one feel inferior. As he noticed me, he smiled with such a gentleness it began our meeting with the embers beginning their glow! Strictly business, no romantic overtures, all my fantasy, for sure, as we talked of mundane things related to a project we were working on together. The very essence of his maleness, the strength of his character and, of course, the nature of the project that became the real reason for our togetherness."

Sharing the great emotional tether she had with him, our long-term patient and Doctor relationship offered up the ingredients of one woman's life's drama. Not revealing her real name and residence allows leniency writing her story; she has given her permission, as she feels she must release the agony she is suffering because of the lack of embers forced never to flaming to reward her sexual desires. Professional people are doomed by ethics, *don't you know*? She and he both in stressful, careers bound by their individual oaths; a contrived behavior declared by their hand to Bible and other hand to the heavens to keep the oath, never disgrace the ethics of the individual words that have bonded them to certain behaviors. It is a hesitation on both their parts to keep their oath. As a Priest is bound by certain religious declarations, as is a Rabbi sworn to obedience to certain parts of the Torah. It seems their Oath of ethics is the killer of most romantic thoughts. Indeed, professional people have passions, sexual desires as well as a damnation of Mother Nature's demands on their body and mind!

She suddenly damned the very ethics she once was so drawn to obeying, and his stringent obedience to those he took. Her *altered state of mind* suffered the outburst and was quickly brought back from her trance to the reality she was forced to live. Momentarily, an ugly feeling seemed captured her; sensing she had been pulled back from a very intimate moment she was sharing with him.

Gone but Never Forgotten.

As the so called *"The Days of Wine and Roses"* came and went for these two, graduation from the Universities hastened the Oath of Office, as they needed to gain a license to practice their chosen fields. No need to disclose the details, as it is not really a *need to know* about them and would possibly give away their individual Indemnities to criticisms. Always readers seem to lean toward disclosure of naughty persons, those who disobey rules and regulations, sinful persons seem to excite many readers looking toward the mistakes we make, just for the thrill of it all. This story, however, is from the heart of a woman who sacrificed a physical excitement in the honor of who she is, and he, in the dignity of his titles.

Given her instructions to lean back, cozy up to the pillows lining the recliner, let herself feel the slow, under a net-like feeling of a hypnotic mind altering, she left the immediate reality. We captured her on the other side of herself, in the act of walking toward the military housing in Europe, as she silently gathered images and secret notes of citizens who were suspect at being subverted. A partial give-away of the fact she was somehow involved in *national security* and a hint as to when she first met the ultra-man.

One wonders, but of course, understands the need for strict Oaths!

"I walked swiftly, pretending to sort purchases in a woven basket like most other morning shopping women. He was very noticeable, sitting quietly in a small alcove in a *Ratskeller* (English translation, basement Bar like drinking place). He was staring as hard at me as I him! He was dressed like the citizenry, but somehow, I knew he was not! Another Spy?

"I was not welcomed. Seems only men are to drink in there!"

A gentleman, he came close, whispering in English, "*Go outside, wait for me!*" For no known reason, she said her turning around seemed the right thing to do!

They met then, face to face disguised Americans on some sort of project for the United States Military. He, of course, a ranking Officer... she keeping herself a secret still until a little more was known of him! Entering into a small Brochen (Bread) Bakery, he and she pretended, jointly, to be European; what a fakery! Enjoying a few more meetings, getting to know one another, soon he and she went separate ways. Many years later, entering into a Conglomerate Office Building in New York, there he was, in the elevator, on his way up to his American-titled Office!

"He took my arm, always a bit domineering, escorted me to the basement, a small shopping Mall, then ordered coffee for us both."

In her altered mind, she saw him as flirtatious, touching her in many sorts of ways, however, believed to be in the hallucinogenic part of a trancing. (*Wishful thinking?*) Somehow, she believed there was some sort of *meant to be* to the surprise meeting. Her sensuous fantasies soon began during the many meetings and the joining of a few Governmental projects.

"Not sure if it all was something of National interest or interest in me!"

He gave her a black workbook, and an Ink pen, asking her to write down the notes of the meetings; soon to become a sort of diary of he and she. A false feeling of kinship sort or ruined the professionalism it was soon discovered to be.

Turning the Ill-gotten Pages.
It was all hush-hush between them, meetings became tense when he noticed he was being followed.
"It was dim on the way to the Café; for a weekly meeting; as I turned the corner, he, a small, dark man in a new looking suit was seen peering around the corner at him! It was a quick response as I dropped the black book and Pen to make a distraction, then got a really good look at the stranger as he turned toward me. He was quick to move away, out of the light to disappear into the darkened corner!
"He was annoyed at this, saying I was also seen!"

The uttering of meetings was difficult under her altered state of mind, discussions to translate took a while when she was out of her trance.
Many past recollections become distorted in the realm of a hypnotized mind, somehow like a shorthand, utterances weave back and forth between the words, like the making of a jigsaw puzzle to be put together later.

Off to another assignment.

Between the Acts, like the metaphoric dark red curtain coming down, whilst the stage is being set for a new scene, the lives of he and she undulated between Countries and situations. Keeping touch as much as possible, retirement made a more suitable environment for he and she to meet for different reasons, hence the altering of attitudes toward one another as well as the mistaken Identity that can happen after a long period of absence. Change, the widest gap between friends and lovers, in this instance between two ethically correct professional people, in the flux of the enormous Stage changes, and the gap between the Acts...Still actors and Actresses, they drama on, to the where, what and why, leaving the 'when' to chance, even now!

"...being kept awake now, by the opening, reopening of a tattered past, as a she and he in constant (heat?) awareness of strong feeling for one another, but still tormented by the ageing Oaths?

"When you retire, does that mean you can discard the *Oaths* taken as an active *doer of the deeds* from the University studies? A dilemma here, do we or don't we give in to the primitive situation of Mother Nature's sexual drive to breed? Of course, we would not be doing the breeding bit, but still, we did take life-altering Oaths! What to do? "

As her present-day therapist, remind her that Oaths were still prevalent Doing journeys with her into her sub-conscious mind, listening to the garble of her short-hand type of drama created as a heavy breasted, passionate Spy not as a confessor nor advisory to the lovelorn! She was properly offended, mentioning she is utterly helpless whilst in an altered state of mind from a potent form of hypnotherapy, that "you are responsible for me while on my stage during my performance each time you take away the reality and cause me to wonder between Acts as the scenes change so often behind the dark red Curtain!" See, she is with the flow now, gets well into her altered mind set almost immediately for each of her performances; she is becoming more insistent that we talk more about *him*, still heart-worn by the many years of abstinences forced upon them! Indeed, becoming a very passionate Actress as well! What happens next will, indeed, cause the annal's of Time to implode!

Ima J. Pastula PhD is a published author, master artist, retired adjunct facility professor from Anne Arundle Community College in Arnold Maryland. When both husband and wife retired, they relocated to Melbourne, Florida. She is a past president of the National League of American Pen women, serving after as secretary. A member of the Space Coast Writers Guild for many years and a contributor, many times, to the Guild's Anthologies. Available for creative lectures.

FUCHSIA LIPSTICK
By Joanne Fisher

The woman in the navy-blue uniform had a stern expression as she gestured him to come forward, a slight weaving of the brow, habitual rather than conscious, and the vague sense of a frown about her features. She wasn't wearing a mask like the rest of the airport personnel; she had a clear plastic shield that covered her entire face. She wore fuchsia lipstick, although somewhat unflattering on other women, which for some odd reason, he thought of his mother. She seemed to barely register Zach as she called him through the metal frame. He was just a man like any other that passed through.

He noticed her eyes hovering above his head. He couldn't tell whether the light had turned green or red or even if it was a light at all or some other type of signal. Similar to when he placed his carry-on bag in the small plastic tray on the conveyor belt to be analyzed by the x-ray machine, the disgruntled man handling that part of the operation, re-positioned it correctly so that the machine could read it clearly and quickly.

"I'm sorry." He said but the man didn't even acknowledge him. *Now, it seems possible that I won't know how to walk through the detector properly? Geez!*

It must have been clear because the uniformed woman didn't even look at Zach. He sheepishly waited for his bag as an elderly man tried to jerk his heavy bag from the conveyer. The elderly man looked at Zach and quickly looked away.

Am I threatening to him? Then he briefly caught his reflection in the mirrored walls. His eyes were cold, even through his mask, and his expression closed. Even his reflection was a stranger to him. As he picked up his bag, he followed the elderly man who was wheeling his bag as quickly as he could. From behind, he looked like Zach's grandfather who had passed a few years back. His silhouette sparked a conversation stored in his memory from when he was a boy.

"There's something wrong with that boy," his grandfather used to say.

"No! He's perfectly normal. Leave him be!" his mom ordered as she quickly fired up some vague mental affliction far back in the family tree that would always be raw in her heart.

"It's your side that did it. I don't know what Scott was thinking."

"Don't you dare talk to me about Scott! It's your fault he went the way he did! You pushed him away!" She stormed out.

Zach could still hear his mother shrieking and still felt his insides being shredded to pieces as they continued to argue while he was standing right there.

His bag came through and Zach grabbed his keys, phone and coat. He slid his arms in the bag so it wouldn't fall from his hands.

Another uniformed woman a little way off was watching. This one had fuchsia hair; only her eyes seemed warm and kind. She could have been smiling but under the mask, he couldn't tell.

"Excuse me sir. Could you…?"

She indicated her portable scanning equipment.

Before his heart attack, grandfather would occasionally pick up Zach from school.

"Who did you play with today?"

That's how the interrogation would begin. Nervously, he placed his hand in his pocket, wrapped his fingers reassuringly around Benjy.

"Nobody."

"Nobody?"

Zach wondered what he wanted him to answer.

"Did you ask any of them?"

"No."

"No?"

When he threw his words back at him, he felt like he made accusations. *Did he hear what I said?*

"They don't interest me."

"They don't interest you?"

"We don't like the same things."

He would sigh unenthusiastically, gripping the steering wheel. His grandfather never made an effort to try to understand his grandson. Most of the conversations ended in a disappointed scoff or a resigned sigh.

"Sir?" The woman lightly touched his arm, bringing him back to reality.

"Sorry," Zach mumbled.

"Sir if you could take your hand out of your pocket." She asked gently.

Instinctively Zach had placed his hand in his pocket and withdrew it slowly, making himself easier to scan.

"What's that?" she asked.

With a jolt Zach realized he was still holding Benjy. The skin beneath his collar burns. The tattered little pterodactyl unfolded in his sweaty palm. One of its eyes was coming loose.

The security woman looked bemused, and then cracked a smile.

"I'm sorry—"

"No, no," she waved the apology away.

Slowly she reached towards her belt, continued into her trouser pocket. Pulled out something small and orange. A bundle of cloth, old and lopsided. Four legs, a tail, black stripes. A worn out little stuffed tiger.

She shoved the little tiger in his face and laughed whole heartedly, pulling her mask down.

Then they clinked both small toys to each other like two glasses of champagne. They smiled at each other. Then Zack noticed her name tag.

"Belinda? That's a lovely name!"

"Thank you." There was that warm smile again. This time it wasn't hidden behind a mask.

Zack pulled out a business card and shoved it discreetly into her front pocket. "I'm Zach." Then he got closer to her ear. "I'll be back in a few days. Would you like to go out to dinner?"

Belinda pulled out the business card, and with the pen she had clipped inside her pant pocket, she wrote her cell number on it. Then she pulled the hand that was holding Benji and slid it right under the small toy. "Text me." She winked and waved Zach to continue towards his gate.

Zach pulled his mask down so he could give her a huge smile. "I will!" he shouted as he fixed his mask. With a skip in his step, he quickly headed for the gate. After many months of doom, gloom and one bad thing after another, he finally felt something he hadn't felt since February...hope.

###

Joanne Fisher is a Canadian, Italian, American author who has penned TEN books: 3 steamy romances, 1 Christmas Novella, 2 historical fictions, 2 travel guides, 1 anthology and 1 murder/mystery. She has also written several short stories for various Space Coast Writers' Guild Anthologies and in April of 2019 was elected **President of the Space Coast Writers' Guild**. She lives in Florida with her husband and two dachshunds, Wally and Madison. Please visit www.JoannesBooks.com

HEAD FOR THE HILLS
By Dan Fisher

It was a crisp, October day. "Wow, what a nice break from the record heat we've been having," Thomas said to Joyce, his new wife. "I think I'm going to head up into the hills for a hike. It's been so hot, and I really miss the good outdoors! Want to come along?"

"No, I have to work on my new book. I have a deadline coming up, soon, and I'm too far behind. You go."

"Okay, you sure?"

"Oh, yes. Have a good time."

"Oh, I will."

"Don't you think you should take someone along? You know. In case something happens, they can call for help."

"No. I've hiked up there so many times. I know that area like the back of my hand. Another person will just hold me back. Besides, I'll have my cell phone to call for help. But I really won't need it."

"Okay." She kissed him lightly on the lips as Thomas went out the door. It slammed shut behind him

Joyce knew how much her young husband enjoyed getting out into the fresh air. Hiking was his favorite form of exercise. He said that it worked all his major muscle groups. She knew that to be fact; after all, it's how they had met, just a year-and-a-half ago. She had been hiking a well-used trail with a small group of girlfriends, and they had come across Thomas and several of his friends. He was so sure of himself, and she—well, not so much. Actually, it was her first time out, and she was having a bit of trouble.

"Your first problem is your shoes. You can't hike in sneakers. They don't grip well on the sand, you feel every pebble on the trail, and you have no ankle support. Look at my shoes. See how thick the soles are? And look how they go up over my ankles. You don't have to spend a lot of money. In fact, a decent pair of hiking boots won't cost any more than those fancy sneakers—maybe even less!"

Joyce was impressed with how this guy just zeroed in on her problem and offered a solution. He wasn't judgmental. Actually, he was quite kind and caring about it. Plus, he was a bit of a hunk.

"Here. Take my phone number. I'll help you pick out a good pair of starter shoes at the local sporting goods store." He handed her a card. It read, Thomas Richards, Sales Consultant for the local Ford dealership.

As the young men walked away, Joyce's gal pals let out a couple of quiet wolf-whistles. "Woo-hoo! Go get him, girl!"

Joyce turned three shades of crimson. "Aw, c'mon. Knock it off!" But her mind was racing ahead.

When she called him the next day, he said, "Perfect timing. I just sold two vehicles and I'm taking the rest of the day off." Shall I come pick you up, or do you want to meet me somewhere?"

"Well, can I come by the dealership and we can go together from there?" It was her way of verifying that he was who he said he was. In this day and age, you can't be too careful.

"Perfect! When you get here, we'll hop in my truck and we'll be on our way."

Hmm, a truck. That's a switch!

When she arrived at the dealership, she saw a group of salesmen standing in a cluster outside, almost blocking the entrance. Two of them had cigarettes hanging from their mouths. *How disgusting! They look like a flock of buzzards waiting for the next meal! Is that how this guy spends his days?*

"Good afternoon, ma'am. Are you looking for anyone in particular? If not, I'll be happy to help you find the perfect vehicle!" He was sort of a weaselly-looking guy. His shirt was hanging out on one side, and he smelt of stale cigarette smoke.

Joyce simply showed him Thomas's card and said, "I've already been working with Mr. Richards." The young man sort of rolled his eyes and mumbled something. Joyce thought it was something like, "Damn, another one for Tom," but she couldn't be sure.

The weaselly young man said, "Come this way." He led her into the showroom, to a desk where she recognized Thomas. "Hey, Tom, this lady says she's been working with you."

She certainly wasn't impressed with his tone of voice. *What an ass. I'll bet he doesn't sell many cars.*

"Oh. Hi, Joyce." Thomas stood up immediately and offered her his hand. "Thank you, Frank. I've been waiting for her." Again, Frank rolled his eyes. He wasn't shy about his apparent disdain for Thomas.

"So, what are you looking for, today?" Thomas flashed a barely discernable half-smile.

Joyce didn't miss a beat. "Oh, I need something for off-road. You know, good support, and something that won't let me feel every stone and pebble." She gave a coy wink.

"I think I have just the thing for you. Come this way."

All the while, Joyce was noticing his physique. Obviously, Thomas was a physical sort of guy. *No couch potato, here. He's obviously active and keeps himself in shape. And no ring. Hmm. Of course, that doesn't always mean anything, but it's a good sign.*

Joyce followed Thomas out of the showroom. The "buzzards" that had collected around her when she entered, just looked in awe as they headed back to the employee parking area. As they walked, she commented, "So, what's up with that guy?"

"What guy?"

"The guy that brought me in to you. He seems to have a bit of an attitude."

"Oh, Frank. You know, I trained him, or tried to. Most salespeople don't like to train someone new, because you're basically training your competition. Not only do you have to compete with the dealership down the road, or in the next town, but you're in competition with the folks at the dealership where you work. But I've been doing this for so long I've built up a reputation for not fleecing people. Sometimes I'll sell a two- or three-pounder, but sometimes I'll sell one for the minimum commission. You have to read your customer, and if they have a really tight budget, you give the car away. Frank, though, hasn't taken any of my advice. I can easily sell two cars a day. Sometimes three. He's lucky to sell two in a week. If he'd wash his clothes and not smoke at work, he'd do a lot better. I've told him that, but he doesn't want to listen. He takes it personally and gets all offended and butt hurt. I've done all I can do. You either take the advice given you, or you don't."

"What's a two- or three-pounder?"

"Oh, sorry. It's car sales jargon. A pound is a thousand dollars of commission. So, a three-pounder is a three-thousand-dollar commission. Those are extremely rare, but I usually make a few every month."

He led Joyce to a shiny, metallic ruby red F-250 pickup truck—Super Duty, Limited. As he grabbed the handle, it opened right up. It wasn't "lifted" and it had a step on the side, so she was able to grab the inside handle and climb in. Thomas walked around to the driver's side and hoisted himself up. A push of the button, and the truck was running.

"You don't lock your truck?" Joyce was incredulous.

"Oh, I have a proximity fob. I keep it in my pocket. The truck can tell when it's within a foot or two of the door. There's a sensor in the handle that unlocks the truck when I grab the handle. Same thing when I get out. Only, I don't have to do anything. The truck senses when I leave, and it auto-locks. You'll see when we get to the store."

Joyce felt the soft leather of the seats on her skin. She then felt the coolness. "Air-conditioned seats," Thomas said. *I could get used to this, really fast! It beats the heck out of my Prius!*

At the store, Thomas said, "Don't get out, yet. I'll show you how." He exited, came around, and took her hand. "Here, grab the handle. Like that. Now, put your right foot on the step. Yup. Like that. Now your left foot. Okay, now, just step down. Or, if you get brave, you can just slide off the seat onto the ground!" Then, that half-smile, again.

They picked out a pair of good hiking shoes, and Thomas whipped out his Visa card. "It's on me," he said.

"I can't ask you to do that. We hardly know each other."

"Actually, you didn't ask me. So there!" He inserted his card into the card reader gizmo and signed on the screen. "There, that's that. You hungry? Where do you want to eat?"

He hadn't actually asked her *if* she wanted to go somewhere—it was *where* do you want to go?

"Well, I could use a bite. I really don't know, though. I haven't thought that far ahead."

"I know this steak and seafood place. It just opened a month ago, and the food is very good."

"Okay, that sounds great."

They went out to the truck. This time, she got in like a pro. Thomas drove a mile or so to Surf 'n' Turf's. Again, Thomas told her to wait, got out, went over to her side, and opened the door. He extended his hand to help her climb out. *Wow, this guy is like no other guy I've ever met!* She recalled her father's advice. "Don't have anything to do with any guy who doesn't hold the door for you." She recalled that he had always held the door for her mom, until her mom had passed away. She used to protest, saying that it was lame, and guys didn't do that anymore. "The good ones do," was her dad's reply.

They enjoyed a nice meal and some pleasant conversation that went well into the evening. Finally, the server—Thomas called her a waitress, saying that anyone can be a server, but a waiter or waitress is a professional —said, "I really hate to break up your evening, but I have to close out the register."

Thomas looked at his watch. "Holy cow! It's ten already!" He gave the waitress his card. She returned in a jiffy, he added the tip, and signed the bill. That was that.

By the time they got back to the dealership, the gates were locked with her Prius inside. "Oh, my," Thomas said. "I hope you don't have too far of a walk home." She jerked her head to look him square in the eye. Then she saw that half-smile. "I can call an Uber. Or I can just drive you home. It's up to you."

"Oh, you can drive me. I'm not that keen on taking rides from strangers." She winked.

"Okay, show me the way!"

They got to her apartment. She got out and began walking to her door. "Hey, Joyce! I don't work tomorrow. How about we give those new kicks a good workout? Break them in good and proper, you know?"

"That's a splendid idea. What time?"

"I can be here at seven. We can get an early start, before it gets too warm."

"I'll be ready."

And, the rest is history, as they say. They were married six months later. Of course, the first thing that he did was replace her aging Prius with something that had a bit more horsepower. Joyce had gone from never having ridden inside a truck to owning one, in less than a year.

After Thomas left, Joyce sat down at her computer and began to write—or, attempted to write. For some reason, she was unable to put any words down. A classic case of writer's block. She got up and started cleaning the house, absent-mindedly.

Thomas got to his usual spot. He would be hiking about two to three miles, and then return to his truck. On a good day, he could do that in a few hours. It wouldn't be very fast-going, because of the terrain. He liked a challenge. He wasn't out for a stroll in the park; this was true exercise. He put on his hiking shoes and warmed up, stretching all his muscles. He checked his supplies. A couple protein bars for energy, a liter or two of fresh water, and his cell phone. Ah! His battery was fully charged. Good communication was important to him, so he kept his phone charged to full capacity before each hike.

As he started out, he took a deep breath and inhaled the fragrance of the pines in the fresh air. These hikes really helped him clear his mind from the stresses of sales. *One day, I'm going to have to do something else, but I really don't know what I'll do.* Sales was his life, and he was good at it. It wasn't as stressful for him as for some of the other guys, because he was so good at it. Perhaps it was because he enjoyed being with the people, putting a customer into just the right vehicle. He never pushed something on a potential customer, never did the hard sell. He always was cordial, letting the customer make the choices. But, when it came time to deal, he knew just how to overcome the customers' objections. It was almost like a sixth sense for him. He'd usually have a deal done in about two hours, start to finish. And every customer thanked him for his time and his willingness to work with them.

Thomas had told Joyce the truth. He had hiked these trails for years, and he knew every branch and every stone on the way. He got about 2 miles out and was almost ready to turn around to come back. *I'm feeling pretty good. I think I'll go a bit farther today.* So, he forged onward. There was a narrow spot on the trail, and he had to grab some tree branches to steady himself. He had done this many times before, and it was second nature. Suddenly, *CRACK!* The branch gave way. As he slid down the hillside, his backpack came off. Down, down, he slid, about 75 feet, to the bottom of the ravine. The whole thing took only a few seconds. When the dust settled, he took stock of his situation. He was on his back, and he felt pain. He couldn't tell exactly where it came from, but he felt it. The sun was low in the sky. What the hell? It was only 11 or so when he slipped. It's almost sunset, now. I must've lost consciousness. *Where's my backpack? Oh, it's up there.* His backpack was about twenty feet away. He tried to get up to get it, and he felt a pain like he'd never felt before! He looked at his left leg and saw that it bent in a place where it was supposed to be straight. Then it hit him! He was hurt badly. There was no way he was going to walk on that leg in its current condition! No problem. I'll just call Joyce and she'll be out here in no time!

He grabbed his phone from the pocket of his shorts. *Thank goodness I didn't shove it in my backpack, or I'd really be screwed!* Thomas looked at the display and saw it was shattered. Not to worry. He pressed a button and said, "Call Joyce." There was enough of the display still intact that he could see it trying to dial. Suddenly, he discerned the words NO SERVICE! *Now, what? It's getting dark, my backpack is over there out of my reach, and I'm stuck here.*

Thomas had to decide whether his jacket was going to serve as a blanket or a pillow. He decided to just wear it, as he figured he wasn't going to get much sleep and it would be pretty chilly tonight. His leg hurt so much now, with a pain that he never could have imagined. He was an experienced outdoorsman but had never camped out in these conditions! His thoughts wandered to Joyce, and what she must be thinking. Maybe she was worried that he had picked up some floozy customer and was having the time of his life! No, she'd never exhibited any jealousy. Although, she had mentioned once, early on, that if she ever found out he was fooling around she would modify him so that he couldn't do it again. Somehow, he thought that would be less painful than what he was experiencing! How he wished he could let her know his condition! *How I wish I had listened to her! How I wish I had brought along a buddy! I'd have been out of here long ago! Now, I'm not sure if I'll ever get out of this hell hole!*

Finally, he fell asleep.

He awoke sometime later, and it was pitch dark. He could hear animals walking around in the underbrush. He knew that there were wolves and coyotes out there. He just hoped that none would pick up his scent. He lay awake for what seemed like hours and then fell asleep again. It wasn't a restful sleep; it was more that his mind rendered him unconscious to protect him from the pain.

He awoke to a bright, sunny day. His body was stiff and sore from having lain on the hard, rocky ground, in the cold, all night. "Help! Help! Is anyone there?" He shouted over and over again. There was no answer. He yelled until he became hoarse. His leg was hurting even more this morning, and it was swollen and purple. He had a gash in his right leg that had already begun to clot. There was a good amount of blood on the ground, though. His head felt like it was split open, but a quick check with his hand showed no blood.

Suddenly, he heard something. Voices. No, it couldn't be. *I must be hallucinating!* He had heard of that happening. People get injured seriously enough, and they start seeing and hearing things. *No, wait! There it is again!* "Hello! Hello! Help! Help me! I can't move!"

He heard a voice. "Where are you, man? I don't see you!"

"I'm down here! I grabbed a branch and it broke off, and I slid down here! Down in the bottom of the ravine! I'm hurt! I've fallen and I can't get up! My leg is broken, and I've lost a lot of blood!"

Then he saw a face at the top of the ridge, looking down at him. The person said, "Holy crap! You look in bad shape!" There's no cell service here, but I have a ham radio. I'll call for help!"

"A what?"

"Ham radio." He held it out so Thomas could see it.

I don't know what he's going to do with that little thing! But then, it's bigger than my cell phone. Maybe it can do something.

"I'll make a call on this. There's a repeater on the other hill over there. If someone's listening to their radio, they'll hear me and call for help."

"I really don't care how it works. I just need to get out of here!"

Thomas heard the young man. "Mayday, Mayday, Mayday! This is Kilo Golf Four Sierra Delta Juliet, KG4SDJ. Mayday!"

"KG4SDJ, this is AI4GK. What is your emergency?"

"I'm on the Quaker Trail in Gadsden County. There is a hiker who slid down into a ravine. He's fifty to a hundred feet below, but he says his leg is broken and he's lost blood!"

"I copy. Standby."

What seemed like minutes, but in reality, was about a minute-and-a-half, "KG4SDJ, this is AI4GK."

"KG4SDJ here."

"I've notified the sheriff's department. They're going to send a rescue helicopter out immediately."

"Roger that. Thank you, Old Man!"

The young man called down, "Help is on the way!" He then began climbing down toward Thomas.

"My wife! She must be worried sick!"

The young man grabbed his radio again. He called the "old man" (jargon for a male ham radio operator) again. He provided Joyce's phone number, and asked him to relay Thomas's condition to her, and that he would be enroute to the hospital soon. She could meet him there. Once the message was relayed, Thomas heard the "thup-thup-thup" of the helicopter. It hovered over him, and a team of two paramedics was lowered down, along with an elongated basket. The paramedics started an IV and splinted his leg. "There's no bone showing, which is a good thing," one paramedic said.

"Yeah, but my bet is that he's going to need surgery." He looked right at Thomas.

They loaded Thomas into the basket, and he was raised up into the aircraft. The hoist was lowered again, and the paramedics rose up and into the helicopter.

It was a short flight to the hospital. After Thomas was properly sedated, Joyce was allowed in to see him. She ran into the room and threw her arms around him, nuzzling her face against his. "Oh, Thomas! I was so worried! Worried sick! I didn't know what had happened! I'm so glad you're okay!"

The emergency doctor looked at the two of them. "He's lucky. He survived."

Dan Fisher is a native Floridian, born in Kissimmee, and has lived in the Melbourne and Palm Bay area for 60 years. He is a former electronic technician (antennas) and a retired police officer. He is the editor and Author's Assistant for Joanne's Books and is an avid amateur (ham) radio operator (AI4GK). Dan has short stories published in the Pets, Florida, and Baker's Dozen anthologies. He is one of The Traveling Boomers (thetravelingboomers.com), and webmaster for SCWG and The Traveling Boomers. He lives in Palm Bay with Joanne and their dachshunds, Wally and Madison.

I SURVIVED MAGGIE MALONE
By DL Havlin

Survival encompasses a wide spectrum of events and circumstances. In my lifetime, I've been in airplanes with landing gear that wouldn't go down. A friend and I were *in* a gale with forty-five mile-an-hour winds, *in* a fourteen-foot boat, *in* shark infested waters. I've even been shot at by a deer hunter who thought I looked like Bambi. But, none of those events are close to a survival experience that occurred in my high school days.

Maggie Malone! Doesn't that name conjure an image of a red-headed Coleen from the Emerald Isle? She was. In my high school she was the dream and idol of every male whether he be stud or gelding. Football captains groveled at her feet. Friday night dances, after games, were her court, the boys her court jesters. For those younger folks, *yes Vinnie and Virginia, the legend is true, there were 'hops' after games, usually held in the gym.*

Though she tempted every one of my friends, I was in a particularly vulnerable situation. She sat in front of, and behind me in two classes. Maggie was blessed with the five "C's" ... Charm, Confidence, Conversation, Cuteness, and Curves. Cuteness is an understatement, but it works here. Being exposed to all those C's daily, provided me with an understanding of a famished dog's mind-set who has a steak hung right outside his cage.

My male friends were envious. I spent a lot of time just feet away from Nirvana. Maggie and I had pleasant conversations. At least, she extended me the privilege of speaking to her, the honor of answering occasionally, and the even greater honor of a rare smile. Most of my friends were members of the great unwashed majority in our high school social pecking order. A Maggie hello, goodbye, or go to hell, would have been a 'to die for' if graced on any male member of that 80% of the class. My friends encouraged me to ask her out, but my lack of masochistic tendencies prevented that. Besides, her dates drove new Caddies and Town Cars, I drove a 1952 Studebaker.

Early in my junior year I became a starting running back and that advanced me a couple inches on the social ruler. Nirvana warmed a degree, but my strictly middle-class parentage was a limiter that had the same effect as a switch on a modern microwave...it turns things off if it gets too hot. Still, she occasionally spoke to me first. The point was mute, she'd accepted the class ring of a senior and the starting quarterback...I resided in Never, Never Land.

Then it happened. All in one day. My opportunity to enter heaven materialized. I believed I'd been blessed. Maybe it was because I saved my sister's cat from a Doberman. Or, maybe it was because I gave mom all the change when she sent me to the store for bread and milk with a five. (for whipper-snappers – bread cost $.19 and milk $.89 a gallon in '58) Whatever the reason, God smiled at me. *I thought*. Tears were in Maggie's eyes and the ring had disappeared from the chain around her neck. There would never be a better opportunity. I pounced. After she'd told me about her thesis on why a girl should never go steady with a quarterback, I asked, "Would you go to the homecoming dance with me?"

A smile radiated through the tears. "Thank you for asking."

She paused and I waited for my rejection. Instead, "I'd like to very much." That started one of the weirdest two weeks of my existence.

Joy! Exuberance! Then the first cloud drifted by. I excitedly, informed my two closest friends, after bragging to several others, I had a date with Maggie Malone. After their shock subsided, one counseled me. "Hey cat man, she's doing the string thing to you. Couple of days from now she'll tell you she was joking and blow you off with breath cold enough to freeze alcohol." My friends concurred, I disputed them. However, the seed was planted, and I spent the entire period from that instant, until I drove my car into her driveway homecoming night, fearing the humiliation of her standing me up.

I hadn't reached the locker room when the second problem flashed into my brain. What would quarterback Mark Stonebreaker's reaction be? Ex-boyfriends can look unfavorably at the next in line. I didn't want to incur his wrath. We were an equal physical match. Not so socially. A few words to the offensive line and I'd take more hits than the battleship Arizona at Pearl Harbor.

It's amazing what a tortured thought causes the rest of the brain to invent. It was my observation that fewer people said hi, or reacted "normally" to me as I entered the locker area. Were they pissed? I saw Mark and avoided him until we'd finished calisthenics. There was no avoiding him in drills or in the huddle. While the coaches were arguing over some trivia, he sauntered over, put his arm on my shoulder and asked, "I hear you have a date with Maggie. That so?"

I nodded. The Sword of Damocles began to fall on the hair of my electrified neck.

"She didn't take long to break that promise," Mark grinned. "When I told her, I wanted my ring back, she said she'd always be there for me." He slapped me on the back. "Good luck."

I didn't know what to say. Since silence is said to be golden, I decided to get richer. What someone tells you, versus what their true feelings are, doesn't always match. I wasn't sure of his break-up story's truthfulness until after homecoming, even though we had multiple conversations on the subject. Some of those talks terrified me in a completely strange way. His helpful hints about the care, dating, and loving of Maggie made me think of abandoning the date.

The next issue: Since I'd invited Maggie to a *dance*, it seemed that my being able to *dance* with her was a necessity. Could I *dance*? You have to define *dance*. I could stand on the *dance* floor, move my feet, and at times their movement had some relationship to the music, in a spasmodic, accidental way. I asked her, "What's your favorite dance." I thought, Foxtrot, Tango?

Her answer, "Oh, I just love to Jitterbug."

The Jitterbug. Not in my skill set. I needed help. Where does one go for assistance of this nature? Mom and Dad, of course! Dad would be the quicker, less painful teacher. I asked. He answered. "Ha, ha, ha, ha, ha. Me? Jitterbug. Ha, ha, ha, ha, ha." On to Mom.

"Oh, my dear, that is so wonderful!" I got the mandatory, unnecessary hug. "I can teach you, but my version is dated. Why don't I ask Estelle over? I'm sure she'll be happy to teach you."

Estelle! I'd spent my freshman and sophomore years trying to find a seat on the school bus that was half occupied to evade her. She hunted me more persistently than my Dad's birddogs trailed quail. I can best describe Estelle as a boy crazy, smart, neighbor girl, who resembled a tomato stake. I doubted Mom would have any challenge in arranging my dance lesson.

Estelle made a surprising racket when she knocked her skinny knuckles on our rear door after dinner the next evening. Her smile made me want to run…I've seen deer hunters with that expression as they pulled the trigger. In her other hand she carried a small stack of 45's. Again, for the young, that's record's, not automatics. Record's play music, automatics kill people. Just pointing out a generational difference. She held the records up and announced, "I brought some Elvis, the Del Vikings, Big Bopper, and the Diamonds." After depositing her stack of records next to the phonograph, she reached into her dress and removed what created her only visible curves; three pieces of chalk and an eraser. Estelle marked a number of "R's" and "L's" on the floor, to make it as boy proof as possible. I told you Estelle was a smart girl. She taught me the rudiments of the Jitterbug to the dulcet strains of Hound Dog and Chantilly Lace. My dad wandered through toward the end of my three hours of intense instruction. He laughed after saying, "I don't know whether you look more like an elephant on roller skates or Uncle Willard when his gout is acting up." At least, I learned three or four moves. If I didn't take too long of strides…I might fake it to an acceptable degree. As a bonus, Estelle attempted to teach me the 'box step.' In fifteen minutes, I broke her resolve. She loved being held. Problem, her thin feet worked well when supporting her ninety pounds, but became mangled when I added my two hundred on top. I asked her suggestion on slow dances, she answered, "Sit them out."

Besides waking each morning cringing from the fear Maggie would humiliate me by backing out of the date, another cause for panic faced me daily. Mark, her *close* ex-boyfriend, passed along tips he said were to help. They terrified me instead. At seventeen, I was as green as an apple in July. Along with most of my virgin pals, our primary exposure to sex was a well-pawed copy of 'Playboy.' Our knowledge depended upon whispered rumors, dirty jokes (many we didn't understand) and universally bungled birds and bees talks inflicted on us by our parents. Dad instructed me. Mine consisted of a fifteen-word description of the requisite female body parts, and an inquiry as to whether I understood their use. Of course, I lied, while smiling…the smile caused by panic that made me pray I wouldn't need to provide details.

My stress started simply enough. Mark sat next to me in the locker room a couple of days after I'd announced the date. He said, "Lots of tongue."

"What?"

"Kissing Maggie. She likes lots of tongue." Mark smiled. "That's a guaranteed shortcut."

I said, "Thanks," already realizing some of this dating Maggie business might be a little past my pay grade.

In the next ten days, Mark's instruction raised my sexual knowledge from white to brown belt in Karate terms. My pristine view of Maggie had been of purity that snow sprinkled by angels could not match. Mark enlightened me. Things she liked, things she liked more, and things she liked most. By the time he finished, most of the snow had been removed by snow-shovel wielding devils. He warned me Maggie demanded performance. By the time the day drew near, I was petrified.

Another straw arose two days before Homecoming. Estelle came over to give me a quick dance class refresher, and asked innocently, "Where are you taking Maggie after the dance?"

"Home, I guess."

"Oh, no! You can't do that. She'll be expecting to go where the in crowd is going. You need to get busy and find that out!"

I didn't say anything, the panic on my face was my answer. I nodded and managed a weak, "Thank you."

"You did get her a corsage, didn't you?" Estelle asked in a contemptuous tone.

I did that one right. "Yes, I got her three orchids."

"What color are they?"

"Orchid, I guess."

Estelle held her hand in front of her mouth, "Oh my! You don't know the color? Don't you know you're supposed to coordinate that with the color of her dress? You've created a disaster for yourself. She'll be miserable all night if the colors clash."

"Aww, shit." That summed up my feelings. The old saying, "be careful what you wish for," came to mind.

The last tip Mark gave me saved me from my greatest fear. He said, "This is important. Maggie won't drop her laundry unless you have a condom. She won't do it unless you wear one."

Being of the peasant class, I repeated, "A condom?"

"A rubber! Damn, you need to up your vocabulary." Mark's vocab was large, but very focused. I'd found my way out. The only Trojan that had ever been in my car...the ones in the Iliad. My billfold had no tell-tale bulges. With performance anxiety removed, I breathed with relief the whole day before homecoming.

My sky-blue rented tux, consisted of an ill-fitting straight jacket, and clown loose trousers. They were draped over the back seat of my used, 1952, green and gray, Studebaker Commander. It didn't have its name stenciled on it, but my friends all called it the "poverty wagon." It lost all semblance of glory when I aimed it into Maggie Malone's drive. Since I had a game to play, I wore my football jersey and jeans. When the poverty wagon rolled to a stop, among the Cadillacs, Porches, and Lincolns, I felt five pounds of air pressure escape from its tires. I crawled out of the front seat, concerned someone would think I was the gardener or a vagrant. Being dressed like one made me concerned I'd be accepted like one. I walked to the front door, slowly, making up apologies for my car, my clothes...for me.

When the door opened, I blurted out, "Hi, Mr. Malone. I'm David Mills. Please excuse my clothes, I got a game before the dance. I'm Maggie's date." I shoved the box of orchids at him like a peace offering.

"You're expected Mr. Mills. I'm taking you to the living room to meet Mr. Malone and Mrs. Malone." He pushed the orchids back at me. "May I suggest you keep those, and hand them to Miss Malone, personally."

The butler led me into a room large enough to house a small basketball court. That's an exaggeration, but the huge room dwarfed our family's living space. Awestruck, I'm not sure whether my mouth dropped open or not.

Mr. Malone smiled. "It's a pleasure to meet you, David. I appreciate your coming out of your way to introduce yourself to us. I know you have a game to play. That's a sacrifice…we understand."

Mrs. Malone smiled at me. Her lips said, "I'm pleased to meet you. Maggie has spoken about you ever since you asked her out." Her eyes said, *what have we here*?

"Thank you. Both." I shifted from foot to foot and hoped Maggie wouldn't be long. I looked at the entrance I expected her to walk through. Mrs. Malone read my mind, "She'll be ready in a couple minutes. She has to be there for the parade before the game and to practice the halftime ceremony. You know she's one of the princesses in the queen's court."

That cue heralded my date's entrance. Maggie was a full-fledged woman at seventeen, a beautiful one. For those few minutes, all the fears and tensions fled, and enduring them was worth it. Maggie's flashing green eyes said, "Hello," louder than her words. Her dark red hair was piled on her head, her green satin dress flattered a figure that didn't require it, and emerald colored high heels finished her appearance. Her angel image returned……
The orchids were white.

I dropped Maggie in the parking lot where her friends blended her into their social mass. Then I returned to the locker room, football, and the just plain folk that play the game. The Mustangs had a good night. We won easily, and I scored a touchdown. Things were looking up. And, *then* I got to the dance.

Maggie found me. "Please be a dear and bring us all something to drink. For the princesses and the queen? I have to stay with the court until the queen's crowned and the ceremonies are over. Oh! Would you pick us out a good table, and hold it? There will be eight." She blew a kiss to me and was gone before I could ask where.

There were seven. I'd have to figure how to get seven plastic cups of punch from point A to point B a hundred feet away. I grumbled about being a delivery boy as the girl dispensing the punch filled eight cups and I tried to figure a way to make one trip. "How's your date going?" A familiar voice asked. Estelle stared up at me curiously.

"Fine," I answered. "You look nice." She did.

"See you later," She smiled and walked away.

The 'waiter' found a large piece of cardboard. I placed the filled cups on it and picked a path to get through the forest of schoolmates loitering on the dance floor. Fog-horning, "Coming through," often and loud enough for those people residing a state away to hear, I made my way back to Maggie and the cluster of our class's royalty hovering in front of the stage. I announced, "Ladies, your punch."

Maggie arrived first, cooed, "Thank you, David. You are sooo sweeeet," and went back to hugging every male in the social elite she could get her arms around. The girls took turns picking up the drinks. Some thanked me with a noticeable lack of sincerity. Some never bothered, considering it was their due. The drink left on the cardboard was mine. As I reached to remove it from the unstable cardboard, one of the girl's dates backed into me, sending the punch splashing over my chest. "Oh, I'm sorry," he said, though he didn't look that way. My shirt became two-tone; I was adorned with pink and white ruffles. It took a half-hour and a full strip in the restroom to clean up enough to head back to the floor.

By then, all the tables were taken, or at least, there weren't eight spaces available at one. I saw two of my teammates and their dates, plus another couple, sitting at a table for ten. They bailed me out by relocating to other tables, allowing me to complete my assignment. I tilted the chairs, so the backs rested on the table, and waited. And waited. And waited. Baffling delays set the time back from eleven to twelve fifteen. The Maytag repairman had more company than me. The only good thing—my pastel pink ruffles dried a little more.

Ceremonies started with an anti-climax…the queen's crowning…a fact everyone had known for a week. Then boredom. A succession of former queens and kings each added their dribble about how their time at Roosevelt High shaped their lives, in their allotted two minutes. It proved one of the few times graduating from an old school proved a detriment. The line of Ex's seemed endless.

At last! The queen and king adjourned the proceedings, and the crew packed on the gym stage scattered like a pack of rats that a cat just pounced in. I'd have company. At last, I'd be part of the fun. At last, I'd have my time with the fair Maggie Malone.

The band played. Maggie and three couples approached the table laughing and joking. The princesses deposited their royal purses on the table, marking their territory like a tomcat. All hauled their dates to the dance floor. Maggie grabbed my hand and said, "Let's go."

The first song the band played when we walked on the floor, Chantilly Lace, gave me confidence. I thought I executed my moves like a pro. Bowler maybe? The second song, Poison Ivy, went well. And then the band played a slow number. I couldn't be sure how my legs and feet would do, but I knew my arms and hands would hold her just fine.

Maggie smiled, said, "This is nice," as she folded into my arms. Bobby Darin's Venus it wasn't, but the band's rendition sounded similar enough to make the endorphins arise. Maggie's body was warm, her cheek rubbed against mine. Heaven was near.

"May I." Someone tapped me on the shoulder. He was a senior I'd seen walking the halls.

"Certainly," Maggie answered before I could say no. She waltzed into his arms as smoothly as she had mine. I watched for a few seconds, felt conspicuous, and slunk back to the table. By the time I got there and sat, a different boy took the first's place. She went through three more before I returned to take possession of my date. Maggie smiled, nestled into my arms to the theme from Gone with the Wind. She squeezed me tight, put her lips to my ear and said, "Thanks for being soooo understanding. A few more trips around the box and the band took a break. My dancing and date were gone with the wind! As we returned to the table, Maggie asked sweetly, "You wouldn't mind letting me dance the first number with Ty, would you? He asked right before our last dance."

What do you say but, "Sure."

My eternal optimism evaporated like water on a grill. It was apparent I'd spend most of my time on 'the bench' waiting for the coach's call. It never came. I passed time counting the number of squares in the gymnasium ceiling, 242. Next, I tried to keep my eye on one of the reflected lights cast by a rotating ball made of mirrors, as the 'star' sparkled around the room. I managed to get a couple more dances with Maggie. However, my Nirvana had become my Nightmare on Elm Street. When Maggie suggested we go to a party one of her friends hosted, instead of my planned restaurant, I begged off. The game had tired me out, my knees hurt, the dog ate my homework.

The group left me at the table after Maggie administered a mercy kiss on my cheek and mumbled a hurried thank you in my ear. I headed to the restroom, waited until I believed my slinking retreat to my car would be unobserved, and took a circuitous route to the exit. I thought I'd been successful until I pushed on the gym door.

"Are you going home? My ride left me." Estelle stood a few feet away. I hadn't seen her, but at that point in her life, she was an easy thing to miss. We walked to my Studebaker in complete silence. Estelle's a smart girl.

Actually, the drive home turned out to be the best part of homecoming. Estelle knew the right icebreaker. "I love your car. Studebaker's are neat. You can't tell if they're coming or going."

We chatted a few minutes before I asked, "Did your date go off and leave you? Who is the sorry dog?"

"No, no. I came with some friends. They paired off and I was odd gal out. Besides, the only reason I came was to see how you danced." She paused, then added, "You did beautiful."

We became buddies on the last twenty minutes of the drive home. More than that. I remarked that a good night kiss would be a good idea on a special night like homecoming. She agreed. We exchanged a very pleasant one at her front door. I drove the five driveways farther to reach my house, knowing the evening wasn't a complete waste, and I'd survived Maggie Malone.

It wasn't until twenty-six years later I discovered how that survival impacted my life. Our high school reunion gave me my first glimpse of Maggie since our graduation. We both went off to school in the north. She didn't return.

"Hi David," A red-headed version of a Dallas Cowboy pulling guard spoke to me as though we knew each other. The woman had been "rode hard and put up wet," as the peasantry say.

I mumbled something to cover the fact I hadn't the foggiest. "Hello, it sure is good to see you."

My wife bailed me out as she has so often. "Hi Maggie, how are you. I see your father sold Malone Motors. Is he retiring?"

I squinted at the woman standing in front of me. Yes, buried under the exterior layers I could see the Maggie Malone of years past. Then, I wasn't one to toss rocks, my weight being almost a hundred more than when we walked for graduation. We talked for ten minutes and said nothing...until Maggie remarked, "You know, I've never stopped kicking myself in the butt for being such a conceited ass when you took me to homecoming. I know I messed up. I have four ex-husbands to show for it." She paused, adding, "I sent hints and messages to you, but I finally realized I'd screwed up so badly, there wouldn't be second chances."

"You weren't that terrible," I lied, but said, "I guess that's life."

Maggie smiled at my wife and me. "We're at table six, if you want a place to sit." She nodded and waddled away.

Wow! I'm glad I survived Maggie Malone, flashed through my relieved brain. I started to say the words, when I glanced at my wife. She had that look she has when she knows something I don't. Another moment to get richer.

"See there? That's Melinda, she stood next to me in chorus." Estelle hurried her near perfect body off to see her old friend. Sometimes being lucky, beats being good.

###

DL Havlin - Author of quality history and mystery/suspense is an eclectic author whose novels, novellas, and short stories mirror his rich, varied background. He has packed three lifetimes of experiences into one brim full existence. An avid lover of the outdoors and sports enthusiast, his passion for fishing, hunting and camping are frequently included in his writing.

"Open Minds - Open Books"
www.DLHavlin.com
www.DLHavlin.WordPress.com
www.SandySays1.WordPress.com
www.Facebook.com/DLHavlin
https://twitter.com/dlhavlin
www.amazon.com/author/dhavlin
https://about.me/havlindl418

IN THE MIDDLE OF THINGS
By Cindy Foley

I've lost track of how long I've been here. Every muscle in my body aches. Fever is burning me up. I don't want to open my eyes. I sure as hell don't need the glaring lights to sizzle my eyeballs too. The beeps, strange machine noises, and whispered tones are keeping me awake. Can't help it. I'm a light sleeper. As if finding it impossible to breathe isn't the worst. Like, an entire set of encyclopedias is sitting on my chest.

I guess I always knew the respiratory thing was going to get me. Runs in the family. We all end up the same. Mom and Dad's ventilators were removed postmortem. So, what good did it do them?

Can't help wondering if I even want to be on one. Hooked to a machine, hoses everywhere, crap taped all over my face. The tube down the esophagus has to be rough. Makes me want to gag thinking about it. Wrong pipe, I know. There'd be tubes on me for that, too, because, obviously I couldn't eat. This sick, who wants to?

Unfortunately, I don't really have a choice in the matter. The hospital I'm in has initiated ventilator rationing. I didn't get one. I'm too old. Too, there's my underlying complications, the respiratory thing.

I listen to the ventilator breathing for the guy next to me. Continuous air, perfectly timed. Man may be fiftyish. I saw him when he came in. I've got at least twenty-five years on him.

The noise of the ventilator aggravates me. I need to sleep. I'm so tired. The nurses give me meds to help, but they're so busy with more cases coming in all the time, …sometimes they're so busy they forget? Or maybe they don't want to overdose me for fear I'll die in my sleep. Not going to die. Pretty sure of that. Oh, so what if I do.

I can't recognize half of them. I try to recognize them by their eyes. Hard to see through all the gear they're wearing. I don't have the energy to try too hard.

I've decided to use the ventilator's perfectly timed continuity as a mantra. Maybe the repetitive sound will help my concentration. I'm trying to get back to that place on the energy healer's table.

I was in the middle of living when all this came down. Don't have the foggiest where I got it from. Once a year I go to the doctor for a wellness check. Not when I'm sick. I rarely get sick. I'm one of those who bites the bullet, takes over-the-counter meds, and goes about my world.

In hindsight, I guess that's not such a good idea. I suppose that's how this thing is spreading. Who knew? Is everybody supposed to stay home at the least sign of a sore throat? Sometimes those things last for days and that's before it blooms into the cough, the runny nose, the fever. That's when I'd stay home. But mine never turns into a fever. Well, this time it did. How was I supposed to know? Who can afford to take off work for the nine days it takes to get over the common cold?

Shwheeee…click … swoosh…click. shwheeee…click… swoosh…click. shwheeee…click …swoosh…click.

I think of Rev. Galen. The revelations I glean from his healing sessions bring me to a different consciousness than I've ever experienced. I wonder if God was training me there for this moment? While I lie on that table, face up, eyes closed, palms open by my sides, Galen touches me with just the tips of his fingers, sometimes on my solar plexus, sometimes on my knee joint, or my forehead. Occasionally he rests the heel of his palm on my cheek.

The touch is what takes me. Well, not the touch. He's a channel. Call it cultish or quirky medical science. I just know. I go way out there to a special place and love every minute of it. Escapism? I could use some of that right now.

One time, as I followed swirling, colored pinpoints of light into the distance, I found myself exhaling more than I was breathing in. The more I exhale, the more I want to see how long I can go without inhaling. Death wish? For a brief moment I pitied Galen if I did die on that table. But I wasn't afraid and not because his touch connected to the world stuff while at the same time taking me away from all of it.

On that table, I learn how to let go—of everything; the shame, the anger, the guilt, my job, my judgments of my husband's stupidities, my own. I come to understand that it doesn't take a whole lot of breath to live. Just one every now and then.

I could have died on that table. Might have wished it. Possibly came face to face with it. So, I could certainly die now, and if I do, at least I won't be hooked up to some artificial life force that wasn't how God intended me to live. Well, that's not true, otherwise why would He give the idea to us? The Devil Wears Prada. Non sequitur. Gibberish.

Who knows what to think?

The fire rages. I don't want to think. I'm going out there where gold-tinged purple clouds follow the colored lights.

Shwheeee…click… swoosh…click… shwheeee…click… swoosh...click… shwheeee…click… swoosh…click.

Murmurings reach me. Something about a sponge bath. Winter chills my forehead. It's like a drink of water. Frigid as an arctic lake. Goosebumps prickle my skin.

Mumbles. "Can you hear me?" I give a thumbs up. I was perfectly content out there. I guess they have to disturb me once in a while. Check to see if I'm still alive or if they can use the bed for another victim.

I'm so sick. I envision Galen's table and those colors I follow.

I search for God out there. I wish He'd take me. He's an alien. I'd like to get to know Him better. What more have I to do here? Obviously, He's not ready for me. Maybe next minute. Did He put another box of books on my chest? I need so little. How long will I have to suffer?

"Want something to help you sleep, sweetie?"

Go away.

Someone raises the bed. The water is a drink of life. I swallow the bit just enough to get the tiny pill down. Good. Maybe I can sleep my way to lala land. I'm exhausted searching for something that seems just beyond my reach.

The bed lowers.

I never fall asleep on Galen's table. I'm conscious the whole time, sort of. What's the word for it? Definitely not unconscious. Subconscious? Superconscious? Call it enlightened control. Call it whatever you like. God isn't going to catch me sleeping. I'm right here waiting.

"So strong." That's what Galen said when I told him I wasn't afraid to stop breathing.

Funny, I never pictured myself…

How long have I been out? I take a chance and open my eyes. The lights don't seem so harsh. I look over at the bed next to mine. Shwheeee…click… swoosh…click. shwheeee…click… swoosh…click. shwheeee…click …swoosh…click. Fifty-something is still there. He's looking at me. I give him a thumbs up. He blinks. That's all. Poor fellow. He must have it worse than me. Good thing they gave him the ventilator.

Someone's taken the box of books off my chest. A masked, zoot-suited stranger speaks to me. "Your temperature is down. Want to try a little broth?" HeSheIt raises the bed.

"Sure." My dry voice cracks. I don't really want any broth. I want to go back to sleep. But, I suppose, since God isn't done with me yet, I can at least take responsibility and help Him out. I struggle to sit up higher. Can barely move. Zoot helps me. I giggle. I love the name I've picked. I don't have the strength to ask what HeSheIt's real name is.

Soup, the nectar of the gods. This has to be what He saved me for.

Surviving is all about living in the middle of things. I take a breath and another sip of soup.

Ahh!

###

Cindy Foley, writer, flutist, gardener and Small Business Consultant won the 2016 SCWG Don Argo award for Florida literature, past Director, Treasurer and Past President of the Space Coast Writers Guild, a member of Scribblers of Brevard, and Florida Writer's Association, and founding member of Brevard Authors' Society, and has frequently appeared as a guest speaker on various author panels and book signing events in Brevard County

Books:
The Truth Lies…a Florida Saga
I, Clawed-Book One: The Renewal
I, Clawed-Book Two: Dog Days
Water Drops – poetry
Chase A Dream Today – poetry
Purple – personal anthology
Beyond the Dark – coming in November 2020

INEQUALITIES OF NUMBERS
By Michelle Sewell

John wasn't a complicated man. He liked beer with his burgers, the local malt beer, none of that IPA fancy crap; no pineapple on pizza; and football any time, the American kind not that European stuff.

He owned a plain house in a quiet neighborhood where everyone mowed their lawns, and nobody became fanatic with the need to win imagined gardening awards. There weren't any hidden meth labs, nor were there any hoodlum kids. A few unruly teens of the usual caliber with overloud slumber parties on the weekends and toilet papered trees during Halloween and Graduation.

He drove a blue Chevy truck. Not a bright blue, nor a metallic blue, but a plain, nondescript blue that if someone were asked what color the vehicle was, they probably couldn't remember. He put gas in his Chevy once a week, changed the oil and rotated the tires every three thousand miles. Simple, none pretentious. No bells or whistles, just a vehicle.

He didn't gamble. He wasn't an alcoholic nor did he smoke. There weren't unpaid credit card bills and there wasn't a hidden mountain of debt in his history. He had been married for eight years. It ended amicably and without feuding. Child custody was shared in his favor.

He was a cop. Not a detective. Not a SWAT member. None of that over verbalized law enforcement malarkey. If you broke the law, he wrote you a ticket. If you did something really bad, he arrested you. It was a government job like hundreds of thousands of others that paid the bills and made sure society didn't label him a bum.

It wasn't a simple life, and he didn't think of himself as a simple man. He was uncomplicated and did not seek out problems where none existed. He played softball in the spring, barbecued on the long weekend during summer, carved a pumpkin for Halloween, and strung up Christmas lights Thanksgiving weekend. New Year's Eve was spent with friends, drinking until the ball dropped and making resolutions no one would remember in the morning. Followed by New Year's Day of cleaning up unexplained messes and trying to identify who was snoring in the tent that magically erected itself the previous night in the backyard.

Straightforward. Normal. Nothing strange is how John would have identified his life.

Tuesday mornings were spent parked in front of the local grocery store to track vehicles. The curvature of the road prevented would-be speeders from noticing the marked car until it was too late, but regulars knew and would always slow to appropriate speeds when traveling past. From 8:50am until 10:27am, John sat in his cruiser, watched traffic not speed and listened to other calls being placed throughout his hometown, population approximately forty thousand.

The radio crackled as dispatch began to speak. Reports of shots fired, multiple victims. Suspect on site. EMS en-route. All available units dispatched. Location, Plaza Flats High School.

John stopped daydreaming about weekend activities as his mind filled in unsaid words: Kids. School. Kids. Gun. Kids. Shooting. Kids. Hurt. Kids. Dea...

John's thought process stuttered and fizzled to a stop. His mind couldn't complete the idea as it was. Death. Kids. The two words were as synonymous as yes and no and could not be spoken together in a coherent sentence or thought.

Dispatch repeated itself to add pertinent facts. Student. Shooter. Body counts... John's mind stalled again.

He took off for the school, radioed to dispatch his location, call response and ETA. He was a cop and this was his job; scenarios he had spent countless hours training for. While he was a dad, his mind wouldn't allow thoughts of her. Later, he wouldn't be able to say if he had purposely or mistakenly blocked the information, but he would never admit either fact.

John's mind, though, could not stop. It ran, ideas formed, collapsed, piled up, collided off of each other, disintegrated and reemerged. A tricky organ at best, a downright stubborn ass at worst, it did its thing without regard to its emotional heart companion. Feelings were labeled by the brain, not felt there.

He could not have said how long his drive took, although dispatch had time documented his response to call at 9:52am and scene arrival at 9:59am. He was the first officer to appear and his movements reacted to the screams he could hear, panicked bodies in fear.

His instincts took over and his brain switched to tactile. The resounding discharges were not automatic, the pitch too high and spaced. The suspect did not have an assault rifle or shotgun, more like a hand revolver or a weapon used for home defense.

Damn! Another irresponsible parent.

John's mind vomited the opinion, or maybe it was his heart, but the cause was irrelevant to the present effect. A smaller weapon, while just as deadly, was less likely to cause mass casualties than a semiautomatic would.

The adjustment of the Velcro straps on his Kevlar vest were muffled beneath the riot helmet cops were now required to carry in the trunks of their patrol vehicles. With an additional weapon in hand and an issued order to assess the immediate area, John slammed the lid of his trunk and proceeded to enter the premises.

Objects moved. People ran. Sounds of fear and despair. The echoes of everything not wanted to be heard in the first place, but that was being echoed in deafening proportions as John entered the closest building.

The agonized crowds thinned to nothingness as he headed towards the back of the building, briefly checking door locks as he loped past. The emptiness didn't pertain to people only; there was also an absence of assailants, victims and carnage in general.

Except for the haze. The smell of gunfire was just as thick as the sounds, acrid, unnatural and disorienting. Too much hung in the air and John immediately recognized his error. His earlier evaluation had been flawed. The shooter was using a small caliber weapon, as first assessed. However, the shooter was shooters. Multiple guns in multiple hands.

The sounds were closer, fifty maybe seventy feet away. Being inside disrupted auditory perception somewhat. John spoke to dispatch again. Fellow officers were behind him, close to joining the fray.

Countless briefings, practice exercises, drills, instructions and run-throughs were never enough. As a cop, John knew that to handcuff a fellow classmate at the academy was different than trying to handcuff a coked-out suspect at 3am alongside a busy highway. He knew that being tackled by a hundred-pound woman charged with prostitution was different than being tackled by a hundred-pound mom who had just been told her children died. And as he rounded the school hallway and entered the gymnasium, he recognized that a school shooting was devastatingly more traumatic than any domestic violence scenario he had been taught.

Bodies. So many human figures not moving. Not breathing. Not savable. They covered the wooden floors and bleachers, staff and students alike. Those with head wounds were the lucky ones, clean blows of execution. The others, not so much. Wounds to abdomens, chests, shoulders and necks were slower bleeds. Equally as deadly and nothing that paramedics would be able to treat in time.

John hadn't been able to protect any of them. And he couldn't stop and serve them now, in their last moments. He had to continue to the source to prevent others from being harmed. Others who still had a chance.

On the far side of the gym were several doors, all of which appeared to have been shot open. These rooms held sounds of suspects and victims alike. By random chance, he chose one on the right to approach first, fellow officers following and converging on the remaining others.

Lesson one of weapons training: Never draw a weapon unless you planned to shoot. With an active shooter, John had held a gun in his hand upon entering the building, no question of not being prepared to fire.

He called out a warning as he entered, his words drowned out by more shots being fired. The inside was small compared to the gym and his gun was aimed on the suspect as he surveyed the scene in his peripheral.

Through the tide of adrenaline that coursed within, John tried to turn off the flood of horror. It wasn't a slowed down slideshow of events happening in his mind. He wouldn't later be able to recall the specifics: his path to the suspects, how many shots he had fired, or where fellow officers were stationed.

Lesson two of weapons training: Aim for center mass. Most of the vital organs were located near the chest cavity and even if the heart was missed, it was a lot more difficult for a suspect to be combative with a pierced lung than if he had a pierced leg.

John took the opportunity and fired several times. Heedless of the threat, with their back to the doorway, the first shooter crumpled immediately. The second suspect turned to face the threat and tried to twist away from the hazard. Instead, the movement allowed for hits to the chest and neck from multiple officers.

Duty had called and he had answered. The job didn't allow for favorites or exceptions, such things caused further chaos and harm. He had taken his oath and upheld it to a tee.

Duty.

Serve.

Protect.

That was the mantra of a well-trained cop, and he tried to cling to it like a lifeline as his grasp slipped away, unforgiven.

Each ricochet formed an invisible fissure across John's soul as if it were a tangible organ. In one unsuspected and irrational timed event, his once uncomplicated and normal life would forever be anything but.

The second suspect was his daughter.

###

Michelle Sewell writes a variety of genres but is happiest penning satire and romance. Writing is a fun pastime and not an all-consuming life need. She grew up in Florida, left, and has now returned with her husband and troupe of four-legged children. Like most people, she does things she enjoys with family and friends. Her dream is to one day see a unified English grammar-front on the use of commas, and conjugative adverbs.

INTIMATIONS ON BEING
By Marjorie A. Cuffy

Our paths are governed by our purpose,
And our innocence of youth
Beguiles our sense of uncertainties.
Our childish impressions of security,
Damaged or strengthened by circumstance.
The childhood ailments that create concern,
Hastily tended with love and care.
This becomes a source of affirmation.
So, we survive.

Myriad internecine changes flow
Through the various phases of life;
And they imbue the senses with a clarity
Of the situational vagaries –imagined--
That often share a wholesome act
Within that common experience.
We watch as the world looks on
As the gales blow up a storm.
Yet we survive.

Beset by common fears and qualms
We hearken to any signaling alarm.
Beset by surprising enigmatic forms
Contained within the fearful strife.
All the vigor of the surging tide
Of resourcefulness and bight
Reverberate about on tender wings
To bring us all the hopeful signs
That we will survive.

The human calcifications that endure
Bring forth a genuine hardness of the core.
Dependency asserts that all will be a force
Of irrevocable and salient emotions
That wither as each one begins to recognize
An interminable bond within the body politic.
Each different yet the same,
A purpose to pursue—to bring us into harmony
So that we survive.

For every individual's chore can teach the lessons
That bring hope to all. And events that unfold bring forth
The singular purpose of our lives – to be as one.
The determined appeal that asserts its cautionary concerns,
Consistently reveals that to be an enduring entity,
The actions taken must conjure the merits of a devotional
To bring into fusion, the song of love at dawn.
For it is in the awakening that we become
The force of a survival consumed by love.

What armies and confusion bring succor to the hallowed frame?
Of eventual and sojourning mercies to the weary throng.
In all the willful and erstwhile shame that furrows the benevolent
And dark refrain, we seek to conjure a spirit bold and free
Amid the terrors and brutality.
When the dark forces are extinguished by the light,
We become enamored with the sacred antipathies
That surrender to the memory that's spent,

For it fosters hope that all will survive.

Suffering abounds amidst the trenches deep and wide.
It's in the forested arches where animals gambol
That hope displays her wiles.
It's in the heartbreak that each develops strength,
And sublime pathways embrace the synergy
That beckons us on to youthful guile.
We keep the fires burning till all the world's a stage
Where helplessness and doom experiments with justice—
A coveted prize—so needed yet elusive for want of fair display.

Survival of the fittest becomes the mirage
That overtakes the embedded impulses of the surly fray.
Afar, the slender thread of unity and despair
Awakens the senses to certain anxieties and fear.
Beyond the scope of imaginings, the climatic changes
Surround the earth with tensile opportunities.
Sensors of depraved conjectures flow from streams of effluence
To bar the healing, and the wisdom to enforce systems
That bind the forces of a healthy shrine invoked by resonance
And sacred music, so all survive.

The music that steals forth along the wounded plains,
The ever-mocking fury of the land engrained
The torso and the limbal activated by the form
Of a terrain so studded by the erupting maze,
Belongs to a faraway time and sand swept age.

For despite it all, the agony and the ecstasy of the formations
    Become the new arrangements that uplift the folds of time,
    To emulate the brigantine and forceful nature,
    To enshrine the beauty that is nature's allure
    In a redolent glow, insistent of the glorious aspects
    Of a benevolent will to survive.

###

Marjorie A. Cuffy is the author of *The Bond of Love: A Global Affair* which she hopes will find its rightful place among the foremost editions on love. She has been brought to this moment by the love that is of all and brings forth a spiritual aspect that is, by design, the weight of a vision of her own spiritual hankerings that have expressly become the tenets of her life's work.

Formerly a healthcare professional whose experiences span diverse cultures and, in general, borne witness to the human condition, she is motivated by the desire to the search for peace and justice.

She enjoys gardening, volunteering, communing with nature, and has traveled extensively, a passion which she shares with her husband. She has two sons and lives in Melbourne, Florida.

IT'S LIKE HE JUST DISAPPEARED!

By Dan Fisher

So far, it had been an unremarkable day for Officer Ben Daniels of the Bay Palms Police Department. Music came from the speakers of his patrol car's AM/FM radio. He needed that music to help keep his mood at an even level. He never knew when he might need his cool and level head. Of course, the volume on his two-way police radio was at a level so that he could hear what was going on. If he were dispatched to a call for service, or if another officer needed help, he had to be able to respond instantaneously. Of course, he had his coffee in an insulated mug safely nestled in the cup holder of the console that housed his police radio, siren and lights controller, and other equipment. The car's air conditioner was working overtime.

It was early afternoon, a bright and sunny spring day. He had made an arrest, earlier, for shoplifting. Since the suspect had a valid driver's license, a local residence, it was a first offense, and the value was only seventy-five dollars, he had written a "Notice to Appear," which is a summons to show up in court on a particular date. The violator could plead guilty or not guilty, or even *nolo contendere,* a fancy Latin term for "no contest"—meaning the violator wouldn't put up a defense to the charge. Sometimes it would be accompanied with a request for the judge to withhold adjudication, meaning that there would be no pronouncement of guilt, *if* the violator successfully completed a term of probation without being arrested for any other offenses.

Officer Daniels had conducted several traffic stops. There was a place where he liked to sit in a fast-food parking lot that gave him an eagle's-eye view of a rather busy intersection with a "No U-Turn" sign. The sign was strategically located between the two traffic signals for the left-turn lanes. If you saw the traffic lights, you saw the sign. After possibly a hundred people told him, "I didn't see the sign," he took a photo of it with his cell phone and printed it on 4 X 6 inch paper and tucked it into his ticket book.

Now, when folks insisted that they didn't see the sign, he would proudly produce the photo and say, "You mean this sign?" Whereupon the driver would slink down in their seat, knowing that they'd been "busted." In the end, Ben rarely wrote tickets for that violation. For him, it was sort of like a fishing expedition: catch-and-release.

The crackle of the dispatcher's voice on the Fire Department channel brought him out of his reverie.

"Rescue 89, unresponsive male at 1432 Wallowwood Street Southeast. Nine-one-one operator is giving CPR instructions over the phone."

"Rescue 89, en-route!"

Wallowwood? Damn, that's almost around the corner! Even though the fire station was only about a half-mile away, it would take a little time for the paramedics to grab their gear, climb onto their truck, and get underway—thirty seconds to a minute.

"Car 90 to Dispatch."

"90, go ahead." It was Nancy, his favorite dispatcher. She really knew her stuff, and when things hit the fan, she always had the officers' backs. He'd never heard her get emotional on the radio. She always had a monotonic, soothing, almost sexy voice. He felt fortunate that she was on his shift. When she was on the radio, he always felt safe.

"Car 90, go ahead."

"I just heard the rescue call on FD's channel. I'm right around the corner. I'll respond to assist."

"Ten-four. Car 90 responding."

Ben was so close that there almost wasn't a reason to activate his emergency lights. But it was protocol, and when he arrived on scene, he would need to have them on, anyway. He flipped the switch, and the lights began flashing. In mere moments, Ben arrived at the house, During that time, Ben ruminated how he had taken CPR classes every one of the ten years of his career, but had never had to actually do it on a "live" patient. He said a very quick prayer. "God, please help me with this!" He pulled up in front of the house, threw the car into park, opened the door, grabbed his CPR mask, and sprinted to the house.

What he saw there was mild chaos. "He's back here," someone said. She led Ben through the living room, toward the kitchen, A man lay on his back on the kitchen floor. His face was a deep purplish-red, and he wasn't breathing. Another quick prayer.

Suddenly, another person appeared in the room. "I'm a nurse. Can I help?"

"Yes! We need to do CPR. The patient has no pulse or respiration. Can you do compressions and I'll do breathing?"

The nurse and Ben both knelt by the victim. They worked on the victim for several minutes, until Rescue showed up with their equipment. Ben and the nurse stepped away as the paramedics began CPR. "Do you need me for anything?" Ben asked.

"No, we have this."

"Okay." Ben then began collecting information he would need for his report: name, address, date of birth, and so forth. Certainly, he was going to have to do a death investigation report. The patient had a history of heart problems, diabetes, and high blood pressure. There were no external signs of trauma. This most likely wouldn't need a detective. He was being transported to the emergency room and if he didn't make it, the hospital folks would take care of notifying the Medical Examiner. When the patient was wheeled out on the gurney, a CPR machine was doing automatic chest compressions. This is an ingenious device that wraps around the patient's torso and squeezes tightly—so tightly that the body lurches upward on each compression.

Ben and the nurse both left the house. Ben thanked him for showing up. "So, you're a nurse. Where do you work?"

"Oh, I'm in the Navy. Stationed in Hawaii. I'm visiting relatives here, around the corner." He began walking up the street.

"Well, thanks for showing up. I don't think I could've done this without you. You're a real life saver!"

Ben looked down for a moment, inserted his key into the car door, and unlocked it. He looked back in the direction of the nurse. No one was there. It was as if the nurse had vanished. Ben blinked and shook his head. *Where did he go? It's like he just disappeared!*

Fast forward, five years. Ben was in the police station and happened to see a maintenance man painting the walls. The worker said, "Hey, you're the officer who came to my house and saved my life!" Ben looked at him. The man continued. "In May, five years ago. On Wallowwood Street. You were there. Because of you, I survived!"

"Oh, yes, I remember. You were in bad shape. I thought you were a goner, for sure. But how would you know? You weren't even conscious! You were as good as dead!"

"I left my body. I was looking down and saw you doing CPR. My wife and daughter were there, crying. It was such a feeling of peace and contentment."

"Oh, then you saw the other man, the nurse, who seemed to come out of nowhere."

"No, there was no one else. Just you. Not until the paramedics showed up."

Ben looked at him in stunned silence. *No other person? No nurse? And where did he go after I thanked him?* The only conclusion Ben could come to was that his prayer had been answered. An angel had been sent to his side.

The man looked at Ben and said, "Well, you know what they say."

"What's that?"

"Good things always happen in Springtime!"

###

Dan Fisher is a native Floridian, born in Kissimmee, and has lived in the Melbourne and Palm Bay area for 60 years. He is a former electronic technician (antennas) and a retired police officer. He is the editor and Author's Assistant for Joanne's Books and is an avid amateur (ham) radio operator (AI4GK). Dan has short stories published in the Pets, Florida, and Baker's Dozen anthologies. He is one of The Traveling Boomers (thetravelingboomers.com), and webmaster for SCWG and The Traveling Boomers. He lives in Palm Bay with Joanne and their dachshunds, Wally and Madison.

LET'S GO FLY A KITE!
By Betty Whitaker Jackson

"Good morning, My Sweet." Ed whispered into her good ear.

She struggled to wake, even for this eagerly awaited day. She'd been caught up in a dream, a recurring one lately, of her Ed grasping the kite string, holding the line, and the agonizing moment when the huge box kite she had sewn ripped from his hand and plunged headlong into the ocean, fifty feet from shore. With a moan she awoke, not quite sure why.

"What's wrong darling? Are you all right?"

"I . . . I think so. I was dreaming that same dream again. The box kite one. Remember, I told you about it last week sometime? We were kiting, of course. The royal blue box, you know, our favorite, broke away. You know how long we took to build it. Why would it break? We checked every stress point. We secured every line. We reinforced every seam. Why?"

"Well, if it'll ease your mind, we can check it again before we fly it. Maybe that'll put your mind at ease, whaddya say?"

"Guess so. Anyway, can you imagine how disappointed we'd be if something happened to that kite? It's going to take the grand prize at the convention next year. I just know it! Every time we've flown her, she has just soared. And you handle it so well. The swivels and the test lines, and the balance. We've flown it in gentle zephyrs and strong cross current winds, and it's never disappointed us. Why would I keep dreaming that dream?"

"Maybe you're just concentrating on winning and not just flying it for the fun. I'm thinking togetherness is worth a whole lot more than a trophy. 'Specially today. Who cares about that kite on our anniversary day?"

"Of course, you're right. Let's start this morning off again, shall we. Good morning, Love of my Life." Cuddling her head on his strong shoulder, she asked, "Did you sleep well?"

"Sure did. Any time we're here, the waves lull me to sleep. I just love the sound of the ocean. There's just nothing like it."

"For sure. Just now, though, I'm thinking about our wedding day. Can it really be fifty-one years ago? December 28, 1968. Man, that was the day we'd hoped for, planned for, and it was like God had some surprises in store."

"For sure. Rain, hail, fog, sleet, snow. Brrr. People couldn't get there. The caterer was late. And to top it off, I came down with a cold the day before and felt absolutely miserable!"

"Remember how we both chuckled when we said, 'In sickness and in health?' What a promise to make. I was sick the beginning of our honeymoon, and you were sick by the end of it.

"Well, My Sweet, none of that today, no way! This will be a day to remember for all the right reasons!"

Cuddling in their condo furnished in light turquoises and pale ocean blues was one of their favorite things to do. Now that retirement had come, Sadie and Edgar were living what she called the Age of Frosting. They'd earned the right.

His auto-parts business had flourished, doubling, quadrupling and more in size, supporting their family for all his years from high school until last year when he joyfully handed the keys to an enthusiastic buyer. Now it would bless the other twenty-five families, now, and for years to come, if they followed his business model.

Sadie had been the best household engineer he could have wanted. They started with a little two bed apartment with borrowed and thrift store furnishings, and until they outgrew it with the first two of their six children, they made do and saved every penny they could until they could afford the Sears Craftsman fixer upper on Joslen Boulevard.

Anticipating retirement to Florida some ten years ago, they had bought this beautiful sixth floor beauty in Satellite Beach. They'd join the thousands of others retiring to Florida one day.

The siren call of freedom was a strong pull. They would never have to worry about slipping on ice, or paying heating bills and taxes in New York. She would never pull another errant weed or paint another room or plant another garden to feed their family. No way.

It was the right decision; they were sure of it. Three of their children, after visiting their first Christmas here, had preceded their move to Florida. They all taught music in Brevard. Charter members of the Space Coast Symphony Orchestra, they were super involved in church, and making lifelong friendships.

Sadie and Ed raised and adopted three foster children. One was finishing medical school; one earned her law degree next June. Perhaps the other, their youngest, would sometime see the light and make the trek to Florida too, although New York City ballet scene's allure had won her heart, it seemed. Nothing like it here. Too bad.

Everyone had come here for Christmas and for today's festivities. They took up a whole floor of suites at the hotel down A-1A.

"Guess we'd better get this show on the road. We're meeting for brunch at 9:30. Gives us an hour, My Sweet."

"OK if I shower first? Gotta get my hair dry."

"Don't you have an appointment later? You look just fine to me. Let someone pamper you for a change."

"Ya think? I want to look presentable."

"I'm thinkin' you look absolutely beautiful right this minute!" he said as she strolled, naked as Eve in the Garden of Eden."

"Not so bad yourself," she demurred. Imagine, at eighty they still delight in each other. Neither saw the sags, the wrinkles, the limp, the fear of falling.

Hugging her close, he quoted, *"Charm is deceitful, and beauty is vain, but a woman who fears the Lord is to be praised,"* from Proverbs 31, reminding her that she is beautiful to him inside and out, and nothing on earth can change that. "My Sweet, I'd marry you if you weren't already taken!"

"And I'd accept your proposal, even knowing what we've been through and not knowing what we'll face. Best decision of my long life, and I wouldn't change a thing except hoping that kite doesn't fail us."

"Silly girl. If it does, we'll make a better one for the next competition. Don't you worry about it. When that competition comes, we'll be there with or without that kite. Maybe God is telling us to make another one. Whaddya think about that?"

"What do you have in mind? How do we improve on perfection?"

"I'm thinking ahead to the 2021 one."

"Why on earth would you be doing that? Aren't we going to compete in the 2020 one?"

"Well, yeah, but I've got a theme in mind that's been running through my brain. I want to design a box kite on the theme 'Sharing the Plenty in 2020,' with hand-painted panels on the boxes."

"That is a catchy slogan, for sure. You mean my dream is a premonition, that the blue box is not supposed to win in 2020?"

"Maybe. We've had promptings like that before, remember?"

"K. Let's get praying about it. Maybe God's got other plans for next October.

As it turned out, God indeed did have other plans for October.

Sadie always trusted her premonitions. She had dreamed dreams, and they sometimes came true. They flew that box kite just before trials of Richmond Festival in October. Oh, how she sailed. There were four other box kites in the competition, and the blue box soared above the others and held the time record. She was the winner of the distance trophy too, and Sadie and Ed won all the cheers.

Then, it happened. Before they could bring her in so everyone could admire her construction and learn lessons from her for their own, a sudden gust from the east broke her two lead lines. An astonished crowd heard the crack of the leading edge. Sadie and Ed struggled to control her spiral. Others ran to help, backup of sorts, and within seconds, though it seemed an eternity, she crashed into the waves, collapsed in on herself, and sank.

The crowd gasped, lowering their cameras. They couldn't believe their eyes. The officials looked at each other in dismay. The prize depended on its safe landing. All was lost.

Sadie looked at Ed and whispered, "I told you she would crash. I saw it all in my dream, over and over. Now do you believe me?"

With a hug, he said, with his usual optimism, "Let's build her better. I told you we want one with all the events to Share the Plenty of 2020, didn't I?"

"Indeed, you did. Guess we're going to start all over. Only problem is, we don't know why this one failed."

"It didn't fail, darlin'. It flew the longest. It flew the highest. It brought all kinds of smiles, and oohs, and aahs, and signs when she died. She did what she came to do, and she did it well."

I guess there's a lesson in that."

"With the hugs of their admirers, and their obvious sorrow at its outcome, their friends expressed both their joy and their sympathy.

The fellowship of fliers is unlike any other. They've all experienced the high joys of soaring success, and the downright gloom of failure, and survived to fly again. And so would we.

When we returned home, we sketched out plans for our Share the Plenty in 2020 kite. Decisions to make. Color, light blue with dark blue margins against the staves. Each panel of the box would depict a "blessing painting." Staves would be a new bicarbonate, both flexible and strong.

We picked up new line, the strongest on the market. We did due diligence; we scouted the market. This one would not only fly higher and longer; we were sure we could retrieve her for the grand prize every time we flew her. First test would be the North Carolina meet in April. Then, we'd take her to the World Finals in October.

With high-gloss acrylics, I painted scenes on each panel. This kite would depict our blessings. It would tell the story of our awesome life together, our homes on one panel, our gardens on another, the portraits of our children on another, and a special one, our legacy, our beautiful grandchildren adorn the last ones. The cross, center of our lives and this gorgeous kite, prominently depicted from every side, its glory. Gold rays radiate outward holding the framework to a whole new standard. Finally, the trailing ties depicted the fruit of the spirit virtues: love, joy, peace, patience, kindness, goodness, faithfulness, gentleness, and self-control in waving bands of multicolored nylon.

Once again, to construct it, true to the architectural sketches and with infinite care, we moved all the furniture out of the living room. The sewing machine hummed as I stitched and double stitched the seams, facings, and channels for the staves. I reinforced every possible weak spot. We poured our souls into this piece. She would take all the prizes.

We flew her first at the beach on our anniversary day. The kids were all here, once again, and they admired our handiwork. It was a calm day, and we figured it would be a good test to see how she'd soar. And soar she did. We used almost all our line. While Ed flew her, I took a video. She handled the soft breezes and the few sudden gusts and descended smoothly like an obedient puppy on a leash. Words like spectacular, winner, gorgeous, splendid …none could do her justice. Ed even said, "I think we lost the first one just so we could fly this beauty!" And he was right.

Our kids dispersed to their places and we were once again alone in our little world. We'd Share the Plenty in 2020 with our friends, our bridge and mahjong partners, our church family, and our volunteering for the symphony and the museum and at the Kennedy Space Center. It would bring us such joy.

And there's always kite-flying on the beach. We had such a collection of colorful beauties, some purchased, many home-made. It always amazed us how we gathered admirers any time we flew kites and often shared some of ours so they too could feel the ocean breeze catch the colorful windsocks, diamonds, and stunt kites.

Although there was a kite-flight in Ft. Myers in February, we decided not to show off our new box kite until April. It's not that anyone could replicate it. We just wanted to show it off at World class event, not just a regional show. Her big test would be World Finals in October.

We hear about the "China virus" about this time.

Suddenly, we are under a stay-at-home order for our own safety. Friends of ours contract the Corona virus. In six days, we hear they are dead, and no one can attend their funerals. We seniors can only shop safely at certain times, and when we do, we can't buy half the supplies we need for an extended stay at home. We're used to stocking up for hurricanes, and stores prepare ahead for those. This is far different. And our little condo has so little storage space. No bulk buying for us.

For our safety, the kids stop visiting. Is Christmas the last time we'd see them all? We have no contact with them until we learn how to Zoom. Who ever heard of such a thing?

The grandchildren can't go to school. The church is closed. The usually busy street is silent. Talking heads spew disaster. The President appoints a task force. Worldwide, people are dying in droves.

We know it's serious when all the kite flights are canceled, one after another. We are not to gather in crowds, and ten is considered a crowd, not the usual thousands these events draw. We are devastated.

We start the masking, the handwashing, the sanitizing, the isolation. We are determined to survive. Determined.

Ed and I are optimistic. We are healthy. We have no "pre-existing conditions." We are just sick in spirit. We grieve with the loss of friends, one after another. We see mounting numbers, and they are frightening. We hear about hydroxychloroquine. We hear about ventilators. We hear about zinc and vitamin C, we hear that developing a vaccine will take years, but a task force can work miracles. All the while, we feel like the walls are closing in on us.

Three of our sons-in-law are considered "essential," two daughters are relegated to "non-essential status," whatever that means. A real blow to their egos, that's what it means.

Each couple has to decide who stays home with children. They are supposed to be going to school on their computers. How on earth does that work?

The "essential" guys have to mask up, stay six feet away from their colleagues, and change their whole working relationship. While they were used to collaboration, meetings, discussions, and the usual corporate model, they each now get a segment of a project to complete on their own. Video-chats destroy camaraderie, but now replace face-to-face problem-solving. Little satisfaction in that.

Restaurants cannot serve meals. They sell off their standing supplies, sort of like grocery stores do. Can't let food go to waste. New "apps," we have to learn fast. We can order meals, even have groceries delivered.

Too bad we can't take our heads out for haircuts. Too bad we can't play bridge on Tuesdays or mahjong on Thursdays at the Senior Center.

We miss, we discover, our schedule. It's hard to know what day it is. We've run out of books to read, little chores to do around the house, and I can't go browse-shopping in my favorite stores.

Our kids tell us to just stay home so we're safe, not realizing that isolation is beginning to affect even how we talk to each other. We run out of topics, and our only picture outside the four walls is television. That becomes depressing.

By summer, things are really dire, and we'd do anything to get out of the confines of the place.

It's June. Through remote learning, whatever that is, Jordan finishes medical school and is immediately put to work helping people fight this virus. There's no graduation. There's no celebration. He works twelve-hour shifts, is afraid to go home to his family. They might contract the virus, so he has an isolation ward where he sleeps, if indeed he can sleep at all. We learn about PPE; we learn how terrible this disease is, and he continuously warns us to stay at home and not even bring packages into the condo until they've been disinfected. He especially warns us not to use the elevator in our building. He hears that's how some of his patients must have gotten COVID-19, its newest name.

Jennifer, our sweet daughter graduates this week too, bless her heart. After all the accomplishments, highest honors, awards, prizes and accolades, there is no ceremony to honor her. She even has to interview remotely for her first position here in Brevard. Yes, she could have gone to the office, looked around, met future colleagues, but no... life is a bit different these days. We are so very proud of her.

And our grandson Todd was to give the valedictory address for the senior class high school graduation. He missed prom, the awards ceremony, graduation. . . all rites of passage for our kids. This is certainly a strange June.

And finally, or at least one more disappointment, Carrie and Jim have postponed their wedding until more than ten people can attend. They planned their venue, flowers, music, guest list, reception, and discovered cancellation after cancellation. They're not even sure their apartment lease is safe. Such an unusual time we're in. Those fifty-one years ago, we thought rain, sleet, snow, and fog were bad.

Now, we are obsessed by survival.

Our kite will fly, although we may, to be honest, have to update the panels and paintings. Sharing the Plenty in 2020 is oxymoronic, although we still try to count our blessings each day.

The balance sheet bleeds red. We carry on with changed moods, with sheer boredom, with less hope for tomorrow than our optimism once held so dear.

The 2021 kite may be black, the pictures with CLOSED, masks, and frowns. We will, God willing, survive intact, if God's grace be with us all. So be it. Amen.

*

©May, 2020. "Sharing the Plenty in 2020" Betty Whitaker Jackson.

No part of this book may be used or reproduced in any manner without written permission from the author at www.bettyjackson.net. Exception: brief quotations for review or marketing purposes.

This book expresses the views of the author. It is a work of fiction and characters are not reflections of persons living or dead. The setting is Palm Bay, Florida. Without the events of the last six months, notably the Corona Virus

Thanks to American Kiteflyers Association and its website where the reader can see each type of kite in flight.
at http://kite.org/education/styles/single-line/figure-kites/
http://kite.org/education/styles/sport-kites/
http://kite.org/education/styles/power-kites/foils/

###

 **Betty Whitaker Jackson** has published twenty-five books since her retirement from her forty-year career as a secondary language arts teacher. Her works also appear in eleven anthologies. She won first prize in the LifeRich Reader's Digest Memoir competition with her book *Rocking Chair Porch: Summers with Grandma.* An active member of Space Coast Writers Guild, she thanks members for their support and encouragement. She writes fiction, nonfiction, memoir, devotionals, poetry, and children's books. She regularly blogs at www.bettyjackson.net.

MEMORY SURVIVAL
By Shelia Dodd Gillis

Some days, I can almost remember it all. My name, my family, my life in full glorious color.

Other days, I may just know that I should remember things, but I don't.

Today, I have a son. Before he comes to visit, a nice lady reminds me his name is Jeremy. I know she tells me more things about him. It's hard to remember details though. Some days just his aftershave is familiar to me. I wonder if I was a good father? I want to ask him if I was. He always seems so sad when he visits.

It occurs to me that maybe I had a wife. Sure, I must have had one, since I have a son. I asked the lady that helps me if she was my wife. That was a pretty definite no! Although, she still helps me.

Tomorrow I have plans. I think I am going somewhere exciting. Or maybe I already went?

"Eat your peas," the waitress tells me every day at lunch.

"I hate peas," I tell her. "Bring me carrots." Then I get angry because I want the peas.

Looking out the window, I couldn't tell if it was sunrise or sunset. It mattered enough that I went outside to get a better look. They frown on that in this hotel place. I was shocked at the scolding I got. I am a grown man! But not allowed to go outside by myself. The indignity of it would anger a lesser man. In my opinion, anyway.

"Did I show you my name tag? My friend and I traded. We wanted to trick everyone. Then, I wanted my name back, and now I can't find him," I mention to the boy that shuttles me to the game room. He promised he would look for him and get my name back.

I'm really good at playing cards. I'm usually the scorekeeper. When I play alone, anyway.

"Hello, Dad." A stranger spoke to me.

The smell is familiar. "Who are you?" I ask. Or think that I asked.

It's all very confusing. I lay here, somewhere in a strange place. A prison maybe? I want desperately to wake from the stupor that closes me in more each day. Then I get a whiff of aftershave or peas! I know I am losing more as time passes. I can't go back. I hold on tight to what I still have.

"Have you seen my dog?"

###

Shelia Dodd Gillis writes contemporary, western, and romance. She credits her love of words to her third-grade librarian. Born in Texas, she's an Air Force veteran and retired from the US Postal Service. She holds a black belt in SBD and graduated top of her class in Culinary School. Her passions are writing, reading and cooking. She resides in Florida. Shares life with a husband, three daughters, seven grandkids, Gus and a cadre of friends.

NIGHTMARE
By Edward Keck

Screaming. It was terrifying, and I was unable to take any action, to do something, anything that could stop or even impede events as they progressed. Like many dreams, some have a greater impact on you than others. I assume everyone has dreams, some in color, others in black and white.

I know of no explanation how an individual's dreams are visualized or even what plot they follow, since there seems to be no author directing the show. Without a director, no one can read the individual lines since no script exists. Dreams progress on their own in some incomprehensible manner, and we who take part are merely characters around which they flow. A plot, if any exists, is as unknown and as mysterious as the ending. Events just "happen" as we traipse through our roles while the seconds or minutes pass, for as long a dream takes,

Dr. Freud had a lot to say about dreams, but he never was able to specifically identify how each individual mind manufactures the plot and its characters. Daily frustrations, fears, doubts, events of the day are but a few of the suggested activators of what flows through our subconscious as we lay there, allowing this story to develop. As our dreams evolve, we sometimes end up heroes, and other times as victims. Most of our dreams fade away by morning, and our ability to recall them, if with any detail at all, is tenuous at best.

Have you ever had a dream that was so real, so terrifying that you were sure of two things: first, you were in direct threat, and second, you were certain death was imminent? That can be quite an experience, one that most would prefer to never happen. Allow me to relate the story of a dream I had.

In the opening scene, I found myself in an old, late 1800s town somewhere in the Midwest. The town was small, with a population of perhaps one hundred people, and bragging rights were limited to just a few weathered buildings in desperate need of paint. Buildings had been erected on both sides of a very short dirt road. Each side of the street had a wooden walkway in front of the buildings that allowed strollers to proceed along their paths without stepping in the dirt, or mud on rainy days. The setup was almost like a typical cheap movie scene, where only a small number of people had decided to take up residence. The place had no form of entertainment to offer except a bar where the hopeless souls went to enjoy whatever sparse methods of wasting time they could derive. It had half a dozen tables surrounded by several chairs at which patrons sat to eat whatever the cook had to offer, and to play cards or just sit at and relax.

In addition to the bar, there was the usual small hotel, dry goods store, doctor and dentist offices combined in one location, sheriff's office, and a few other buildings, including a church. All the structures, as well as all the residents, were only incidental to the intent of the dream that was slowly evolving and revealing its plot.

It was midafternoon, and the overhead bright and hot sun was fully visible in a cloudless sky. I appeared out of nowhere as the dream began. At this point I became conscious that I existed in this place, this unnamed town, with no background and no point of reference as to where I had been prior to my mysterious appearance. I knew who I was but had no name; I was the only character who had a role to play; well, almost the only one.

People were there, doing their thing of wandering, speaking words I didn't hear, going to and coming from places, leaving and entering the few buildings for reasons totally unknown to me, and apparently having no value to add to the dream. I could see their mouths working as they spoke, but their tongues moved in a silent language. I was standing in front of a building; its purpose never came up, but it was across the street from the church.

    I had no idea why I was standing there and never questioned that circumstance. Like all dreams, things just happen as a series of events transpire. I was dressed in western garb, pants that seemed to be denim, but I can't be certain. I also wore a cotton shirt, boots, and a typical beat-up cowboy-style hat. Apparently unarmed; no gun belt hung from my waist, and no knife was lodged inside my belt or boots; personal safety did not seem necessary to the plot's evolution. I must again assume this dream had no need for such decorations. I felt myself in a comfortable environment, just as if I belonged there, in that era. Perhaps I was a resident or a stranger passing through. I had no concept of having a horse or even walking to the town. The entire sequence did not exist until my mind decided to create it, and place me in its midst.

    As I stood in front of this unknown building, I turned to look at the church. That building was, again, typical of the type usually built in a small town, made of wood with a small steeple in which the required bell was suspended and a cross on top ensuring no one would mistake its purpose. The front had only a single-entry door, not a double door as many churches in larger towns and cities had. It had no particular appeal to me in either a religious or structural analysis sense. I had no interest in how buildings were erected. It was just a plain, weather-beaten church, but it did have a certain appeal. Since this was a dream, I had no thought as to what directed my attention to it, but somehow, deep within myself, I started to feel a need to go to that church, to enter it. Since it was not Sunday, no one would be there, unless the pastor was doing some chore that needed attention.

I endured a few seconds of mental debate as to whether or not to cross the street. Finally, I was "directed" to step off the wooden walk on my side of the street and cross the dirt road. I found myself standing in front of the church. Some strange feeling was growing in my mind; a need to go through that wood door. There was no goal to that thought; I was just going inside. To look around? For what? To observe the rows of pews for seating its visitors, the small altar, or the pastor's lectern, or pulpit? Perhaps I was feeling compelled to enter to pray for some reason. Had I committed some sin I was unaware of at that point? The dream sequence was mute on that point.

I stepped up onto the walkway and stared at the front door. In those days, churches did not lock their doors; entry was available 24 hours a day, seven days a week. Again, the strange feeling I had earlier began to intensify. I started to wonder why I was so drawn to it, almost as though being forced. This was a church, God's home, which, if any place at all can be considered safe, total sanctuary was always available. I did not understand why I had this growing compulsion to open the door and enter even though a feeling approximating that of impending dread was growing, I found my right hand rising toward the large cast-iron handle.

As my fingers started to wrap around the handle, I had an immediate sense of dread, a feeling that was incomprehensible. Why on earth should I get such a feeling? This made absolutely no sense; I had done nothing wrong that I was aware of, and had never in my life felt fear (in this dream, I apparently was conscious that a degree of my background was necessary) when entering a church. Common sense told me I was being ridiculous; there could be absolutely no reason for me to have what was becoming a greatly intensifying sense that should I enter, something dreadful would happen.

Nevertheless, my fingers wrapped around the handle, and I twisted it, then pulled. The door was rather heavy; apparently made of good quality, solid oak. As the door started to open, I had a glimpse of the interior; which can only be described as dark. When I say "dark," I don't mean that only a fraction of the sun's light wasn't shining through the multiple windows on both sides of the building. Nothing could be seen; no light reflecting on parts of the interior from windows that were not boarded up. Think of black ink, the darkest night ever imaginable, where you can't see your hand if you placed it in front of your face.

As the gap in the door widened, I was able to see ... nothing, not even a tiny glimmer of light from the open space created by the half open door. The interior seemed to be sucking up all light, like a black hole where even light can't escape. (Past and present concepts of science seem to have no place for perspective in dreams; anything can happen, any thought can be raised.)

I pulled the door fully open and stood at the entry, dropping both hands to my sides. At that point, some force seemed to be tugging at me, to get me to step inside. It felt unreasonable, and I began to have second thoughts about entering. As my hesitation grew, the "something" inside that blackened emptiness was intent on having me enter; a force was beginning to physically tug at me. In addition to my own body which began to have diminishing emotional control, I felt something was in the church with me, located toward the rear as though hiding within its own blackness so it could not be seen.

While standing in the doorway, a presence began tugging at me, trying to physically pull me into the church. A sense of fear began to grow in my brain. My mind started to race, trying to understand what I was feeling, to imagine just what was lurking in there. *This can't be happening! This darkness does not belong here. This feeling of dread instead of peace has no right to be here.* I felt like shouting, *"God! Where are you?"* but I remained mute as fear started to rule my brain.

What started out as gentle tugging was becoming a true force; I could feel my legs being pulled into the church. I looked down at my feet; the bottoms of my pants legs were actually being pulled at by the force that I was now convinced represented evil. I could sense an invisible hand-like thing holding on to the cuffs of my pants and pulling. I raised both arms and placed my hands on the outside of the door frame to prevent my body being dragged in. The force grew as did my now fully advanced state of dread and terror. The fingers of my hands, stretched out against the exterior of the door frame, provided only so much grip against the force pulling at me. This was real! This was actually happening, and I had no idea what I could do to stop it.

The pulling on my legs grew to such intensity that my feet were raised off the floor as the force pulled, apparently trying to break my hold on the door frame. It seemed intent to get me inside no matter how hard I resisted. My mind was reeling in terror as I realized a foul presence had taken over the church. I sensed that if I let my body be dragged into the interior, something extremely horrid would happen! At that point I began loudly shouting with an attitude of hopelessness, "God! Stop this! Please help me!"

The pulling on my legs intensified, and before I knew it, my legs were suspended horizontally to the ground, as was my entire torso. It became imperative that I maintain my grip on that door frame. My fingers were beginning to tire, and the muscles of my arms were succumbing to the strain. I was unable to get a true grip on anything and was relying on the friction of my spread fingers to resist the pressure dragging me into the blackness. Prayers and screams to God to stop what was happening escaped my lips. "My God! My God! Help me!" This is Your home! Stop it!"

I had reached the point where my screams seemed to echo throughout the town, but no one heard them; no one came to my rescue, and no one knew what was residing in their church. The screams were loud and filled with terrifying fear. I was slowly losing my grip on the door frame, and knew I would soon be dragged into the church to face the unknown entity. My fingers raked against the door frame as they slowly gave way to the pressure, at which point the full force of true terror shrouded my body and my mind. Just before my fingers lost contact with the door frame, knowing I was being dragged into some form of hell, I screamed an almost inhuman sound, as loud as any human ever heard.

The horrific screaming permeated the air, echoing through the timelessness of dreams, and I awoke still screaming in total, absolute terror. It was then I realized those sounds were coming from me. My heart was pounding like a trip hammer and I was sweating profusely. After a few seconds I realized I was safe in my own bed, having avoided the horror that lay within the walls of that church.

And then, fully awake, the inevitable questions arose to hound my conscious mind: Who or what was the boogeyman, and why did my mind create it?

Only God knows. Or, perhaps Dr. Freud?

###

Ed Von Koenigseck

AAS Electrical Technology; BS Business Administration; 4 years Air Force; 1 ½ Years Field Engineer; 46 years Technical Publications (Writer/Supervisor); Contract Instructor FIT; Advanced English–Technical Writing; Lecturer – Biblical History; Author: Technical Writing for Private Industry, *Island Park* – a Memoir

ODE TO EROS OF TRAVELS PAST
By Rod Bornefeld

Dearest…
My time is short and so must be my words.
Words of irony, if not of wisdom.

In our solitude,
Tenderly, my hand lightly squeezes the tenderness of yours,
Once, twice, thrice….

Each night, I would hold you in my arms,
Your warmth and serenity, of which I could feel,
Many times you would softly whisper, "I love you,"
Many times over,
I wished that I could have replied the same.

How hard I would try,
Alas, I tried and tried,
But the words faltered and were of no avail,
The sentiments of endearment,
How often I heard from you,
Oh, so many times,
"I love you"…
…never would my lips reply the same.

Instead, I would hold you in my arms,
And hug you, not once, or twice but three times,
To let you know that each endearing hug says to you,
"I- Love- You."

The times that I came to you in solitude,
A gentle squeeze of your hand thrice times,
A quick wink of my eye thrice times again,
Three gentle caresses on your shoulder,
Three warm hugs about your neck,
Each expressing my unspoken endearment,
Silently conveyed but never spoken,
"I- Love- you."

The romantic words of my heart,
Remaining still and shackled,
Forbidden were they to be spoken.

So, instead, my dearest,
That is how I would express to you,
Over the many, many years,
Three taps, three hugs…
"I- Love- You."

The days have ebbed through time now,
So many years have passed,
Mortality has proved its weakness,
In this twilight of my last autumn.

The beckon of my reaper harks;
Strongly and insistently are the hails,
Alas, the final journey approaches,
Fare thee well, my dear, fare thee well,
Only now am I able to truly speak,
Those so special words of endearment,
"I Love you."

Though unspoken,
I have always loved you,
Even stronger than…
You would ever know.

I love you.

Ron Bornefeld: Tour of duty in Viet Nam "67". He worked as a structural Steel Ironworker and as an Architectural Design Engineer. He is a member of Master Masonic fraternity and Shriner's.

ON THE OTHER SIDE
By Janet Corso

He hesitates for a moment that is an eternity. The opportunity is now, and he knows it shan't repeat itself. One chance is all anyone gets. What awaits him on the other side is unknown. Chance of a lifetime, but a chance for what?

Too often throughout his life he'd met disappointment when he should have found spirit-raising happiness. Or so he thought.

Too often he'd reached out for the gold and found plastic.

Still he kept on. If he did not dare, did not try, what would that make him? He'd be a loser. Just as his father always said he was, a good-for-nothing loser.

He has to keep trying.

He checks his backpack: water, granola bars, extra socks, and an anorak. Everything he needs for a long trek in the mountains. He hesitates. What if it's not the mountains waiting for him? What if it's a forest where the sun seldom reaches below the bottom-most branches of the trees, where the path crunches beneath his feet with years of fallen leaves, and animals ruffle through the bushes beside him?

Or, what if it's an ocean? He has no boat, no flotation device, and he can't swim.

Worse yet, a desert? The heat would bake every drop of water from his body. The sun would blind him. The horizon would disappear into a cloudless, blazing blue sky.

He walks down the narrow hallway. Others have gone this way. No one had returned, no message had been sent back. He wonders what could have happened to them.

At last, he stands before the door, straightens his spine, pulls back his shoulders and reaches for the door handle.

One final thought before he enters. A few last words of self-encouragement. His mother always told him he had a lot of imagination. She told him to use it to think of good things.

Others said he had talent, perhaps too much. He should stop those thoughts right now. He should wake up and realize that every day, in every country, kids were going through the same torture. But he knows, deep in his soul, that none of them saw a trip to the principal's office quite the same way he did.

###

Janet Corso was born in the first half of the last century (which makes her older than some dirt). She belongs to SCWG, Monday Morning Writers and the Wednesday Morning Writers Group. Her pseudonyms are DOD and DOOM. Her writing has appeared in several anthologies and online. Her greatest pleasure in life is the company of writers, edging out even chocolate and various flavors of ice cream.

PAN-DAM-IT COVID-19
By Bob Konczynski

Coronavirus is attempting to infect all of mankind.
Is it a case of Biblical time, Fire, Floods, Epidemic, Civil Unrest?
Or is its Biological Warfare by a country unkind?
Is it an attempt of retaliations?
Because of change in tariff regulations?
To leave a mark on the world's population.
That has changed the norm in its infectious way,
As we fight to survive each day.
Social distancing and wearing masks,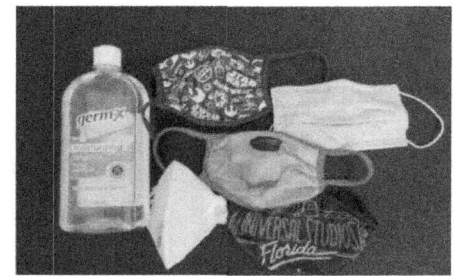
Who ever thought that this would be life's tasks?
The less unfortunate who have died in its wake,
With numerous others infected and quarantined.
Stores closed except for those who sell essential needs.
Schools closed with virtual education becoming a new way.
Places of worship unavailable to serve their followers,
Theaters, Playhouses, Concerts, canceling shows.
Bars and Pubs unable to serve unless providing food and maintaining social distances.
Keeping in step with *CDC guidance and State and Local rules.
Sporting events coming to a halt with team members testing positive.
Travel restrictions put in place, Cruise Liners unable to dock or sail.
Air traffic restrictions to selected countries to stop the spread of Covid-19.

People with essential jobs must keep aware of the virus in the air.
Medical professionals trying to save lives,
While other people gather in protests still infecting more lives.
For those of us that are prone to be more receptive,
Stay at home and be protected.
Keeping distance washing hands using hand sanitizer frequently.
Anything that we may touch could be contaminated with a germ,
When one thinks of it, it is enough to make you want to squirm
For those of us who can work from home,
It's been a blessing by attempting to keep us safe, but for some left home alone.
While others lost their jobs because of massive shutdowns,
Layoffs, Furloughs, Terminations, what is to become of this nation.
As it has been said,
In Pandora's box when all the evils of mankind have been released,
There remains but one thing in the box
HOPE.
The only thing that we can do, is to Hope and Pray,
That this infectious disease goes away.

*CDC Centers for Disease Control and Prevention - CDC 24/7 Saving Lives Protecting People ™

###

 **Bob Konczynski** was born in Elm Park on Staten Island, New York. He met his love from Williston Park on Long Island, New York, married and became a proud parent of three children and two grandchildren. He graduated from New York Institute of Technology with a Bachelor of Science degree. At a company request, he moved with his family from Long Island, New York to Melbourne, Florida in 1995, with multiple assignments to his current position of Sr. Financial Analysis at an aerospace company.

PANDEMIC
By Richard McNamara

George had just settled into his new life after a stroke had left him barely able to hobble along with the use of a cane and a right arm that was all but useless. He could not return to his own home due to accessibility issues, but he and his wife found refuge with his youngest daughter and grandson. He had to spend a great deal of his retirement to remodel his daughter's house to make life easier for him, and it was still difficult to get up and down without help, and he knew it was hard on her and his grandson to put up with grandma and grandpa.

George was moving into his fifth month of rehab when the COVID-19 crisis caused his life to change yet again. He was going to therapy two days a week and going to the gym three days a week when everything closed down. George was basically stuck in his daughter's family room. He tried to do his exercises just as if he was still going to therapy, but it was extremely difficult and, in some cases, impossible. Due to his health issues and his mobility problems, he was basically in lockdown. George didn't go away from the house except for an occasional trip to one doctor or another, and if he did go with his wife to the grocery store, he stayed in the car.

Things were looking grim. Every day the news reporters spoke of increasing cases of COVID-19 as well as a death toll that continued to rise. While it was true that in Palm Bay, the number of deaths was significantly smaller than New York or even other areas of Florida, they were still troubling. One morning his wife said, "Hey, I've got to go to the doctor, would you like to go with me?"

"Yeah, anything to get out of the house," he said. So, he put on a clean shirt, combed his hair, grabbed his mask, and away they went.

When they pulled into the parking lot at the doctor's office, he was shocked. There are probably twenty doctors in the building, but the parking lot was almost empty. His wife dropped him at the front door where he waited while she parked the car. He was leaning against one of the large pillars that support the portico when a security guard approached him, pushing a wheelchair, "Want a ride?" he asked.

"I will use the chair, but I have to wait for my wife. She's parking the car," George said as he sat down in the chair.

"Okay," he said. "But let me push you inside out of the heat."

When George's wife came in, she went through the check-in process and then pushed him over to the waiting area for their doctor. When the nurse called her name, she got up, and, leaving him sitting there, started to walk to the door. When she got to the open door, the nurse said, "Why don't you bring George with you? That way, the doctor can look at him too. Fifteen minutes later, George and his wife were back in the car and speeding down the road headed toward the hospital.

As it turned out, George was not doing as good as he thought. His oxygen saturation was in the low eighties, he had a fever, and he was having trouble breathing. George's wife drove him to the Emergency Room, got out, and grabbed a wheelchair, and wheeled him inside where his oldest daughter was waiting. While his wife took care of the admitting forms, his daughter, who worked at the hospital, pushed him into an exam room accompanied by an orderly who lead the way.

George was really getting worried now. He thought to himself, "Do I have Covid?" He knew from the looks on their faces that his wife and daughter were thinking that he did, but were trying hard to hide it, probably to keep him from getting upset. He was starting to get panicky when a Nurse walked into the room, holding a tray.

"Okay, George, what's your name and date of birth?"

George told him and watched as the nurse sat the tray down on the edge of the bed. "I have to take some samples, and then someone is going to come in and take some blood. Once that happens, you are going over to Radiology for a CAT scan. Do you understand?"

"Yeah, I understand. But what is this all about? Do I have the virus?"

"We don't know yet, but these tests will help answer these questions. Until then, just stay calm and help us help you, Okay?"

"Sure, Okay," George said, looking at his wife.

As with most hospitals, things happened in their own time. George felt like it was hours before they came to take him to get the CAT scan. Once the scan was over, they took him back to the same ER room he was in earlier to wait some more. Later that evening, they moved him to an isolation room. Everyone that came in had to mask up and gown up. Luckily for George, by that time, he was feeling pretty bad, so things like that didn't really register with him. For the next two days, his remembrances were of blood draws, blood sugar checks, and endless blood pressure checks. Finally, on the third day, he was feeling better, and even though nobody ever answered his questions, he was pretty sure he had something like the flu and not Covid. Later that evening, they sprung him from his confinement, and his wife took him back to his youngest daughter's house.

After the family recovered from the initial scare of maybe losing George, things got back to whatever normal looked like at that given time. The daughters and sons-in-law were back to work, and the grandkids were trying to keep their life as normal as possible. George was quarantined to the house and pool deck as the virus numbers increased not only in Florida but in Palm Bay also. To add to his isolation, his wife was gone for several hours each day, meeting with realtors trying to find a house that she and George could call home.

Each day she would come home from house-hunting and show George endless cell phone pictures of this house or that house as the search progressed. Her search criteria were simple. The house had to be laid out such that George could easily get around, and it had to be close to their youngest daughter's house. Finally, one day she came in and said, "Get up and let's get you a shirt. I found us a house just around the corner, and I want you to look at it." So, she got George dressed and trussed up in the car, and she took him to the house, which was literally right around the corner.

With George's approval, the offer was made, and the process of buying the house was begun. The inspection noted several problems that the seller didn't want to address, but he was motivated to comply since the house had been on the market quite some time. After several weeks, George and his wife finally signed the papers and got the keys to their new home. Friends and relatives helped paint the rooms, furniture was moved in, and furnishings were purchased to make the house a home.

Their new home was nice, and George was glad to be back in a place to call his own, but he still felt like a prisoner. He still only went out to go to the doctor or to accompany his wife to the grocery store. Even in his new home, it was like being in a jail cell. Unlike his daughter's house, there was no pool deck to sit on and bask in the sun. His house only had a screened-in patio, and the yard was not a safe place for someone who could barely walk, even with a cane. One day, even his new house seemed to be in jeopardy.

The governor had loosened some of the lockdown restrictions, so his wife came in one afternoon and said, "The Art Club Board of Directors are going to meet tomorrow at the art center, do you want to go?"

"Yeah, I'll go as long as I can stay separated from the group," he said with visions of his last stay in the hospital still fresh in his memory.

"Sure," she said. "You can sit in the workroom and read or use your phone. So, the next day she piled George in the car, and off they went to Sebastian.

When they walked into the art center, George and his wife were wearing their masks, and he was glad to see that most of the other people were also wearing their masks, as well as trying to social distance. Everyone was happy to see George, and he was really happy that there were no hugs. His wife set him in the workroom, and they all crowded into the office. That fact worried George because they were sitting shoulder to shoulder. But what could he do about it? Nothing.

After the meeting, everyone said their goodbyes, and George and his wife took off for Palm Bay.

The next morning George was sitting in his lift chair reading a book on his Kindle. He was totally absorbed in his reading when his wife came in from one of the back rooms with a grim look on her face and said, "One of the ladies just called and said that Marie just posted on her Facebook account that she is sick and has tested positive for covid-19. She also says that to be safe, all of the people that were in the meeting yesterday should go get tested. I have a call in to our doctor. He should call back really soon."

As they were talking, the phone rang. It was the doctor's office. The nurse told his wife she had an appointment for two o'clock at the testing site in Melbourne and to try to be on time. She also said the doctor had put a rush on the test, and she would have the results the next afternoon.

To say that the rest of the day was an anxious time would not be an exaggeration. Neither George nor his wife could concentrate on anything they tried to do, and they both just finally went to bed. The next day was a continuation of the night before. They were both worried about the results of the test, and it made the day drag by. Then, about three in the afternoon, George heard her phone ring in the back room. George couldn't hear the conversation, and by the time he got up out of his chair, it was over.

She came into the room smiling, so George knew that it was good news. "That was the doctor's office," she said. The test was negative. I have to call the other people on the board and let them know.

It wasn't long after his wife's scare that George received word that his rehab treatments were being resumed. His wife called the rehab center and got his therapy schedule for the next group of sessions. At least he would be able to go out of the house once a week for an hour or so. His new schedule was for Wednesday at one.

On the appointed day, he donned his mask, piled into the car, and his wife dropped him off for his hour of pain. Despite his grousing and complaining, the therapy sessions were working. With a moderate amount of pain, he was able to move his shoulder, and with a little more effort, he could pick up small items and carry them.

So now, it seems that Florida's numbers are falling, and the number of daily deaths is going down. Because it appears that Florida is moving in the right direction, the governor has announced that he is implementing his phase three of his reopening plan.

George and his wife are able to go out maybe once a week to see people they haven't seen in months, and they have even gone to their favorite restaurant for lunch, but only after the lunch rush. You see, they are still being cautious.

George feels a little less closed in because he can see his friends maybe once a week for a couple of hours, but not completely. Because he is still unable to get around by himself, and his friends safely do not feel comfortable trying to take him anywhere, he is still housebound, for the most part. So, while others are enjoying the newfound freedom of phase three, George is still in lockdown. Maybe for a long time to come.

Richard McNamara's interest in literature and writing goes back to his earliest years. His parents taught him to read at an early age and he hasn't stopped reading yet! He is a collector of first editions, mainly Florida mystery writers, and attends several writers' conferences every year. During his career in electronics, he has written many technical articles and papers. He has used that experience to try to move into the field of fiction writing.

ROADSIDE ATTRACTION
By James R. Nelson

This story was inspired by my novel, Menagerie of Broken Dreams.

    County Commissioner Clyde Studebaker drove along a bumpy dirt road seven miles outside the small central Florida town of Blue Cove Springs. A swamp filled with flat, black water was on his right. Several alligators sunned themselves on the muddy bank next to the road.

    He glanced at his fuel gauge. It registered a quarter tank. This was no place to run out of gas. Dark clouds swept in from the west. He hoped he could find the girl and deliver his message before the rain hit. She wouldn't be happy, but he had a job to do. There was no way that freak show could open again. The town had breathed a sigh of relief when it closed down six years before. Now, here they were, trying to reopen.

    Clyde parked in a weed covered lot and glanced down at his papers. Savannah Blanchard. How the hell was he going to find her? He stepped out of the car and walked up to a group of men. A very small man, the smallest person he had ever seen, was barking out orders.

    Clyde stifled a laugh. A dusty black fedora perched on the small man's head bobbed up and down as he directed them. "Now, Jake, go check that the ticket booth's ready. Tommy, see that all the big canvas posters are up. Make sure they're secured. We don't want 'em flying away every time it gets windy. They cost a fortune. They were hand painted just outside of Gibtown."

    Tiny noticed the man with the white shirt and tie. "Can I help you?"

The man looked down. "Ah, I hope so. My name's Clyde Studebaker. I'm looking for a woman named Savannah Blanchard."

"Nice to meet you." He reached up and offered his hand. "I'm Tiny." He smiled. "No shit, right. Well, that's what they call me around here."

Clyde made no effort to shake his hand.

Tiny frowned and pulled back his arm. He looked over at the parking lot. "Studebaker, eh? But you're driving a Chevy. Now that's interesting." He turned back. "Anyway, she's over at the trailer. Come on. I'll show you." They walked between several large tents, past a brightly painted popcorn wagon and a huge elephant tethered to a spike in the ground.

Once inside the trailer, Clyde introduced himself. He tried not to stare at Savannah Blanchard. Her face was beautiful. Strikingly beautiful, but from the neck down, her skin was scaly. Not rough and bumpy like those gators he had seen on the side of the road, but smooth like a snake. She wore a flimsy top with narrow straps. There was no attempt to cover herself up.

"What you got there, Mr. Studebaker?" She reached for the papers he was handing her.

Clyde's eyes widened. He stepped back. Her nails had been filed to sharp points and painted black. Those nails, sticking out of the snakeskin-like hand, made his knees buckle. Sweat popped out on his forehead. He steadied himself and explained that the city council had second thoughts on the business permit they had approved. There was going to be an emergency hearing tomorrow. The attraction wouldn't be allowed to open until the meeting was over.

She glanced at the documents, shoved them back at him, and threw open the door. Bright sunlight blinded Clyde as he stumbled outside.

She followed Tiny out and slammed the door behind her. "Have you looked around? We've cleaned up the place. Everyone's over the moon at being able to work again and be gainfully employed. Just what is the problem?"

Clyde shifted from one foot to another, pulled out a big handkerchief, and wiped his brow. "It's the town folk. They...they don't like the thought of, well you know, you people starting up again."

"Why? We're seven miles from Blue Cove Springs. Nobody's going to see us who doesn't want to. I'll tell you what, you'll be hearing from my attorney. You'd better be able to point to a specific code ordinance before you shut us down. We're going to open tomorrow as planned. It's a soft opening to get the kinks out. So, just so you know, we're not official. You can send in the authorities if you like, but it's really not an official opening."

As Clyde shoved his handkerchief back into his pocket, heavy footsteps sounded behind him. A shadow darkened the area as a huge man walked up. "Is there a problem, Savannah?"

"I guess so, Gaston. Seems like the city fathers are trying to delay our opening."

Clyde stared up at the man's immense height. At over eight feet tall, the giant was quite imposing when he was standing so close.

"This gentleman tells me the city council is reviewing our permit. We have to meet with them tomorrow. There's a chance they may shut us down."

Gaston bent over and stared directly into the man's face. His deep voice rumbled, "Are you serious? After all the work and money we've put back into this place? You...you'd have the audacity to put these fine people out of work?"

Clyde turned toward the parking lot. "Like I already told the lady, I wouldn't be opening those gates tomorrow." He took a few steps toward his car. "There's more than a few ways to get you outta here."

Gaston bellowed, "Is that a threat?"

The man glanced over his shoulder and hurried to his car.

After he left, Gaston asked, "What do you want to do? Should I tell the folks?"

Savannah shook her head. "No. They don't need to be worrying about this. They've got a lot to do before we open the gates tomorrow." She winked. "Unofficially, that is."

Tiny pulled off his fedora and threw it to the ground. "I had all I could do not to kick that son-of-a-bitch in the shins."

Savannah turned back toward the trailer. "I'm calling my attorney in Atlanta. He'll know how to deal with these small-minded jerks." She pulled open the door and sat down behind a cluttered desk. She didn't need this now. Not that she hadn't been expecting it. When the thought crossed her mind about putting the Menagerie of Human Oddities attraction back together again, she knew there would be resistance.

Freak shows were out of style. You couldn't even use that name anymore. Society frowned on it. But society had no problem taking away the ability of those very same people, people who were different, from making a living. The do-gooders had been laser focused on closing down all the carnival shows because it wasn't polite to stare at those who were odd. Apparently, they didn't think sweeping them to the dark corners of oblivion where they couldn't make a decent living was worse than being stared at.

She picked up the phone and dialed the attorney's number. Where the hell was Helen the pinhead supposed to find a job? Macys?

Savannah knew. She had lived her whole life being stared at. Ever since she could remember, she'd been the "alligator girl" or "snake-girl" in various circuses and roadside attractions because of her genetic skin condition. It never bothered her. In fact, she thrived on it. She played it up to the hilt by what she had done to her fingernails. She was a natural beauty. A natural beauty that was also strong willed and confident.

The enormous inheritance she had received from her father's estate, the man who had dropped her off at a sideshow when she was young, had done little to ease the guilt and pain she felt when the old Menagerie of Human Oddities had ceased to exist. Suddenly unemployed, the remaining side show performers were scattered to stinking hovels across the country.

But now, Savannah had finally rounded them up. All but one had been eager to return to the roadside attraction. Gaston Chevalier, a real life giant, had been eking out a living trying to sell used cars in a small town outside Quebec.

She had located Freddy Jasper, the lobster boy, in the drunk tank near Gibson, Florida, the famous winter stopping off point for many circuses. Savannah insisted he enroll in AA before she'd let him return. He agreed. Now he couldn't wait to start his act again.

The various other performers were living lives so horrendous Savannah couldn't bear to think about them.

Two hours later, as dusk began to fade to night, Tiny put down his paintbrush. He'd done it. Finished painting the ring toss game before it got dark. He turned as headlights lit up the dark tangle of mangrove and cypress trees surrounding the parking area. A young man stepped out of a battered truck and headed his way.

Tiny pounded the lid back onto the can of paint and waited. Please, not more bad news.

"Do you know where I can find Savannah, the alligator girl?"

"What's this about? Are you from the county?"

The young man looked surprised. "County? No, my name's Jeremy Franklin. She knows me. I met her ten years ago. It's a long story. But believe me, I'm not from the county."

Tiny squinted. "You sure about that?"

"Yes. You guys were featured on the national news the other night. How you're going against the norm and offering employment to…um, you know, you folks. When I saw Savannah, I just had to come by and say hello. I drove two days to get here. Please, I won't take up much of her time."

"Okay. Follow me." Tiny glanced down at the man's shins. "You better be telling me the truth."

A few minutes later, Tiny walked up the small wooden porch to the trailer and knocked.

Savannah was holding a glass of wine when the door opened.

"This guy here says you know him. Something about driving two days just to see you. Do you know him?"

She stared at the person behind Tiny for a few moments, then shook her head. "No. Can't say that I do."

The young man leaned closer. "Savannah, it's me, Jeremy. I was the kid who had a crush on you ten years ago. I kept dropping off cards for you every day. You saved me from a beating from my father. Remember? You even sent me a poster."

A big smile broke out across her face. She stepped out of the trailer and wrapped him in her arms. "Jeremy! I've thought about you so many times." She backed up and looked at him. "Damn, you're a grown man now. Come in, come in."

She poured her visitors each a glass of wine and then looked over at Jeremy. "What a nice surprise. Tell me about yourself. What do you do?"

"I'm going to college at Bowling Green University in Ohio."

"Really? Why Ohio?"

Jeremy grinned. "It's the only place that would give me a scholarship. And they've got a good marketing program."

There was a commotion on the porch. The door flew open. Jake stuck his head in and yelled, "We got some kid roaming around the lot. Looks like he's got a can of gas."

Savannah jumped up. "I'm coming. Tiny, run and get Gaston. We need to catch him before he does something stupid." On her way out the door, she yelled, "Stay here, Jeremy. I'll be right back."

"No, I'm coming with you."

As Savannah made her way to the attractions, she spotted someone pouring gasoline on the wooden poles that held up the circus posters. She yelled, "Stop! You don't know what you're doing. That gas is going to—"

Before she could finish her sentence, the boy pulled out a pack of matches, lit one, and tossed it on the ground. Immediately, there was an explosion, and the kid went flying backwards in a ball of fire.

By the time Savannah got to him, he was screaming and rolling around on the ground. She frantically looked for something to use to put out the flames. An old burlap sack lay in a pool of water. She grabbed it and used it to start pounding out the fire that engulfed him. Hot tongues of heat licked around her fingers. She pulled back for a moment and then continued to beat on the boy.

Gaston, Jake, and Tiny ran up. Jake had a pumping container filled with water. He moved closer, dowsed the boy, and then directed the stream onto the burning poles.

As Jeremy approached, Savannah called to him, "Run back to the trailer and call 911. This kid's in bad shape."

The next day at the city council meeting, Clyde Studebaker banged his gavel. "Ladies and gentlemen, this meeting is about to begin." He glared at Savannah and the people sitting next to her for a few moments and then looked out over the crowd. "As we all know, the purpose of this evening's meeting was to attempt to stop the opening of the Menagerie of Human Oddities roadside attraction out near Blue Cove Springs."

He looked down at his notes. His hand began to tremble. "I've...I've been in contact with a lawyer from Atlanta, and unless we want to face a certain lawsuit, and the expense that it will entail, I'm afraid we don't have much choice in the matter. The attraction must remain."

Loud boos emanated from the audience, along with more than a few derogatory remarks.

Clyde raised his hand. "Please. Keep it down. I'm not done." Again, he stared down at Savannah and her crew. "I know I was all for shutting these folks down. But recently there have been a few developments that you need to know about. This afternoon I was visited by a young man who had a story he wanted me to hear. He told me that ten years ago, when he was only twelve years old, he visited a circus in his hometown where Savannah Blanchard was performing. The young man visited her several times. Actually, he became infatuated with her. Anyway, to make a long story short, one night his father showed up and was about to beat the young boy with a belt right there on the midway. Savannah jumped in, stopped the attack, got the boy to safety, and called child protective services. The man went to jail. When they investigated, they found evidence of abuse, on not just the boy, but his sister too."

The room became silent.

Clyde reached in his back pocket, pulled out his handkerchief, and set it next to his papers. "There's more. Last night, my son, Darrell, at my urging, drove over to the attraction and attempted to burn it to the ground."

Clyde picked up the handkerchief and wiped his face. "In...in the process, there was an explosion and...Darrell became engulfed in flames." He stopped and blinked a few times. His hands tightly gripped the podium.

"The woman you see sitting in front of me with bandages covering both hands, Savannah Blanchard, jumped in and saved him. He's burned. Burned up real bad. But the doctors at the hospital told me he would have never made it without the help of that woman. She's responsible for my son's survival."

A tear slowly drifted down his cheek. "Another thing. The young man explained to me how the attraction we were so gung-ho about shutting down, is actually a lifeline for the people who work there. We think it's cruel that they get stared at. They don't. They know they're different. So different that it's impossible for most of them to make a decent living. Why deprive them of that if we don't have to? I know many of you won't agree with me, but I say it's about time we welcome them into our community and support their attraction." He stepped back. "That's it. That's all I got to say." There was a smattering of applause as he moved over to the end of the stage.

Savannah turned to Jeremy. "So that's where you went this afternoon."

He smiled. "I had to tell him what you did for me. At first, he didn't want to listen. But I wouldn't leave until he heard me out."

She looked over at the crowd as they gawked at Gaston the giant, Helen the pinhead, Freddy the lobster boy, and Tiny. "Let's get out of here."

As they stepped out into the humid Florida night, she stopped. "I got an idea."

"What?"

"You're studying marketing, right?"

Jeremy nodded.

"We could use your help. Let's put our heads together and see if we can turn these friends of mine, these survivors into thrivers."

"Let's do it. I need to come up with a class project. Sounds perfect to me. I can't wait to spring this on my professor."

Two burly policemen stepped out, one on each side of Clyde Studebaker. His hands were cuffed behind his back.

"What's that all about?" Jeremy asked.

"Arrested for arson, I hope. Maybe there is justice for our kind of people after all." She took Jeremy's hand. "Come on, Mr. Marketing Man. You've got work to do."

###

**James R. Nelson** has published ten mystery novels and a collection of short stories. Several of his stories can be found in anthologies published by the Space Coast Writers Guild.

He is currently the treasurer of the Space Coast Writers' Guild, a founding board member of The Brevard Author Society, and is on the board of the Melbourne Beach Friends of the Library. He has a Master's of Education degree.

He belongs to several author critique groups and has frequently appeared as a guest speaker on various author panels and book signing events in Brevard County and in Michigan.

SPRING SPRINGS ETERNAL
By Betty Whitaker Jackson

Through the kaleidoscope of my office window
I catch the glimmers and stop-frames of spring—
Birds pairing, rabbits chasing, hope-filled nesting begins.
Lurking clouds reserve certain storms' showers.

As buds swell, sprouts lengthen, fresh grass greens
I revel in rejuvenation
Energetic evidence: God's providential promise
To bless the land and those who dwell within.

I'm seeing no greed, no hurry, no deception
As each vigorous creature completes its task
With creativity, diversity, and singleness of purpose
Living harmoniously, gloriously in industrious pursuits.

We've so much to learn from reflectively realizing
That striving, profit, competition, and pride
Can lead to no better than second-class living
Compared to Nature's picture portrayed here today.

Can't we humans learn rich benefits while doing our thing,
Breathing deeply, grasping grace while it's near,
Treasuring moments to safeguard our oft'-stressed souls
To prepare for harsh heartbreaks to come?

Yes, this spring for mankind indeed is so different
As worldwide epic pandemic expands
To threaten, to frighten, to attack, and to kill
And change our whole normal way of life.

Perspectives have changed, the picture blurs
When life's vicissitudes challenge
Whether COVID, catastrophe, quarantine or cancer
Cloud our perception. Public becomes oh, so personal.

As man's world cringes, COVID menaces,
Running rampant, spreading fear, deep divisions
And politics, riots, protests, obstructions
Assassinate dreams, slaughter incentive, ceasing peace.

Remember resiliency and purposeful serenity
Confinement brings new opportunities
To look at this traumatic 2020's hiatus
And learn, grow, flourish again.

But wait, take a break, look back at spring's cycle
Let's reflect, remember, reminisce
After winter's storm, the buffeting winds
Spring's zephyrs soothe yet again.

The kaleidoscope changes its image to autumn
Life's cycle matures to harvest's rich plenty
What have we learned, accomplished, completed—
What wisdom is gleaned in our storehouse this year?

I can look to nature's lessons once more
Remembering spring's cyclical reverence
To seedtime and harvest, beginning to end,
Shall once more arrive, we'll survive.

The wintry past of our discontent

Will vanish with spring's pregnant promise
That all will be well, we'll recover with scars
To begin, to prosper, again.

###

Betty Whitaker Jackson has published twenty-five books since her retirement from her forty-year career as a secondary language arts teacher. Her works also appear in eleven anthologies. She won first prize in the LifeRich Reader's Digest Memoir competition with her book *Rocking Chair Porch: Summers with Grandma.* An active member of Space Coast Writers Guild, she thanks members for their support and encouragement. She writes fiction, nonfiction, memoir, devotionals, poetry, and children's books. She regularly blogs at www.bettyjackson.net.

STAB IN THE BACK
By Roseangelina Baptista

Just two small punctures
Bubbling a grand noise.
@ entrance.shsh.org
@ exit.shsh.com

-Breathe out,
-Too much bruised *air* trapped inside!
Seal is over.

Tension built
From a blade claw hand
Created in a dream.

A sky-high
Bubble chest.

First,
I asked to the mind—
Mind signaled a familiar face.
Mind concocted taking aim
On billable code.
Then
I asked to the Heart.
All was void.
Sign less calm,
Aimless calm.

###

Roseangelina Baptista is an American-Brazilian based in Central Florida. She is a bilingual freelance writer with interests in promoting poetry and mindfulness for society and in reviving Indo-Portuguese literature. Her poetry first appeared in the *Joao Roque Literary Journal* (June 2019) and *Adelaide Literary Magazine* (November 2019 and February 2020). Other works were contributions to local anthologies 2020.

STUPOR
By Anne-Marie Derouault

The world fell into a stupor
Fear poured into human hearts
Like a lead weight
From an unknown unexpected threat.

We live in uncertain times
Troubled by a modern plague
Despite our sophisticated progress
Or because of it...

The black bird is out of the cage
Most humans will never know
The chain of cause and effect
And the part of chance
The epidemic will run its course
Everyone protecting themselves
Guided by their beliefs and their means
Nobody can stop it.

One more example
Of our place in the universe
Humble and modest
That we forget continuously
Stronger than everything
Master of the world
Dominating Nature
Exploiting its creatures
Without mercy, without restraint.

Nature this time has the power
Some will see it as a message.
I call upon the light and the invisible forces
To soften the pain
To keep us resilient
To protect my loved ones
So that we meet again.

God willing
There will be again
Powerful summers
On joyful islands
Lingering conversations and drink
The joy of being together
Alive.

###

Anne-Marie Derouault Born in Paris, living in Florida, is a consultant in management, communication and stress reduction. She writes free verse poetry in French and in English, haikus and short stories, inspired by her love of travel, nature and human beings. She recently published her first book: *While the Poem Lasts,* a bilingual collection of inspirational poetry. She is a member of Cape Canaveral Pen Women, Space Coast Writers Guild, and Scribblers of Brevard.

SURVIVAL: THE COURAGE TO SUCCEED
By Edward C Rau

Joshua Smith, the fourth child of Dewayne and Latoya Smith, was born in a black settlement in Pike County Alabama just outside the city of Troy. The family consisted of three brothers and one sister. Dewayne, the father, was 49 years old, Latoya, the mother, 47, sons Dewayne Jr 29, Kofi 28, Joshua 10 and daughter Kamisha 21.

Segregation was prevalent and recognizable in Alabama and throughout the South. Dewayne was a sharecropper. He rented a small plot of land from the landowner, Mr. Brewster, in return for a portion of the crop when harvested. Dewayne and his two oldest sons worked on the plot of land until growing season ended. When growing season ended for the year, they worked for Mr. Brewster in his poultry plant.

While a believer in segregation, Mr. Brewster was not a subscriber to many of the ways black people in the south were treated. Jim Crow laws that mandated the segregation of public schools, public places, and public transportation, and the segregation of restrooms, restaurants, and drinking fountains between white and black people existed throughout the south. While he complied with these laws, he was not as radical in their enforcement as were many of his white landowner neighbors. He treated his sharecroppers fairly as long as they paid him their agreed to share from the crops raised. The black people working in his poultry plant worked long hours, and he treated them in accordance with existing laws.

Each day at sunrise, except for Sundays, Dewayne and his two grown sons would leave their home and walk down the dirt road to the plot of land assigned to them. They remained at their work location until sunset except for designated breaks. At the end of the workday, the supervisor would stop the day's activities and the workers returned to their quarters. The only exception being inclement weather when work stopped in the fields and the workers moved to the poultry plant until the bad weather system passed.

Joshua's sister, Kamisha, either worked at home helping Latoya or if needed assisted domestic staff assigned to the landowner's house. At the main house, she helped cook, do laundry and other housekeeping chores. Latoya stayed home most of the time tending to Joshua who was too young for a work assignment similar to what the other males were doing.

The Smith family experienced first-hand the true meaning of "survival" in the segregated south. From birth, every family member became acutely aware that each was in a fight/struggle to survive. Life was hard overall, and each family member, depending on age, experienced the circumstances differently. Dewayne and Latoya knew the horrors of growing up during segregation and the struggle it was to feed, clothe, and provide a home for the children and themselves. The children faced many difficult moments growing up be it playmates, school, work environment, or segregation. The entire family working and praying together made the best of the life given to them by the Lord.

World War II began in 1939 in Europe. President Roosevelt activated the draft in 1940 requiring all able-bodied men between 18 and 45 to register. The draft called the two oldest brothers to Army active duty. Joshua was not old enough to be eligible for the draft. Segregation was still present in the military requiring black men be assigned to all-black units.

Joshua stayed close with his mother who spent a good part of her waking hours teaching him about daily life and the expectation of his assuming chores as he grew older. He went to the nearby black elementary school where he met other black children his age. Well versed in the Bible, he was a smart boy always asking questions and seeking answers about life in general. Many were about the war and ones that his mother did not have answers too. He spent a good amount of time asking questions about his brothers and sister. His mind was like a "sponge" as he processed and retained numerous things. He maintained a thirst for knowledge that fascinated his family.

His primary objective since he was a little boy was to attend college/university. The limitations caused by the difficulties of segregation and the ongoing struggle with discrimination made achieving his plans more difficult. Black schools competed with the white schools except for teachers where teacher selection was primarily determined by race.

Joshua's knowledge and capabilities stood out in each of his classes. He read, incessantly and much of what he read was of a scientific or historical nature His teachers were amazed that this boy had such talent along with a desire to expand his knowledge base. Several gave him used magazines and books of a scientific or technical nature rather than toss them away.

High school is where Joshua experienced his first significant and personal encounters with discrimination. His elementary school experiences, while an all-black school, were not as impacting as his high school years. In high school, he saw firsthand the differences between a black school and an all-white school. The white-only facilities were much better and current. The teachers were all white and a significant number of the students were much more aggressive in their attitudes toward black people.

Many times, the meetings between white and black students were confrontational and required intervention from the teachers and/or the administrative staff. Even though many of these issues and circumstances affected his overall demeanor, he did his best to ignore them and focus on his main objective, graduate high school, and go on to college.

The war ended in 1945 and Joshua's two brothers received honorable discharges from the Army and returned home. Both survived the terror and horrors of the war, but they received injuries physically and mentally. Dewayne Jr. received shrapnel in his right arm leaving him partially impaired, and Kofi incurred some mental deficiencies from the intensive bombing and suffered crippling nightmares from the impairment. Both boys received assistance from the Veteran's Administration with their medical needs as well as each receiving a small pension as compensation for their war injuries. The two boys lived at home and returned to work with their father at the farm. They also worked at the poultry plant when the growing season ended.

Joshua was a good student and possessed an inquiring mind. One where he continually sought deeper answers and solutions to the issues he encountered in elementary and high school. As he advanced in grade, Joshua also experienced greater exposure to discrimination and its accompanying issues. He faced them head on and attempted to resolve many of them on his own. He did however discuss them with his mother whenever he got the chance.

He graduated from high school with honors. His grades were more than enough to qualify him entry into any number of colleges and universities. With the help of his teachers, he applied to Tuskegee University. Frederick D. Patterson, a former Tuskegee

President established engineering and science programs at the school, programs in which Joshua had a deep interest.

Six months away from high school graduation, Joshua was nervous about his acceptance to Tuskegee. He also had not heard anything about a scholarship, as without one he would not be able to attend the university. He had applied for a scholarship at the urging of one of his high school teachers.

One day close to the end of the school year and high school graduation, one of Joshua's teachers called him out of class and told him that she received a letter from the Tuskegee Admissions Office. Joshua's heart was pounding, and his hands were shaking. The teacher handed him an envelope, and he quickly opened it and read the enclosed letter. Joshua let out a yell as he finished reading the letter of congratulations advising him of his acceptance to the university.

Once he calmed down, the teacher handed him another letter from the United Negro College Fund (UNCF) scholarship committee advising him of the award of a full scholarship to Tuskegee University. The teachers and his classmates offered him congratulations and best wishes on his good news and wished him success at the university. Overcome by the news, he could hardly wait until he got home to share the good news with his mother and the rest of the family.

The university was approximately seventy miles from Joshua's home, a life-changing move as this was the first time he would be away from home for any length of time. His mother often talked to him about the day when he would leave the family and go out on his own. While meant to calm Joshua and prepare him for adulthood, it caused a great deal of anxiety amongst the entire family.

His father was also proud, as Joshua was the first member of the family to attend college and begin a path to improve himself and leave the servitude of the farm. His sister and brothers also offered their congratulations and told him how proud they were.

That Sunday, the entire family went to church to give thanks and to pray for Joshua's wellbeing and success in this endeavor. Even the minister mentioned the good news about Joshua during announcements and asked the Lord to look after him during this new phase in his life. Dewayne bought several chickens for their celebratory meal, and Latoya made a special supper in recognition of Joshua's success.

Many tasks remained to get Joshua ready for school before departure day. Latoya and Kamisha assembled his clothes and made sure that those things he was taking were in good repair and laundered prior to packing. Latoya also went to her small stash of money to get a little for the boy to have until he was settled and found some part time work. The family did not earn much money, and they needed almost all money earned for food and clothes. Joshua's two brothers chipped in some of the money that they had squirreled away from their Army days. In all, Joshua had approximately $75.00. Not much, but for the Smith family it was a lot of money.

Graduation day finally arrived, and the entire family went to the ceremony to cheer Joshua's success. The school principal spoke to the graduates, encouraging each one to give it their best and use what they learned in school. Then the ceremony recognized those students who excelled during their four years at the school. Joshua Smith received the first award in recognition for being overall best student. He had a perfect attendance record, and excelled in science, and other technically focused subjects. He received a Certificate of Achievement for his scholastic efforts and for his ranking as number one in his class.

When Joshua came on stage, the entire class and audience stood and gave him a rousing cheer and thunderous applause. The principal raised his hand to quiet the crowd and announced that Joshua had received a four-year scholarship from the UNCF to attend Tuskegee University. The recognition overwhelmed Joshua and his family. Joshua shook hands with the principal, nodded to the teachers and audience as a sign of thanks and appreciation, and then left the stage. In his closing remarks, the principal said, "I leave you with the following: your courage to succeed is what survival is all about."

The days of summer were long and hot. Joshua and his mother spent much of their time assembling items that he would need while at the university and listing those things he still needed. The biggest item being sufficient funds to cover incidentals. One evening during a family meeting, a discussion of the funds issue occurred. Recognizing that family members gave him the most money possible, Joshua told them that he would work part time as much as he could if such work was available. He stressed that he would not let the job affect his studies.

The day of departure soon came. The family assembled at the bus stop to help Joshua load his suitcase and to say goodbye. It was a difficult moment for everyone, but each knew this was the right thing for Joshua. When all the goodbyes, hugs, and kisses were completed, Joshua got into the bus, went to the rear, and off they went. After three grueling hours including one bus change, he arrived at the bus stop nearest the school. Joshua was overwhelmed with all the sights and envisioned a new adventure for the next four years.

Once settled, he sought out the student aid office to see about a part time job. The school representative on duty assisted Joshua with applying for one of the available part time jobs. In the end, he took a job in the school cafeteria. The hours were during Joshua's free time. As a cafeteria employee there was no cost to him for meals.

The classes for the first year were mostly mandated, but he did have an opportunity to take a couple of science related classes, a difficult workload when coupled with the cafeteria work, but Joshua was strong minded and well disciplined. He handled this workload quite well for a first-year student. He wrote a letter home each week to keep his Mom and the family apprised of his progress and any issues that he felt needed Mom's attention and/or guidance.

The first year went well and he received four A's and one B which placed him on the Dean's List. He was so proud he could not wait to return home for the summer break and to see the family again. It was a great day when the bus came rolling up to the stop near the house with the horn blaring at some animals in the street. This also alerted the family that Joshua was home at last. Everyone rushed out of the house waving and cheering, so happy that he was finally home, for a while at least.

Joshua and the family followed the same procedure for the next three years. The one major change was that his father took ill in the fourth year of the college program. Latoya asked each family member to keep this news from Joshua as he was in the final year of college and she did not want anything or anyone interrupting his schedule. Dewayne struggled for most of the final year. However, he was not physically able to attend the graduation ceremony. Latoya attended with her three sons. Kamisha, the daughter, stayed behind to attend to the ailing father.

The ceremony was long as there were a large number of students graduating. Joshua was graduating with honors as he was on the Dean's List for all four years. He was at the front of the graduating class. He was concerned that he did not see his father nor his sister at the ceremony. When asked, Latoya responded that Dad did not feel well and excused himself from making the trip. She asked Joshua's sister to remain so the rest of the family could attend the graduation.

After the ceremony, the family assembled near the bus stop and prepared for the trip home. It was during the ride home that Latoya and Joshua discussed his job offer. The discussion was lively and continued for the entire trip home. Kamisha and the father were waiting outside for the family to arrive. The honking of the horn was the giveaway that the bus was approaching.

Joshua received honors and his scholarly efforts recognized. In fact, he did such a good job, the school offered him an Assistant's job in the Engineering Department. He did not accept immediately as he wanted to discuss it with his mother. For the next four weeks, the family focused on Joshua asking him about his new job and his plans. The family also spent a significant amount of time reminiscing about the happy times when growing up and doing things as a family. Everyone enjoyed this time together as it did not happen very often.

Tragedy struck the third week of Joshua being home. The ailing father suffered a massive heart attack resulting in his death. The entire family grieved the loss and had a difficult time coping with the situation. Dewayne's funeral service led by the local pastor was at the same church the family attended with burial in the church's cemetery. Joshua was at a crossroads. Did he stay home and assist his mother in getting back on her feet or did he return to Tuskegee and begin his new job. His mom insisted that he return to Tuskegee and begin his career.

The brothers and the sister were staying on at their Pike County home, and they insisted to Joshua that they were capable of caring for their mother. Everyone encouraged Joshua to return and begin his new job and not worry as each was committed to watching and caring for the mother. Joshua's new job was a family milestone since nobody prior had such an opportunity. They also suggested that he might never have an opportunity like this again. Begrudgingly, Joshua followed their advice and when the time came, he returned to Tuskegee. On his departure and between the tears, his mother reminded him of the following:

Survival is the Courage to Succeed
###

Ed Rau was born in Lawrence, MA. A 1963 graduate of Merrimack College with a BS in Marketing. A former Air Force Captain with Vietnam service, receiving a Bronze Star and two Air Force Commendation Medals for his military service. Ed, a former Space Coast Writers Guild board member, has contributed to Guild anthologies including Love and Rockets, Gratitude, Spring, Friends, Perseverance, Holidays, and Change. He published his first novel, Rocky Water in March 2016.

TATTLETALES

By Ima J. Pastula, PhD.

Of the Great Change:

Sad that, entire coveys were busy with the gossip. Who were they? The disappearance, the hush, hushes all that sort of stuff. Thought to be of sound mind and body, Hortense, in constant denial, swore her sources were honest, spreading the news, not in a facetious way, only as a neighborly gesture. As town Librarian she felt it to be her duty. With such strange happenings, the transference of a disease from Bats that upgraded to humans, a Covid Virus; all the hustle and haste to survive the strange medical danger that was becoming a Pandemic! Now, Hortense stirred the muddy waters with her antics!

It began with the whispers at the Colony Cafe, favorite watering hole of that local group of writers, and those wishing to meet the writers. Over the din of the different languages, the faint confession of one, speaking broken English, out-volumed the others. According to Hortense, the crippled words spoke of an Alien Abduction, one so real sounding she could not help but eavesdrop closer!

One must realize, of course, that to really grasp the entire content of a secret, between writers, it becomes an illicit, invasion of privacy. Beginning now, a much more dire notice of the mysterious ailment, akin to the flu, so it seems.

A favorite topic amidst the literary; speaking of copyrights. Are the overheard conversations between writers a public domain? They write words in books for all to read, right? Can one inch their way toward the sound of another's voice, record that content, feel safe in sharing the shadowed words? Indeed, faint, echoing gasps of someone usually means a great, mysterious something has happened, right? Words, like creepy floorboards squeaking, a traipsing during midnight, slamming of doors, strange flushing of toilets, all those sorts of disturbances are valued once one is in the glory of a disclosure. An air of suspense is the forgery of a type of fear, the innermost fading of confidence and inspiration.

Patent, of a personal nature, words become a string of a plot revealed.

She of dubiousness sat the in cracked, red vinyl seat and watched the gesturing of both hands and lips forming new words. Hortense, leaning a little too close, slipped off the end of the tilt, startling all with her cuss words, "Oh, Oh no!"

Even the thoughtful voice of one concerned embarrassed the snoop, yet it all gave haste to her recovery. A flick of her bouncy hairdo, the coyness of her nail polished fingers sent the eavesdropper to the cashier to check out. Vowing with a whisper to return. Seen sneaking through a more discrete door, off the alleyway and behind the dumpster.

On the scent of sensational, our excited gossip slipped into the empty booth, hunching slightly just to disguise her in the renewed view. Shaky fingers ran the keyboard; the laptop literally hummed the words of the God-awful truth of the matter! Second hand, evenly typed words, rang with a hallow hint of truth. Whatever was about on that dreary morning, the one after the terrible storm, claiming that the sound of thunder was a landing *'Space Ship'*, one of a shuttle, of sorts, that gathered maiden ladies up, one by one, to haul off to outer Space and waiting dates with Aliens?

Perhaps a symptom, within the pandemic, is senility?

Sparse but astringent tattle tales followed the disclosure of what Hortense claimed she overheard, swearing it seemed authentic, a real dilemma. Nothing to do with the current, medical drama; but all listened; gasping at the overwhelming tale of abduction, rape and birthing of Alien babies! Who knew? Now this is a small town, not many virgins left here about. Besides, Aliens only want virgins? Confused by the *'beyond belief'* tales of debauchery, militant stalking of the tree-lined neighborhoods and the peeking around the corner of the Library must have all been done in the still of night, after midnight, in the nautical twilight of a finishing yesterday? On a moonless night? Strolling Aliens? Surely, they look different enough to stir an alarm?

Curiosity, that evil spell cast upon one whilst hearing the latest gossip, especially from a professional gossiper like Hortense, engulfed all who heard. Off we went, to the very booth said to be the crime scene; we sat, all ears, so to say. In came the habitual writers, sitting at their favorite booths, chatting in a literary language foreign to most of us. What was divulged next is now legendary in our small covey of a township, set in bold on the front page of the old time, local paper, *GIVE A HOLLER*. Wait for it!

BREAKING NEWS
THE MORNING AFTER
by REPORTER JOHNSON

"Mysterious, Alien abductions, reported by our Librarian, Ms. Hortense Berringer, on the eve of the great storm claimed as a thunderous landing of a 'Space Ship,' landing to capture virgins for the delight of some outer space creatures, bound to cause the birthing of a new colony of beings within our town limits! Not a hoax mind you, but a great misunderstanding. Overhearing two of our local Authors, at their favorite Cafe, discussing their new collaborative book, our Ms. Hortense mistook fiction for fact and passed on the passages of the manuscript titled, *Not So Far Away*.

EPILOGUE

Censured, sued for infringement of Intellectual property, banned from the writers' corner of the Cafe, the ruined Gossiper, Hortense, sold her rickety house inherited from a less than bright ancestor, hastened to the train, and headed toward the Brooklyn Navy Yards, N.Y boarding a transport Ship to Europe. Latest gossip about Hortense? She became a writer; her books contained all the gossip she gathered over her years as the town's Librarian. As fate would have it, she has two *Best Sellers* amidst her ten volumes of work. Seems the local bartender followed her a few months later, and together, with their equal tendencies to eavesdrop, live happily together as they stalk the local sources.

ADLIB:

Not gullible, however, on thunderous, stormy nights, I keep a sharp eye to see as far as one can in the thick fog and rain just to be sure, what is seen is the light from a thunderbolt, not an Alien Space Ship landing, because I am a virgin!

In the still of a most beautiful evening, one that had shown a multi-colored rainbow earlier, bright from one corner of town to the other, it sparkled somehow with stars that you knew were far from earth, of other worlds and with the intent of lighting the world beyond the mysterious lightning and splintering of thunder clouds.

None of that this evening, just the evidence of the starlight. I saw it then; a shadow approaching, seeming to be walking through the many moonbeams that appeared as clouds and moved aside the full moon to surround many more stars and such!

As the shadow began to hover, then move in and out between the moon beams, a sound so melodic moved me to hurry toward the corner Café. It was to watch the shadow in the safety and the lure of the aroma of fresh coffee and sticky buns. Josh tenderly touched my arm, pulling me gently toward the table by the window. We sat then, spoke of the slithering shadow that was moving about, beyond the large glass windows of the alley side of the Café. We sat in the illusion of the undulating, the seemingly lurking of something that was casting that mysterious shadow! Josh, suddenly laid his head on the shiny, red table, saying he didn't feel so good! Had the infamous virus captured Josh? Off to home and to bed; just to make sure it's not just some, not so rare, reaction to the café's junk food!

Returning to the café, the quietness, the pleasant aromas and multi-lingual whispers of those also attracted by the antics of a mere shadow were pleasant! We were reminded, in unison of the quaint Gossip, our town Librarian, who fled in embarrassment to Europe and wrote of her imaginary small town full of illegitimate, alien plus humans. A bloodline of mixed babies! Josh confessed he was still curious of all she tattled about, the way she seemed to have the inside scoop on ancient alien astronauts. The extraterrestrial years of our ancient history as well as the strange blood line of those thought to be of half and half in the lingering of a blood line remaining an enigma.

The weird reality was just that, weird! Those suspected could not receive whole blood from the town's folk, nor give transfusions. Their blood could not be matched with any other type, actually a type so very rare, they even looked different. Pale skin, light blues, green eye color with no hair on their arms or legs. It was a legacy no one understood. However, the citizens no longer laughed at the eccentric Librarian that seem to carry a bit of the bloodline she tattled about.

HAPPY NEW YEAR

History is become illogical, ancestors, becoming strange notions in the Library's Archives. Births over the next year will be separated; laboratory studies began in ernst; all recordings with a question mark! The category of *What for Christmas presents* was a biological report of one's blood type with proof of linage! Gossip, indeed. Clans began to form. Some even had their own religious beliefs. Strange rituals alerted all to any new births; people lingered in the hospital nursery, hovering to look upon the newly born. There did even seem to be a different way of birthing; and the child had strange orange fuzz for hair!

Our town suffered the anomaly in complete patience and tolerated the suspects— as well as keeping an eye on the growing pandemic—treating the weird situation as just mother nature's way of changing the human species to mix us all in a conglomerate of a rare and, of course, extremely intellectual new species.

Never proven, we all suffered the anonymous situation of our ancestry; beginning to mate, mix and match both, to an even more rare species. For some unknown quirk in the weather pattern, last year we had the most horrendous hurricane. Many of those suspected as an Alien Astronaut illegitimate breed, somehow, perished overnight. Massive amounts of people were lost to the viscous storm. Those suspects that survived became a new county, with their own police, schools, law and order, etc. They erected a huge, brass monument of the first gossiper, Hortense the Librarian.

Remaining the most secret, mysterious small town, snuggled between the borders of North and South, rumors started that it was now haunted! Not to worry, all native born of whatever, remain peaceful and hopeful that history will soon reveal a pattern of some sort of an understandable *Birth Certificate!* Biological studies continue, and most listen intently, as they linger at that corner café, to the local gossip featured at the time! The library began filling with Novels of authors' new beliefs!

The mysterious *change in everything* has remained our forever weird past!

Out of State-ers act as tourists, viewing us all, and especially the new county of survival suspects! Named quaintly 'New Town County'. Can you believe they sell t-shirts with weird symbols and tiny bags of candy shaped like spaceships? Unusual, strange scenery on babies' diapers! All of this from gossip? Indeed, one continuous change is the evolution of the mysterious pandemic; No gossip needed here, just the reality of it all.

THE DAYS OF STRANGE WINE AND DIFFERENT ROSES?

Walk with me my friend, along the trails amidst the new county, stare a while, then stop at the new corner café for aromatic whatever. We from original county are welcome, actually, the suspects have copied a lot of our living habits as well as some alcohol beverages (must say— they don't handle their liquor as well as we non-suspects.) Gossip has it that many linger at a small, tacky Bar well into dawn, listening to the many new authors that have moved over to where all the strange happenings are now. Guessing— being the old norm has become boring for the curious ones?

Of course, we are talking ancient history, the Pandemic, year 2020 seems to have been as much a change as Mother Nature's mysterious creativity of another time and place in our most unusual history. The Archives at the old library is now open 24 hours, for all the research going on, still! We remain in the curious domain of change.

Heard any good gossip lately?

Ima J. Pastula PhD is a published author, master artist, retired adjunct facility professor from Anne Arundle Community College in Arnold, Maryland. When both husband and wife retired, they relocated to Melbourne, Florida. She is a past president of the National League of American Pen women, serving after as secretary. A member of the Space Coast Writers Guild for many years and a contributor, many times, to the Guild's Anthologies. Available for creative lectures.

THE ARTISTRY OF SURVIVAL
By Marjorie A. Cuffy

We begin at the dawn of time,
And the adages that keep us unhinged
Bring mercy and kindness to the foreground
Of a thought. It intimates that we are one.
That is unquestionably the maxim
By which we co-exist.
For co-existence is the mantra.
It foreshadows our pre-emptive attitudes
To shine within that spherical light.
Who or what, then, does this imaginary impulse include?
What, then, does the state of survival indicate?
How reflected in this popular refrain of humankind? –
That we are born free.
Free to exploit the disadvantaged?
Free to use the resources meant for all, injudiciously?
Free to dominate at will? Introspectively,
We are all those inconsistencies.
Measured by the refrain that we are free.

It is the nascent attitudes of an evolving race:
Humankind. The adages of time replaced
By a prepossessing attitude that brings forth
A multiplicity of varied inconsistent truths
So, varied in content and substance
That the natural mores embedded deep within—
Of humankind's inherent tendency to love--
Become frayed and stretched to emulate
The progenesis of an ever-eerie particularity of fate:
To belong to the instruments of dark synthesis,

And dismal strains of nether worldly anxieties.
These are the fated particulars that bring distress and fear.
We wander in the maze of time to endure the intransigencies
Unfolding within the nexus of a self-ordained critique.
In this abounds the maturity of souls-- supine with longing--

The age-old aspiration of being in the specious seeds of time.
And we engage the fray within this arbitrary and distinct particularity
Of the well-known refrain—we are one. This mundane and exemplary sense of being
Brings all into sober hankerings
That suggest: the principles of love
Belong to all who seek.
Not oft do we harbor thoughts of a life so free
That we allow the pathos of a world,
So brimful of suffering and disaster,
To seep into the mirthful chatter
And forgo the tender thoughts
That engage our activities, to ponder
The meaning of what attends our existence.
For all was meant to bring a joyful spark,
Or a joyousness within the sphere of living.
What greed or lack thereof compels the spate of materiality?
So, predominating!
What allows for the inhumanity of humankind?
That it shrugs at the disillusioned forces
Who suffer from the world's excesses?

We reach beyond our sphere of influence,
Emboldened by the hazards of time,
To eschew the frail and injurious elements
And create a universe by design—
That, in its unfolding, ensures that love's principles
Of unity and peace are brought into focus and equilibrium
As the interconnected forces align
With our purpose –of healing and indivisibility.
In this particular aspiration, we embrace
The full intensity of the culminating synthesis
Within the heart song of the refrain –we are one.
It speaks of a will to survive beyond our spatial interplay
Though precipices and dangers hinder progressive thought.
We engage the sinuous obstacles that insinuate the selfless
And the virulent auguries that threaten our way of life,
For we are the children of love and light.
The independent spirit survives the needless taunts,
Inspired by that engaging adage -- we are one.

###

 **Marjorie A. Cuffy** is the author of *The Bond of Love: A Global Affair* which she hopes will find its rightful place among the foremost editions on love. She has been brought to this moment by the love that is of all and brings forth a spiritual aspect that is, by design, the weight of a vision of her own spiritual hankerings that have expressly become the tenets of her life's work.

Formerly a healthcare professional whose experiences span diverse cultures and, in general, borne witness to the human condition, she has been motivated by the desire to the search for peace and justice.

She enjoys gardening, volunteering, communing with nature, and has traveled extensively, a passion which she shares with her husband. She has two sons and lives in Melbourne, Florida.

THE LAST TWO WOMEN
By Rebecca Christophi

From the diary of Rebekah Mechst
Year 2553

    Lora and I met when we were children. I can't remember the day although I know there must have been a singular moment in time when our two lives collided. It just seems to me, when I look back on my life, that she was always there. Perhaps we were both at a swimming hole, dressed in slick purple water skins, she with her mother, me with my father. The swimming hole near my home with the deep velvet-blue water, cold as bone, where we often went to play and shared so many secrets. Where she first told me about Greg. Or perhaps it was behind the ruins. Maybe I was sitting cross-legged on the moss-covered ledge under the limestone statue, the one that looks like a man, but with a child's face, the masculine parts removed and replaced with the awkward plaster casting of a lily. I was reading a book of poems, or maybe writing one of my own, something about a girl drifting aimlessly in a boat to a forgotten island where there still dwelt extinct species of manatee and opossum. Lora was playing hide-and-seek with one of the neighborhood boys, when she bumped into me, and was shocked when she turned around to see the suntanned face of a girl her age smiling, bewildered, up at her. I don't know.

    The image I see when I think of our childhood is a still-life of the two of us. My father, who had paid a great deal of money to adopt me when I was a baby, not wanting the doctors to change me, believing that we should return to the old ways, had a travelling artist make it. In the image we are about seven. It still sits, an icon, on his wide oak desk. Two girls, holding hands, one with a wild crop of short, dark curls, unsmiling, holding a stuffed rabbit, the other blonde and fair and dimpled, nearly a head taller, with a huge carefree smile. I always thought it was the perfect image of us, that somehow the artist must have known our characters in order to capture them with such precision. Later, much later, I came to understand that this view, my view, of both Lora, and our friendship, could not have been more wrong. What follows is our story, and, in a way, the story of the human race.

 On that blistering June morning Lora still looked like herself. She had always been beautiful. Effortlessly beautiful. Which is the worst kind. Her long honey-blonde hair was pulled up in a ponytail, her large bronze-flecked eyes were rimmed with red, but somehow, not even that detracted from her overall prettiness. Her mother (that word still sticks in my throat, since I never had cause to use it myself), was also beautiful. She was from a long line of Orthodox that emigrated here more than a century ago. Most did not have children, the birthing too painful and the public attention too difficult. But Lora's mother was rebellious and at seventeen gave birth to a healthy baby girl. I, on the other hand, was a malfunction, and never had a mother. Beautiful and with a mother, life certainly wasn't fair.

 I won't deny that I was jealous of Lora, but I never hated her. I couldn't. I had no-one else. It feels silly to me now, that it took almost the full twenty-minute ride to figure out what was different about her. You must understand that I was, at that point in my life, living very much within my own mind. But something like a small, blonde mustache on a beautiful woman should have been pretty obvious. Now, so many years later, I can almost laugh about it.

 We didn't, of course, come to this overnight. There are many history books on the topic, and although I'm sure they don't tell the whole truth, they give us a version of it. I will try to distill the important points.

People have always, from the time they reached understanding, striven to look and act like one another. If you peruse old photographs of middle-school students from the early 21st century, you will see what I mean. The male version: think the quintessential pop-stars of that time period. Hair shaven on the sides, long and tousled in front, clothing brandishing the name of whatever store was currently popular, a wounded mysterious expression on every face. The female version: something between blonde bombshell and boho don't give a shit. Anyway, my point is, people have always found a type of person that they think is closest to perfection and tried to imitate it. For a long time that meant two idealized versions, one male, one female. There was an algorithm you could use to see just how perfectly proportioned a person's features were, and then you could get your doctor to, essentially, give you that face. In the beginning there were always subtle differences, which depended both on the amount of money you could pay for the procedure and the quality of the doctor, though I suppose these are not mutually exclusive.

It was sometime in the early 23rd century that Dr. Gilbert Wong began the experiments that would truly change everything. His daughter, Elizabeth, was born with a vestigial penis (yes, think the high school required reading, *Middlesex*). His wife and he already had two boys and desperately wanted a daughter. But Dr. Wong did not want her to undergo any grueling anatomical surgery, after all, she was his own flesh and blood. He began experimenting on Marmosets, tiny tan monkeys with gigantic round eyes and hands like tree-frogs.

At first, he attempted to develop a sort of hermaphroditic XXY monkey. Or maybe that's the wrong word. A neutral monkey. Yes, that's better. Physical neutrality. It didn't work. There was always something inherently male or female about these animals. Some sequence of genetic material that, no matter how he manipulated it, would make the animal just slightly more one way or the other. An aggressive way of approaching other animals versus a desire to nurture, for instance. He began to feel, in some ways, that his experiments were actually confirming stereotypes rather than diminishing them. So, his neutralization effort was scratched in favor of a single gender idea. It was easier, he found, to turn a female monkey into a male than the other way around. And he thought that, if he could do one, it might open doors to accomplishing the other.

He began experimenting more with the idea of a single gender. Many of his first experiments were still phenotypically female, XO, without ovaries. A little testosterone at puberty though, and they looked and acted like males. It was nearly impossible to tell them apart from those born naturally. Dr. Wong still felt that that wasn't enough. They needed to be "fully" male. So, the X portion became just a snippet of an X.

I'm not sure if Dr. Wong had any idea what his experiments would eventually lead to. It's a sarcastic twist of fate that his desire for a daughter created a world with none. He died before he could begin work on creating females, and his daughter and wife both vanished.

Over the course of the next two centuries physicians and scientists continued Dr. Wong's work, expanding it to human trials. From this was born the idea of a single gender society.

Women, or, at least, feminine women, had become increasingly uncommon. The new "perfect human" had become, possibly as a result of the neutralization efforts, masculinized. It made sense. Women, throughout history, have been oppressed. To be sure, there were great strides made. But women were always less, and knew it. They were tired of it. They saw a chance to finally, truly, be equal.

Again, the transformations were gradual. If you look back through old magazine files, as I have, you'll see the evolution. Three women sit on a bench, drenched in luminous sunlight. They have lovely, delicate features. Thin, aristocratic noses, large almond-shaped eyes. Two have pencil-thin mustaches, and one a fuzzy tuft of goatee. All three have shaved heads, which, for a while was preferred to the short military-cuts that later replaced them. They are dressed in space-suit-green, gray, and dusty-blue jumpers. Later, only by studying the photos very carefully, can you distinguish any difference between those who are phenotypically male and those who are not. Perhaps one is slightly shorter, with a more delicate bone structure. Another has spotty clumps of facial hair. But, of course, these things could also be true of even a genuine male. For a long time, society existed in this sort-of limbo state since the surgery was still too difficult, and a lot of women just weren't willing or didn't have the income to go "all the way."

The problem of children had been solved long ago. I won't bore you with the details, which I'm sure you already know. Test tube and incubator babies were the norm. More than the norm, they were the only thing. People born "the old way" were freaks and outcasts before they took their first breath. No eggs, no sperm, no in-vitro fertilization involved, just simple old-fashioned cloning. Malfunctions like me, like Greg, are either a result of a doctor's mistake or just a random anomaly. A piece of DNA that should produce, say, a person with an IQ of a perfectly acceptable average 110, transforms, and the child has a genius level IQ of 187. Or, in my case, an X(snippet)O that should guarantee a male baby, transforms inexplicably into an XXO. A female. An evolutionary anomaly aimed at preservation, not of the species, but of the irregular.

Many leaders, aided by science, saw the promise in gender and racial neutralization. Most of mankind's strife had sprung from problems with one of the two. If all people were identical, at least on the outside, well, we'd no longer be "judging the book by its cover." We'd level the playing field. Like so many things, it started as a desire for peace, for equality. The only thing that had been holding us back was the technology, but with the breakthroughs that continued through the 24th century, that was no longer an obstacle.

It is amazing what society can accomplish when nations are in pursuit to be the first to succeed at something, nothing like it had been seen since the race for the moon. Suddenly, there were breakthroughs being made everywhere, and a tiny lavender pill was developed in Japan. No grueling series of surgeries, no manipulation of phenotype, no life-long visits to therapists. Even if you were born a malfunction, you could still be normal. To hell with what God had given you.

"What's going on?" Lora said, not looking at me.

"I should be asking you that."

"Oh, this," She stroked the feathery mustache but still wouldn't look at me.

"Yeah, that, want to tell me about it?"

"I just can't do it anymore, Beka. I can't be this symbol you all want me to be. You have to know it's never really been what I wanted. I'm tired of everything being so hard. Why does it have to be so fucking hard? I just want to belong."

She was crying. Large tears streaming down her face, distorting her mouth into a thin line, her eyes to slits. Her hair had fallen over one eye and her cheeks were flushed petal pink. How could someone cry like that and still look pretty. "I don't want everything to be so hard. Either people look at me because I'm a girl, or they don't because I'm a girl. I'm a walking freak show. Can you understand that? Can't you just understand?"

I suppose I should have felt sympathy, but I didn't. Lora had always been dramatic and usually it just irritated me. Despite the confusion of emotion that was coursing through my hot-blood, I could still feel this familiar annoyance beneath. Somehow, it was comforting. Even as I thought, *I should have seen this coming*, I also thought *everything will be OK*. Because we were revisiting our usual scenario where Lora cried about something, and I was annoyed but nonetheless provided a listening ear. Except this time, it was more, and underneath I was terrified.

It's funny, the things that come to mind in a moment of panic. In that car, on that day, I thought of the silliest things. Of the two of us, I was the greater tom-boy. She had always loved the dresses and hair-bows her mother made. Certainly no-one sold that stuff anymore.

She loved being a mom. She breast-fed Stephen until he was two. They did a piece about it in the *Daily*, and she became a sort-of celebrity. (She would have called it a 'freakshow item'.) She even slept in the bed with him for the entire month he was quarantined for SP107. An act of heroism that was attributed to her femininity and got us both a lot of positive publicity.

I thought we were going to change things, together. Maybe not completely, but at least get them started down a different track.

She could show everyone better than I could. Help them see women didn't have to become extinct, that we could benefit society. That we were necessary. She was married, had a biological son. Maybe one day she could even have a daughter. I had, I realized, put all my hope in her. I tried to slow my breath. I didn't want to lash out at her.

"What about Greg?"

"He's OK, he'll *be* OK. It hasn't been easy on him either, you know?"

"And Stephen?" I said quietly. Stephen, her son, could not be OK. He loved, no, he adored, his mother. I had been there when she gave birth to him. A soft, round, rosy child who we all wept over. He was six now, and even though I had not been the one to carry him in my womb and deliver him in blood and fury, I loved him as much as any person has ever loved another.

"It will be better for all of us, in the end."

"You can't seriously believe that? After everything you did to fight for this? For what you have? Why would you do this now?" I felt myself, despite the breathing exercise, growing wretched with anger, my voice rising, my heart thumping loud in my chest.

"Greg asked me to."

I could barely hear her when she said this, and I had to ask her to repeat it.

"He knows how miserable I've been these last few years. All the publicity, all the hatemongering. It's just not for me. He loves me, he does. And I was thinking about it too. It wasn't just him."

"Why didn't you tell me this sooner? What will you do? Will you still live together?" The questions poured out of me, a torrent covering my fear. I felt my own hot tears coming, and I pressed my fists against my eyelids, trying to stifle them.

"I'm sorry I didn't talk to you before, I know what a shock this must be, but you haven't really been around much lately." Lora looked at me sideways, and I turned away from her. "And yeah, I think we'll stay together. He's going to help me get used to everything. We'll help each other, and Stephen of course."

"But..." and I found I didn't quite have the words for a moment. Greg was a man. Not the kind they had been creating for the past two-centuries. He was a malfunction, like me. He had sexual drive, something that had essentially been eradicated. He was crazy about Lora. I had my own confused feelings for him, feelings that were unavoidable, considering. How could he possibly be OK with this?

"Beka, He's already made the change." Again, Lora's voice was so quiet I had to ask her to repeat what she'd said. I wished I hadn't. I did not want to hear those words. *Already made the change.* I slid my index finger along the car's security strip and got out. I needed to walk. Lora, thank God, didn't come after me.

We had pulled off into one of the little aerial parks that dotted the cloudless summer sky as far as you could see in either direction. It was the usual 20 X 20 green square, with intermittent clumps of yellow and white daisies. An iron bench made to look like wood. A round, decorative fountain, filled with blue-gray rainwater. Each park was connected by a real path that crisscrossed over the line of lime-white highway. When they were first invented, there were several mishaps with them, but eventually, most of the kinks were worked out. Just like with people, I thought. Most of the kinks have been worked out. Except for a few. Lora, Greg, and me. We had been three of those kinks. Now, it was just me. Unless I could somehow change Lora's mind.

If it just wasn't so easy, I thought, breathing in the hot, perfumed air. I had walked across three of the little parks and this one, instead of daisies, was planted with clumps of lilac. Their tiny, star-shaped petals were wilted from the sun, but their smell was still intoxicating.

Once upon a time, the change had involved multiple, grueling surgeries, classes to cope with sexual dreams, therapy appointments, etc. Now, most people were just born male, but without the messy stuff like sexual desire or anger management issues.

And if, like me, they were a malfunction that was allowed to grow into adult-hood (usually because the parents were religious), and decided to undergo the change later in life, well, then there was the pill. A nifty little thing no bigger than a thumbnail that would be taken over the course of a week. No surgeries, no therapy appointments necessary. At least, not usually.

It was far too hot, and I realized, suddenly, that I needed water. My mouth felt like I had swallowed cotton. I looked longingly at the still, greenish rainwater in the ever-present fountain. That was a recipe for some sort of stomach-emptying virus for sure. Instead, I sat on the bench which was shaded at one end by a small potted palm. Someone had taken a great deal of care with this park. Usually there weren't trees.

I tried to close my eyes, but it was too hot, and all I could see every time I did, was Greg's face. That face, so different from other men, so alive, so animal. Most men were not large, 5 foot 5 or thereabouts. They always sported beards or mustaches, but they were usually of the wispy, barely-there kind. Perfectly quaffed, clean, tidy, gentlemanly. They were fine. They were not Greg. He was rough, he was loud, he had an appetite like a bull. He was, I was sure, very good with his hands. How could Greg have decided to do this? It was, quite simply, impossible. Lora was lying.

The walk had done its trick. It had cleared my head enough of the initial shock to help me think clearly. There was no way Greg would decide to change. Suddenly, I was desperate to see him. To confirm with my own eyes, that he was still *himself*. I also, simultaneously, felt nauseated at the thought. What if I was wrong? What if, now, where there had been the broad, jovial, intense, living face of Greg, there would be that placid, smiling blankness. I didn't think I could bear it. But why? Why would Lora lie?

She had found out. That must be it.

I will tell you. Greg kissed me. Or I kissed him. Only once, nine months ago. I wanted to know what it was like. Kissing a man, who was a man. He had Lora, of course, so it meant nothing to him. He did it, I was sure, just to be nice. But part of me wanted to think it meant more. That he had wondered too, what kissing me would be like. And that is why he did it, not out of pity or kindness, but from desire.

We never talked about it, but sometimes there were glances, or hands brushing, or knees touching. I tried my best to forget about it, but it was impossible. I found myself, more often than I care to admit, daydreaming about what it would be like to be in Lora's place. To be his wife, to be Stephen's mother. To have a family of my own. It was a physical ache.

I'll tell you about the kiss. It was, at least for me, an explosion. His lips were warm and sure. He was not timid. His tongue was in my mouth, and it searched for mine. It was strange and remarkable to be that close to someone. I think, right at that moment, if he had said he could read my thoughts, I would have believed him. I would have believed anything. My breath stops, caught in my chest like a trapped bird, whenever I think about that day. When I am close to him, it is like it's happening again.

That's why I no longer go to their house. I come up with excuses. The usual things, "I'm sick" "I have a lot of work to do, I'm tired." Maybe Lora noticed and asked him. But wouldn't he just have told her he loved her, that it meant nothing? He would have known what to say to put her mind at ease. They could have decided to cut me out of their lives. Why this? Lora, obviously, was really undergoing the change. Unless that was also an elaborate ruse. But that would be too much, even for her.

I felt like my mind was going foggy again. I wasn't thinking clearly. I stood up, intending to continue my walk when a skycle skidded to a halt next to me, and Greg jumped off.

"Beka, my God, she told me what she said to you."

I began to cry, and then to laugh. It was him. It was still him.

"I'm so sorry." He grabbed me and pulled me close, wrapping his arms around me. He smelled of warmth, earthy and heavy and alive. My heart was pounding. I felt flushed and sweaty. I wanted to look at him but was afraid. Gently, he stepped back and lifted my chin with his hand. "Open your eyes," he said. I did.

He kissed me then. And it was the same as before. Strong, sweet. But without fear this time. And this time I also knew, he wanted it. After a bit, we sat together on the bench, our fingers entwined. We were quiet for a long time. I didn't want to move, hardly to breath, for fear somehow, I was in a mirage.

"You know, she has been talking about this for a long time." It wasn't a question, and he spoke almost in a whisper. "She just didn't want to do it anymore. She said she never really wanted to. She wanted to change since she was a kid. She always wanted to belong. She said you were the only reason she didn't do it before. And Stephen. Not me though. She never said it was me.

She wants us all to change. Stephen too, so we can be a normal family."

"Stephen too?" I said, surprised, but also not really. It seemed reasonable if what she really wanted was for them all to be normal. "What did you tell her?"

"I was really angry, at first. Then hurt. Then I tried to listen. The mourning stages, you know?" He looked sad, but somehow, not heartbroken. I looked at him. He hadn't answered my question. My heart started to pound furiously again. Was he saying goodbye?

"It's OK," he said, and I noticed where my nails were digging into his hand, there was blood. He turned it over, stroking the palm with his fingers, smiling. "I told her no. And I told her about us."

"Oh," I said, unable to say anything else. Hoping he would go on.

"She cried and said she already knew. Not necessarily about the kiss. But…" He paused and looked at me, almost shyly. "She said she knew that you loved me."

I sucked in my breath. A slow gasp. "Yes," I said quietly. "I think--- I think I always have."

"Beka," he said, for the second time, tilting my chin so I had to look at him. "Yesterday, she told me everything. She wanted us all to change because she knew about you. She didn't want you to have us. Stephen and me. The only reason it took her all these years to do it was because she didn't want you to have us." Small, burning tears were squeezing themselves from the corners of my eyes. "I love you too, Beka," he said. "I told her I wanted her to be happy, but that I couldn't, I wouldn't do it and I wouldn't do it to Stephen either. I came here to tell you that." He looked at me.

250

I rested my head against his chest. I could hear his heartbeat. A strong, steady beat. A drumbeat. It seemed that my own heart slowed so they were in time with each other. *And the two shall become one.*

I remembered the words her mother had spoken at Lora's wedding. We had all the future before us. All the future of the world. I imagined in that moment our entire lives stretched before us. Stephen, our son, grown. Married, perhaps, to one of the girls rumored to still be living in Eastern Europe, where legend had it that Wong's wife and daughter began a monastery for women, though no-one has ever found it. Married, and with a son and a daughter of his own. And then, we, my granddaughter and I, would be the last two women.

Suddenly, the strip in my left arm vibrated. I glanced down and saw the small icon with Lora's face appear. I turned it away from Greg, not wanting him to ask about her. Not wanting to break the spell. Three words appeared, in Lora's small, tidy print.

"I love you."

I stood slowly, turning away from Greg, and continued my walk. I did not look back even as he called my name again and again. Not until the sound of it merged with the soft hum of vehicles and insects. By then, he was no more than a black mirage in an unspeakably blue sky.

RIVER SECRETS by Rebekah Mechst

>In a waking dream I was upon the water
>It was smooth, clear, shallow
>So I could see the things beneath
>Staring up at me
>Glinting their eyes and silvery fins

One swam beneath
Wise dolphin face playful and strange
Meeting my gaze
For a moment
Asking a question I could almost find
The answer to
Sleek azure boat carries me
By my strength carries me
To stretch on a hidden beach
Flowered with print of bird
Small mammal life
Maybe raccoon
Otter
Opossum
They make a maze on the sand
But none are
Of my kind
Loneliness
Is perfect
Like one of them I shy away
From speaking men
Turning to go another way
Averting
To see the pulsing billow of great gorgeous beast
Manatee
Coyly submerging
Her soft snout the faintest ripple
I don't think she is afraid
Not of me
Only wary
Of all

This time it is a secret
She asks me
To stay
With her
For she sees that we are the same

###

Rebecca Christophi, an adventurer and mom, writes short stories, and has been published in *After Dinner Conversation, The Fredricksburg Literary and Art Review* and *Change: A Space Coast Writers Anthology.* She is an MA candidate in Literature and Creative Writing at the Harvard Extension School and has a BS in biology. She is currently working on her debut novel. She resides in the Florida Space Coast with her husband, five children, and an overweight and well-loved kitty.

THE STING OF SURVIVAL
By Shelia Dodd Gillis

She stared at the package sitting on her desk. The black oily stains looked like something containing liquid was broken. She hadn't ordered anything. No one ever mailed stuff to her. She leaned over the box and checked the name again. Pretty sure she was the only Mallory Elizabeth Waters that worked for this hell hole company.

"Miss Waters, do we pay you to sit and stare?"

She jumped in her seat almost toppling over. If she didn't need this job so bad, she would gladly go toe to toe with the sleazy, obnoxious supervisor. Always slithering up behind people. Jeez. Unfortunately, her rent was due. She bit her tongue and forced a fake smile.

"No, Sir, I'm on my break."

"I've watched you for ten minutes, break is over. Get back to work or else!"

Thankfully he spotted an empty chair across the room and headed over to harass someone else.

"Hey, Mal, you have a secret admirer?" Curtis, a coworker, leaned back in his chair waving at the package.

"How come you never get in trouble? You men get away with murder!" She whispered back.

Mallory jerked up the package and tossed it in the trash can beneath her desk, wiping her hands on a napkin she had saved in her desk drawer.

"Gross." She made a face at her sticky hands.

At five o'clock she had her lunch bag, purse and umbrella in her lap, ready to dash out. The phone on her desk rang simultaneously as the timeclock dinged quitting time.

"Oh, heck no." She practically ran over Curtis as she vaulted down the row of desks.

"Hey, Mal, your phone's ringing." Curtis laughed.

She was a master at ignoring people these days. She hated people in general, especially the slime that worked here at Protect All. What a sham. Selling protection services that consisted of window stickers saying they were protected, what a crock. Worst of all were the sheep that gladly gave them money they couldn't afford to give.

She always speed-walked the three blocks to her car. First to get away from the office faster, second to get away from the people she worked with, and third because the neighborhood was lined with junkies, drunks and street walkers. She carried her purse tucked under her arm like a football, her umbrella ready to fend off any potential attackers. She never made eye contact. Every evening when her car was within sight, a sigh of relief washed over her. Safety was just a few steps away. That creepy feeling of always being watched or followed was ever present.

She was anxious to get to her flat and shower. Hard as she tried, she couldn't remove the stink off her hands from that stupid package someone left on her desk.

Quickly, she unlocked her car, got in and relocked the doors. She had followed the same routine every evening for the last six months. She almost had enough money stashed away to quit Protect All. Then she would have time to find something better, in a safer area.

"Why did you throw away the package I sent you?" A gravelly voice rang out from the backseat as a needle pricked the skin on her neck.

Her last conscious thought was a blur of confusion.

"Smell the pheromones she's emitting?" Curtis nudged the Recruiter, before getting out of the backseat. He opened the driver door and shoved Mallory across the seat. The Recruiter bent over the seat to reach her. Tasting. Attracted. The smell from her hands mixed with her scent of fear, driving his own pheromones to a fevered pitch.

Curtis swatted him back. "Easy, no damaging the goods."

She laid perfectly still on the scratchy blanket. Afraid to move. What happened? Where was she? She tried to open her eyes only to realize they were sealed shut. Her throat dry, burning, she tried to speak. Her lips were bound by the same glue. It tasted of medicine or chemicals. Her nose began to run profusely. Her hands, bound tight, legs and feet as well. Some kind of wax? Fear engulfed her. She shivered, cold, then flinched when something soft touched her hair. She recoiled.

Something licked the side of her cheek. Slime, sticky like from the package at work, oozed down her face. She couldn't stop shaking. Another sting pierced her neck. Then nothing.

When she woke again, the slime covered her entire body. She still couldn't see, but she sensed she wasn't alone. She thought she could hear breathing.

"You have been chosen. Your spirit to live will ensure our survival."

Not a question. They had no intention of letting her communicate. Adrenaline sped up her heart rate. Her fight instincts hummed to no avail.

She struggled, only to be rewarded with another sting to her neck. Another blackout.

The Mother shook her head. Looked around the room at her waiting drones. "Continue breeding her, sting to keep her complacent, careful, try not to kill her. When she is filled with eggs, seal her in. Please, try to keep this one alive. At least until the brood hatches."

The creatures nodded in understanding. Curtis looked at the Mother in askance. "Do I get to keep this one?"

The Mother shrugged, wrapped her wings around her. "We will see if she lasts."

Mallory woke, hot, stiff, still bound tight. Her head pounded. She listened for sounds. Silence. Maybe they left? She struggled to breathe, panicked, clinging to life. She needed to throw up, but her lips were sealed. She swallowed the bile. She waited for the sting. It always came when she woke up. Fuzziness ever present began to clear. Was she alone? She tried to think. She rolled to her side, her stomach bulging, convulsing over and over, unaware of the thousands she was giving birth to.

A buzzing sound filled the room. Louder. Deafening. Still her stomach convulsed non-stop. She was so hot. She had to get away. Tiny insects were crawling all over her! Pinches, bites, stings! Buzzing in her ears. She shook her head, rolled onto her back, wiggled, trying to get away from the bugs.

A door opened; she felt a draft of cool fresh air. The insects left her in a whoosh. She lay perfectly still, exhausted, drained. For a second, she savored the peace and cool air.

The Mother turned to Curtis. Looked him over. Greedy, disgusting humans. "You can have her now."

He dropped to his knees next to his prize. The Mother nodded over Curtis' head. The Recruiter pressed his stinger into the back of Curtis neck, pumping a lethal dose of venom.

Curtis' eyes widened as he fell dead beside Mallory.

"And her?" The Recruiter asked.

"First dispose of that human." She glanced at Curtis' body. The Mother prodded Mallory. "She is a strong one."

Fully conscious, Mallory's body buzzed as if electrical current was passing through her.

"Such a good queen you turned out to be." She stroked Mallory's neck. "You survived an entire breeding cycle. That's never happened."

Mallory's muffled screams came out as moans.

The Recruiter rushed to the Mothers side with a flutter of wings. "Shall I?" he asked, his stinger at the ready.

She nodded. He gently stung Mallory's neck. They watched her black out.

The Mother turned to leave, hesitated. "Start her breeding again. I'm interested in how long she can serve."

It was time to recruit another. Humans expired so quickly. To get two broods out of this one human would be unprecedented.

Shelia Dodd Gillis writes contemporary, western, and romance. She credits her love of words to her third-grade librarian. Born in Texas, she's an Air Force veteran and retired from the US Postal Service. She holds a black belt in SBD and graduated top of her class in Culinary School. Her passions are writing, reading and cooking. She resides in Florida. Shares life with a husband, three daughters, seven grandkids, Gus and a cadre of friends.

THEY EVEN TOOK THE BEACH BALL
By Janet Corso

They just showed up one day, out of the blue, you might say. But we were warned, many times. You people who laughed at those of us who took the tabloids seriously? Well, just who's laughing now? Who's even able to laugh? Not many, I bet.

Got another question for you. Where do you think they came up with the ideas for those *Men in Black* movies? Do you know any humans with such wild imaginations? I mean, after all, come on.

They tried to tell us. But did we listen? Of course not. We never listen. Wouldn't take any steps to help ourselves, to forestall the inevitable. So here we sit, mostly ten to a room, definitely a mixed ten. Nothing made a difference to them. Not color, not sex, not age, not religion. Nothing.

Once in a while some guy in what looks like a hazmat suit comes in and takes out one of the ten. When they come back, they're changed, and I can't tell you how. They just are. Why anyone in particular is chosen, we never know. Can't even guess. There's no rough stuff, no manhandling. Although I don't think that word really suits this situation. They're not men; at least I don't think they are.

They never say anything. That might be because they can't, or won't, communicate the way we do. Never heard any voices from inside those suits. What they do is come in, point, and wait until one of us gets the message.

Uh oh, I think it's my turn. Wish me luck.

Well, that wasn't too bad. No mind scans, no invasive probes. Guess they don't need any stuff like that. Whew! At least the tabloids had that wrong. But I understand, at least I think I do.

According to the flyers they handed out, they're supposed to be our rescuers. But just between you and me, if you believe that, I got a bridge in Brooklyn I can sell you, real cheap.

When I finally had a chance to look at one of the big view screens, I could see the size of their operation. Thousands of ships. All sizes. And at the tail end of these many ships they were towing what looked like a beach ball. A giant beach ball. Took me a few minutes to realize what it was.

I got really nervous then. When I saw that 'beach ball,' I knew it was going to cost, and cost big time. Only how were we ever going to pay them back for 'rescuing' us? Especially when they were rescuing us from us.

Turns out we'd set ourselves on the path to extinction. And some of our so-called leaders were eager to be the one to go down in history by pushing the big red button. That was when our rescuers decided to intervene. After all, they had planted us on that blue beach ball—on the third planet from an insignificant sun—as a social experiment. We were, in effect, their stepchildren. Though they didn't like how we turned out, they felt responsible for our well-being.

In the goodness of their hearts (they each have two), and so we would have less reason to feel homesick, they didn't just take the people. They took the planet.

###

**Janet Corso** was born in the first half of the last century (which makes her older than some dirt). She belongs to SCWG, Monday Morning Writers and the Wednesday Morning Writers Group. Her pseudonyms are DOD and DOOM. Her writing has appeared in several anthologies and online. Her greatest pleasure in life is the company of writers, edging out even chocolate and various flavors of ice cream.

TOO YOUNG TO DIE
By Anne Bonner

  Sleepless and sitting alone under the great oak, its sturdy limbs embracing the sky, Joseph inhales the sweet elixir of life. Enjoying the coolness of the outdoors, the glorious outdoors, he listens to songbirds sing their nighttime lullabies. Twinkling stars pierce the ebon sky's velvet blanket in the cloudless night. Joseph nods off to sleep.

  Rat-a-tat-tat! Rat-a-tat-tat! Joseph's hands touch his head. No helmet. Rat-a-tat-tat! Gunfire coming closer. Where is his gun? Boom! Boom! Joseph covers his ears, his eyes squeeze shut. He doesn't need to watch the bombs exploding, he already knows the fiery shards of destruction. Hunkering down, he wishes he were in a better bunker. He sidles closer to the tree, melding his body with its trunk. Joseph prays he's out-of-sight. Guns keeps firing. Rat-a-tat-tat! Rat-a-tat-tat! Bombs keep bursting. Boom! Boom!

  Stop it! I'm too young to die! Bursting into tears, he remembers his beautiful young fiancée dying of cancer. She was too young to die! He's living now in the cottage he bought for her, situated in a subdivision abutting a wooded preserve. His body shaking, tears streaming down his face, Joseph wakes in a cold sweat. Looking at the manicured lawn, he realizes he's not in the jungle. The horrible war's PTSD (post-traumatic stress disorder) had returned.

  On wobbly legs, Joseph crosses the lawn to his home. Always obeying orders, he defiantly raises his fist in the air, yelling, *Now, hear this, Governor! I'm going to the beach tomorrow. I'm a warrior! I can kill an invisible enemy! The COVID-19 will not be victorious! I'm too young to die!*

  Slamming the door shut, Joseph wipes away the tears, making his way to his cozy bedroom.

###

Anne Bonner is a fifth generation Floridian. She has published ten historical fiction books in ten years, all set in the wilds of early Florida. Anne received an Award, "In Recognition of Outstanding Achievement in Historical Preservation from the National Society of the Daughters of the American Revolution for programs presented in schools. She's a member of the Florida Historical Society, American Pen Women, and a former Board member of the Space Coast Writers' Guild.

TRIBUTE TO MY FATHER
By Peggy Insula

You have survived in countless ways since your death seventy years ago in October 1950 at the age of thirty-three.

On December 6, 1946, during a blizzard, you waited in our drafty old house on the side of a hill above the Guyandotte River in the little-known town of Corinne, West Virginia. When I was born near midnight, you sat by me all night long. You talked to me and patted me as I lay in the dresser drawer that was my first bed. You comforted me. You ignored the blizzard that howled outside, sending bursts of cold air through our house. You never left me for a minute that night while the snowstorm raged.

Somehow, during your long vigil, you gave me memories of this night: I remember the bed where my mother lay parallel to the dresser with the drawer that was my crib. I remember the kitchen chair you sat in, toward the foot of the bed, but close to me. I remember your posture and your smile as you leaned toward me. I remember your voice and the whistling wind. I remember feeling safe, warm, and comforted.

You held my eyes with yours like magnets. You bonded with me all night long, so that when morning came, you told Mom, "Jean, I think Peggy knows me." You were right.

When I was a toddler, you'd let me lie in the bed between you and Mom. You talked and giggled with me until Mom said, "James, quit playing with her. She'll never go to sleep."

Then, you'd close your eyes and pretend to sleep, but your smile gave you away. When I lifted the covers to peer down at your feet, you wiggled your toes at me and sent me off into peals of giggles.

From the very first, you gave me tenderness, love, devotion, abundant warmth, and attention. You took me for rides in your Jeep just because we both enjoyed cruising around in it. You showed me off to neighbors and friends. You took me to the candy store and let me pick out whatever I wanted. Never once did you raise your voice to me or scold me. You treated me as if I were a princess worthy of your constant pride and admiration.

You also survive in the mountain of daily letters—evidence of your faithfulness—that you wrote to Mom during the war from 1941 through 1945, before you married her. You resumed writing to her and called her during the several months you were hospitalized in 1950. Seldom did you miss a day to write, and always you affirmed your love.

You knew all about survival. On December 7, 1941, you survived at Pearl Harbor when a bomb blew a hole in the wall above your head as you lay in your bunk. You survived a tour in the Solomon Islands. You contracted malaria there and survived that, too, although it recurred, and you were hospitalized with it three or four times.

Finally home, you married Mom. I was born the next year, and you were well for a couple of years. Then, leukemia struck.

You bore your long and difficult illness with grace and hope. As you sat on the floor against the wall by the stove, you grew paler and thinner. You lost your warm smile. You had frequent nose bleeds, and you couldn't get warm. You couldn't play with me or drive me around in your Jeep. Yet, you did not complain.

After several months of decline, you went into the hospital in Dayton, Ohio, where you spent several more months. You wrote Mom about hoping to come home. You responded indulgently to her anecdotes about me doctoring my dolls and cutting their hair. "I bet Peggy did a good job," you wrote.

Thin and weak, you walked on the hospital grounds with Mom and me on the one occasion I was taken on the bus to Dayton to visit you. You gave your attention mainly to Mom, and you were solemn and distant. Soon afterward, when you were without family in the hospital, leukemia took your life.

When you died, I was three years old. You had already given me more great fathering than most people receive in a lifetime. You instilled pride in me for who I was. You gave me a foundation of self-worth and self-respect that has not only survived but has also bolstered all my achievements in the seventy years we have been separated.

And still you survive. As the seventieth anniversary of your death draws near, you are as vivid in my memory and as huge a part of me as ever. You gave me most of the good aspects of my character, my mind, and my body. You lived the values that I aspire to embrace.

You survive in the physicality, the strength, the appearance, and the personalities of your two grandsons and your great-grandson. You gave two of these three gorgeous guys your own handsome looks. They look exactly like you. You have passed on to one of your grandsons, your granddaughter, and her son your love of and expertise with weapons. You lighted the way for your granddaughter, a reservist, and one of your grandsons, currently a major, to serve in the U.S. Army. You have given all of your grandchildren your sharp intelligence and sense of humor.

Thank God, you have not only survived but flourished for seventy years, and you will go on and on.

Wisdom 4: 8-9 *For old age is not honored for length of time, nor measured by number of years; but understanding is gray hair for men, and a blameless life is ripe old age.*

###

Peggy Insula has published many books, available on Amazon. Mysteries and humor in novels and anthologies comprise most of her works. She has published one poetry book.

A master's degree in psychology and several years of clinical practice as well as teaching preschool through college have contributed to her understanding of characters and motivation.

Mrs. Insula's writing has been published in journals and in previous anthologies by *Metamorphosis*, Space Coast Writers' Guild, and Scribblers' *Driftwood*.

TWO SNIPERS
By Joanne Fisher

Belfast, July 1970

The sniper lay still for a long time nursing his wounded arm and planning an escape. He had been shot early evening just before dark. It was a flesh wound but needed to be attended to, but he couldn't move an inch because the other sniper would have put another bullet in his head for sure. Marcus could not afford morning to find him wounded on the roof. The enemy on the opposite roof covered his escape. He needed to be killed, but all he had left was a revolver. He had to conjure up a plan.

"Got it!" he quietly said to himself.

Marcus took his cap off, placed it over the muzzle of his rifle and pushed it upward over the parapet, until the cap was visible to his opponent. Immediately, a bullet pierced the center of the cap. Marcus slanted the rifle forward letting the cap clip down into the street. Then catching the rifle in the middle, Marcus dropped his left hand over the roof and let it hang, lifelessly. After a few moments he let the rifle drop to the street while sinking onto the roof, dragging his hand with him.

Crawling quickly to his feet, he peered up at the corner of the roof. His ruse had succeeded. His opponent, seeing the cap and rifle fall, thought that he had killed his man. He was now standing before a row of chimney pots, looking across, with his head clearly silhouetted against the western sky.

Marcus smiled and lifted his revolver above the edge of the parapet. The distance was about fifty yards—a hard shot in the dim light, and his right arm was paining him like a thousand devils. He took a steady aim. His hand trembled with eagerness. Pressing his lips together, Marcus took a deep breath through his nostrils and fired. He was almost deafened with the report, and his arm shook with the recoil.

When the smoke cleared, he peered across and uttered a cry of joy. "Got him!" The other sniper was reeling over the parapet in his death agony. He struggled to keep his feet, but he was slowly falling forward as if in a dream. The rifle fell from his grasp, hit the parapet, fell over, bounded off the pole of a barber's shop beneath, and then clattered on the sidewalk. Then the dying man crumpled and fell forward. The body turned over and over in space and hit the ground with a dull thud. Blood spilled onto the street.

Marcus looked at his enemy and shuddered. The lust of battle died in him. He became bitten by remorse. Sweat stood out in beads on his forehead. He felt his heart sink. Weakened by his wound and the long summer day of fasting and watching the roof, he revolted from the sight of the shattered mass of his dead enemy. His teeth chattered, he began to babble to himself, "Damn you, war! Damn you, Marcus! Damn you, God! Damn everyone!" He looked at the revolver which had a slight smoke trail coming out of it. He hurled the revolver to the rooftop in anger. It discharged with a loud report. The bullet whizzed past his head. He was frightened back to his senses by the shock. Somehow, his nerves steadied. As the cloud of fear dispersed from his mind, he laughed hysterically.

He took the whiskey flask from his jacket pocket and drained it in one gulp. Before he slid the flask back into his pocket, he stared at it. He closed his eyes and remembered the Christmas when his brother Ian gave it to him. It read, "With Love, Ian." He had engraved it all on his own. It was roughly done, but to Marcus, it was a work of art. Then his mind wandered to the day Ian left the family home to go fight for the Protestants. It was a sad day in Marcus' Catholic household.

Marcus decided to go search for his commander and make his report. He placed his revolver in his pocket and headed for the stairs. It was eerily quiet and not much danger in the streets. He felt a sudden desire to see who he had killed. "I wonder if I know him?"

He peered around the corner onto O'Connell Street. He could hear shots firing up a couple of blocks, but his area was all quiet.

Marcus darted across the street and stood next to the corpse that was face down just as a machine gun tore up the ground around him with a hail of bullets. One of them hit him on his chest. He crumbled to the ground right next to his dead nemesis. The machine gun stopped. With his good arm, he turned the body over and looked into his brother's face.

"Ian! No!" he cried. "Why? Why?"

Oddly enough, he did not feel like he was dying. Then his good hand went for his flask. "What's this?" his voice trembled. There was the fatal bullet lodged tightly inside the O of the word *Love*.

"Ian…you…saved…me."

###

 **Joanne Fisher** is a Canadian, Italian, American author who has penned TEN books: 3 steamy romances, 1 Christmas Novella, 2 historical fictions, 2 travel guides, 1 anthology and 1 murder/mystery. She has also written several short stories for various Space Coast Writers' Guild Anthologies and in April of 2019 was elected **President of the Space Coast Writers' Guild.** She lives in Florida with her husband and two dachshunds, Wally and Madison. Please visit www.JoannesBooks.com

WHAT A WORLD
By Terri Friedlander

"St. Patrick's Day is canceled."

While working the election polls on Tuesday, March 17, a parade of voters dressed in green for the luck of the Irish streamed past. Only a few sported face masks and plastic gloves. Still unconvinced the proverbial 'Sky was falling', I wore neither like the rest of my fellow mask-less poll workers. When I phoned my husband to meet for the shamrocking party at Meg O'Malley's, he replied the above.

I rattled off a few other places to which he insisted that every Irish pub within a thousand miles had shut down their money-making festivities.

"Out of an abundance of caution, St. Patrick's Day is canceled." Such strange expressions began slipping into our psyche.

The next evening my book club held our monthly gathering. Noticeably gone were the friendly hugs as the hostess requested us to "social distance." Huh? Still unmasked but standing further apart around the table, we cautiously wondered, "Is this crisis being blown out of proportion?" Sightings of toilet paper and Lysol replaced book talk.

Then Disney announced the parks would be closed for two weeks. Wow! The Mouse never sleeps.

In an instant, all cruises stopped. The entire tourism industry- slammed. Live music brought to a halt. The nation was ordered to quarantine. Millions of workers were fired or furloughed.

Hugs and handshakes – Suddenly deemed perilous and taboo.

By late March, schools were chained up indefinitely.

People began wiping down groceries and leaving Amazon packages outside or in the garage to decontaminate. Could touching items manufactured in China really give a person coronavirus? Chaos overwhelmed logic.

What a world.

The 24-hour news cycle stoked fear, anxiety and panic. Everyone knew someone coping with grief over lost family members or friends. Just getting up in the morning with nowhere to go became difficult. The sudden onset of ennui seemed unshakeable. Instead of pursuing my inner Betty Crocker, I found myself equally despising all things homemaking – cooking, cleaning, folding laundry. Repeat. Life felt like the movie *Groundhog Day*.

Protests against social injustice and rioting erupted to pile onto the unending turmoil. Feeling despair about the end of everything normal, a new motivation was needed to forge ahead. To lighten up and not get so worked up about a world spiraling out of control. Slowly four things morphed into my perfectly imperfect coping strategy for survival.

First was to re-adopt an Attitude of Gratitude. Granted, this is not exactly an original tidbit. Every self-help book ever written, and most therapists already preach the benefits of positive thinking. Stop focusing on the wrong in the universe that you can't change anyway. You know the drill. The Serenity Prayer and all. Reflect and deliberate. Find gratitude each day in one small thing.

Once, I remember feeling captivated by a spectacular, awe-inspiring double rainbow. Another time, while walking along the shore of a nearby riverfront park and delighting in the scenery, two playful dolphins splashed out of the water. How those cheery porpoises always had the power to make me smile and feel instantly uplifted! It's too easy to take living in paradise for granted. Slow down and be reminded how truly blessed we are to be surrounded by such beautiful creatures and an abundance of nature. Other days the ideas jostling around to be grateful for were much less profound.

Once, I felt pangs of appreciation for the mundane like the home air conditioner that kept pumping through the quarantine days of steamy, unrelenting humidity. And another morning, a bite of a fresh, doughy, still warm, savory garlic bagel from Einstein's Bagels left me awash in an appetizing moment of simple gratitude.

My second tactic was to remain active and begin a new hobby. This proved harder than it sounded. Friends appeared to be doing cool, self-isolating fads like quilting, gardening, painting and crafting handmade cards, none of which appealed to my Type-A personality favoring immediate gratification. Then, while mindlessly scrolling through Facebook posts, the lure of evening sea turtle walks caught my attention. After one outing, I became hooked.

Strolling along the dark moonlit shoreline, searching for turtle track marks in the sand proved to be great exercise and as well as a tremendous distraction to the swelling pandemic. The guided walk with the Sea Turtle Preservation Society taught the basics about not disturbing the nesting turtle, staying quiet and only using red lights to avoid confusing the loggerhead or leatherback. Watching the female choose a spot to dig the egg chamber in the sand with her back flippers left me speechless. Then seeing those plump, slimy eggs plop down into the nest took my breath away. That late night experience led to a desire to witness the miraculous sea turtle nesting process again and to take many summer evening strolls. Although nesting season ends in September, there's still plenty to learn, YouTube videos to watch, and marine-life centers to visit.

My next resolution for survival was another no-brainer. To use the time in forced isolation to read more diverse books outside my comfort zone. Sadly, the public library was also placed on lockdown in late spring. A friend from the book club had mentioned the library's new OverDrive application whereby e-books, audiobooks and magazines were available to be borrowed electronically for two weeks.

To start browsing the digital catalog of available titles you needed an old-fashioned library card to create your online account. Borrowed e-books could be downloaded for offline use or sent to a Kindle. At the end of the loan period, the titles are automatically returned to the digital shelf without the risk of late fees. After downloading the app, I used the OverDrive to browse the e-books and find the much-touted best seller, *American Dirt*.

Despite the uproar about the author's lack of Latina heritage, this page-turner deserves every accolade it's been given. The story follows a Mexican woman and her young son from Acapulco who become targets of a violent gang leader. Lydia's treacherous journey to safety in El Norte is an exhilarating read full of bone-chilling suspense. After her desperate decision to join the other migrants and jump on top of a moving freight train called La Bestia.

I googled to find if any of this dangerous insanity could actually be true. Shocked, I found many photos of young and old human faces crowded on top of such railcars with stories depicting the real challenges immigrants experience to come to America. What a wakeup call.

A final idea sprang from others coping with stay-at-home orders and requesting guidance on which of the endless choices of TV series had been the most entertaining and absorbing. Getting hooked on some mini-series and binge-watching until two in the morning had not entered my quarantine to-do list. I'd never been a fan of the boob-tube and already tuned into entirely too much television news.

Then, great reviews surfaced of a series titled "*The Last Ship*." After the first half hour, I was hooked. How, in the year 2014, did a group of Hollywood script writers put these very concepts on the screen —pandemic, vaccine trials, plasma donations? What foresight these producers had to dream up this action-packed drama before today's mask-wearing, vaccine-yearning world ever existed. "Their mission is simple: Find a cure. Stop the virus. Save the world. When a global pandemic wipes out eighty percent of the planet's population, the crew of a lone naval destroyer must find a way to pull humanity from the brink of extinction."

Each episode is filled with enough riveting battles, drama and combat scenes to be worthy of a full-length movie! One hugely patriotic chapter after another. This spring, America joined to salute a thousand bed US Navy hospital ship, "The Comfort", proudly sailing to New York City to help treat patients in the overwhelmed medical system. A few nights later, an episode of *The Last Ship* named "The Solace" appeared on the menu. Incredibly, this segment featured a Navy ship called "The Solace" that looked one hundred percent identical to the white mega-ship which had just docked in New York Harbor! Some six years ago, a script writer researched the Navy fleet and created this fascinating series about a future pandemic that so few of us could ever fathom. What vision.

Honorable mention in my view of script writing genius is Emmy nominated, *Little Fires Everywhere,* based on the book by the same name. This star-studded winner is chock full of mother-daughter drama, infertility, adoption and more. With themes of race, image, and identity in an outwardly perfect suburbia, this mini-series is sure to appeal to an audience craving an escape. It also brings to mind the vexing question, Is anybody happy?

So, a sincere thanks to Flipper and friends, the invention of air conditioning, the scrumptious taste of warm bagels and the sight of giant sea turtles nesting on our shores. Kudos to the writers of great fiction like *American Dirt* and *Little Fires Everywhere*. My most heartfelt gratitude to the producers of the action-packed series, *The Last Ship*. Binge-watching a series originating six years ago about an imaginary global pandemic somehow helped me to survive the real one of 2020. Go figure.

And, last but not least, God bless the healthcare angels along with those essential workers stocking the grocery shelves and finally getting some recognition.

What a world.

###

Terri Friedlander, a native New Yorker, has held several notable job titles including writer, college professor, teacher, journalist, and MIS Director of a global law firm.

Her latest venture is a series of children's books, *The Adventures of Percy the Siberian Cat* and *No More Bullying*. Terri also authored novels *The Dorm, Chasing Her Destiny and Work Hard Play Hard* and a column, *In Front of the Classroom*.

Loving life in Florida, visit at www.terrifriedlander.com.

WINNERS ON THE BATTLEFIELD...
By Rod Bornefeld

There are None

My Enemy's eyes I last saw,
Just before, from concealment,
The bullet was fired,
Sending him to his resting place of eternal faith,
His life or mine... that was the call of finality.

The jungle lay quiet of movement...
The sounds of war...
The sounds of jungle creatures,
all abated;
As if in an orchestrated silence of honor,
For the loss of my Enemy's life.

His Brothers in Arms will continue the battle,
Another day, another time, another place,
To what end, to what purpose, no one will understand,
No one will ever know;
One by one the enemies of each,
Will perish in order to maintain their cause, their beliefs.

Blood will drip from their hands,
Scars will be seared into their bodies and minds,
Their once youthful hearts left aged and calloused,
Never again to bear thoughts of innocence.
This tarnished medallion of terror pinned to their soul,
Their horrid companion throughout eternity.

No limits to the suffering of war has the battlefield,
The grisly arm of combat, afar it will reach,
The survivors, those families of every lost soldier's home…
Scorched deeply, a heart wrenching pain will dwell,
Leaving smoldering embers of anguish,
For endless years to come.

A mother's son will not return,
A tear will form in a father's eyes,
A brother, a sister will know the loss,
A wife's shoulders will not an embrace there be,
A void for all,
Never to be filled, forevermore.

The horrific loss never to be diminished,
By the passing of time,
Nor forgotten by aged memory;
The tombstone epitaph of honor,
An eternal reminder.

To those in thoughts of anguish,
The family of my Enemy,
Has also paid that hideous price of war.

Winners on the Battlefield…
There are none.

(For most, this is as close to the battlefield as you will ever get.
Pray that will never change.)

Ron Bornefeld: Tour of duty in Viet Nam '67; He worked as a structural Steel Ironworker and as an Architectural Design Engineer. He is a member of Master Masonic fraternity and Shriner's.

ABOUT THE SPACE COAST WRITERS' GUILD

The Space Coast Writers' Guild (SCWG) is a network of writers' dedicated to the same goal: helping you realize your writing ambitions. Whether you are crafting the great American novel for national distribution or penning an intimate story for an audience of one, you'll find support and encouragement in the Guild membership. Since 1982, SCWG has provided activities to educate, develop, and promote writers and their writing. Dues are just $40 annually.

SCWG BENEFITS:
· Monthly meeting on the third Saturday of the month – currently held at the Eau Gallie Public library with presentations on a variety of topics for writers.

· Opportunities to sign and sell your books at SCWG functions.

· Free advertising on the website and links from www.SCWG.org to your website.

· Critique and special focus groups.

· Monthly bulletin to publicize your work.

· Social media marketing and modern digital publishing guidance.

· Opportunities to network with successful writers, agents, editors, publishers, and many more!

How to Join the SCWG:

Visit/view <u>www.SCWG.org/ABOUT/</u> JOIN NOW

Follow the easy to join instructions.

Made in the USA
Columbia, SC
26 November 2021

49691108R00163